Faber
A Mason Briggs Mission

Annette Goeres

This is a work of fiction. Any resemblance to real people or events is both bewildering and unintentional

To M.M. (still your fault)

And B.G. of course

Prologue

Mason Briggs walked into the restaurant. It was right before the lunch rush on a brisk Tuesday morning. He had been recommended the place by someone knowledgeable.

"Hello, may I help you?" Coming to the podium was a brisk young hostess.

Mason returned her easy smile. "Yes, I am here on recommendation."

"Oh? May I ask who recommended you, sir?"

Mason leaned on the podium with an easy air of casualness. "You may ask. It was a Smith, a Mr. James Smith who recommended this restaurant. He told me also to try the fish soup. It is really lovely, he said."

The hostess paused, her smile seeming frozen. "Ah! Yes, Mr. Smith! He does enjoy our fish soup. I am sorry to say that the chef isn't preparing fish soup today. May I offer you a menu so you might look over our other fine dishes?"

Mason put on a grave face. "Yes, I suppose I had better look at the menu after all. Will the chef be preparing the fish soup at a later date? Say, on the 22nd of this month?"

Again, the hostess seemed to pause and then she replied with equal gravity, "I am not sure, sir, but I can certainly find out. However, this chef will be leaving on the 9th and won't be back until the 14th."

Mason nodded. "I suppose I had better look at that menu now."

The hostess reached under her podium and handed him a sealed plain envelope. Mason didn't even look at it as he slipped it into his coat pocket. "Thank you, madam. I am very sorry to have missed the soup. Give my regards to Mr. Smith when he stops in again."

The hostess nodded after him and he left the restaurant.

Mason walked calmly down the street. He was conscious that there could be someone shadowing him, even as he glanced into a store window along the way. It just wouldn't do to get caught at this stage in the game. It was still too much fun to play.

Mason noted that he was across the street from *The Diamond Nest*. He thought that he might have a look and see if the lead jeweler was in. If he was, perhaps there was a chance for a beer and extended lunch today.

Crossing in the middle of the block, Mason opened the unassuming door of one of the best jewelry stores around. The beautiful woman working the counter glanced up.

"Oh, hello, Mason. This is a lovely surprise!" She said. Turning her head slightly, she called back through the velvet curtain, "Porter! You have a customer!"

"Sienna, I thought I told you to only let the people I want to see know I am here." Porter came from behind the curtain. He was tall and quite handsome.

Sienna smiled mischievously up at him. "Oh, so you did. How forgetful of me."

Porter rolled his eyes at her. "Hello, Mason." He greeted his friend. "What brings you into this haunt, anyway?"

"Probably not your good looks. Sienna might be another consideration, there."   Mason said as he shook Porter's hand.

"No, probably not my good looks. Nor yours, for that matter. Is this a social call?"

Mason shrugged. "Sure, it can be that. Have you made a lunch date yet?"

Porter looked curiously at Mason for a second. He knew him better than anyone else, and he caught the hint. "No, I haven't yet. It's early for me, but I can go with you."

Sienna smiled. "Get out of here, both of you. Since when do you need to be so formal? You great silly boys."

Porter bowed to her with a grin. "Well, when you put it that way..."

"I do, now get going."

Within five minutes, Porter and Mason were out on the sidewalk. "Where to?" Porter asked as they started up the street. "I

6

gather that there might be more here than just a lunch date."

"There might be." Mason glanced at his friend. He cleared his throat a little uncomfortably. "How are you doing? Since the last job, I mean?"

Porter didn't say anything for a moment, but he tensed noticeably. "Why don't you ask Doctor Mitchel? You hired him; he works in your building."

Mason sighed. "Because, Porter, he has doctor/patient confidentiality, he is your therapist, and I fucking asked you. Now, how are you doing?"

Porter relaxed a little. "I'm okay, I think. Some days are better than others. I think it will always be that way."

"Probably true. I was asking you as friend, Porter. I care about you, you ass. You don't have to fucking bite my head off."

Porter winced. "I know. I'm sorry, Mason. It still hurts a bit to talk about real stuff, like feelings. You should probably be glad you aren't my therapist. The session before last was awful for him."

"Good. He's earning his pay then."

"God yes. I really made him work that day."

They walked a little farther before Mason addressed another topic. "Where are we going to eat?"

Porter squinted up the street they were on. "Well, you kind of sounded like you might want somewhere private, to discuss something important. How about Sadie's? They have a private room. For a price of course, but I have had a good few couple of months. I'll get it for us. Then we can order and be undisturbed."

Mason nodded. "I like that idea. Plus they have a very good wine menu."

"That was the other reason to go there."

"You never change, do you?"

Porter shrugged. "Sometimes I do. But I like drinking with friends. I don't do it alone anymore."

"You don't? That is a big departure."

7

"I've been working on it in therapy. It's not good for me to be too alone. Of course, it fucking sucks to be dry, but Doctor Mitchel and I agreed that I am using it as an escape too much. Still fucking sucks. Then, there is Sienna. I've been trying to bring her into my darkness more."

"She is enough to light up midnight."

"Damn straight."

They had gone a few blocks from The Diamond Nest when Porter glanced back. Mason noticed the slight frown.

"What is it?" Mason paid attention to the cues around him as much as possible.

"We might have a tail. I can't tell, since he seems pretty good if he is one. I hope Sadie's is safe."

Mason frowned slightly. "It might not be. But I bet that Franz, across the alley from Sadie's, is. We almost never go there, and they have an upstairs room that I have used once before."

"They do? Good job, Mason. I didn't even know that. Let's go in Sadie's and duck out the side door. The hostess let me do that once before."

"I wonder why you would have needed to use a side door." Mason said sarcastically.

Porter ignored him loftily.

In Sadie's Porter spoke softly to the hostess and slipped her a bill. He turned and gestured to Mason. They slipped through the coat room to a small unobtrusive door. It opened into an alley and they moved across to the other restaurant without trouble.

After they had been seated in the discreet upper floor and had ordered, Mason looked at his friend with extreme interest. "No, really, how did you find out about the side door?"

Porter laughed softly. "A few months ago, I was there by myself and some bloke came in asking for one of my aliases. I didn't think I wanted to see him, so I asked the hostess to help me out. She has a weakness for me since I always tip her well, so she showed me the side door."

"I bet she thinks you're hot."

Porter shook his head at Mason. "I doubt that, Mason. She is not my type."

Mason snorted. "Fuck that, man. She probably thinks you are hers. Anyway, I am not arguing with you. You don't notice how women look at you, which is half the fun of watching. Sienna isn't an isolated incident. Besides, I had a proposition today."

"Really? Was she cute?"

"Wrong proposition, idiot. A job."

Porter became briskly businesslike. "What is it?"

"I don't know; I haven't opened it yet. But, Porter, are you sure you want to hear it? Are you ready?"

"Let's see what it is and then you can help me decide. I promise to listen to you and what you think. Is that fair?"

"I think so." Mason pulled out the envelope and opened it. There was a small tape player and several pictures. He pressed play and set it on the table.

"Good afternoon, Mr. Briggs. The man at whom you are looking is named Emanuel Patos. He is currently living and operating out of Hong Kong, China. He is a high-end forger, especially of diamonds and jewelry. He copies authentic pieces and sells them at a slightly lower price to unscrupulous buyers who do not care that the pieces are not genuine.

"Recently, Patos has expanded into art and literature forgery. We think he has a sweatshop somewhere turning out false paintings and etchings. There has been an upswing in high-end forged masterpieces. None are of the most famous in the world, but several are of lesser masters, such as Rembrandt and Fra Angelico. There have also been, not coincidently, several daring and well-orchestrated robberies of these artists from museums. Patos is paying to have the items stolen so that he can copy and sell forgeries. We can't get him, and we can't prove this.

9

"Patos is a connoisseur of more than just beautiful things. He is also a collector of beautiful women. He is especially drawn to platinum blondes, and he is most attracted to those who resist him initially. Like a true hunter, he wants to stalk and trap his target, and the harder he has to work, the longer his attention is held and the more focused he becomes.

"Your mission, Mr. Briggs, is to get Emanuel Patos. You have to bring him, alone and without his security forces, to the embassy. That is not enough, however; your team must also provide irrefutable evidence of the operation we know exists but have no first-hand evidence of yet.

"Patos has been floating the money he has from these jobs for various political enterprises, including supporting regimes in some of the most unstable areas in the world. You and your team will have to work through an embedded agent in Patos' inner circle. She has been there for years and knows the enterprise better than any outsider we can find.

"Good luck, Mr. Briggs. Should you or any of your team be discovered, there will be no official acknowledgement of your existence. You have at your disposal five million dollars and a private jet. You know the channels to go through for both.

"Please destroy this tape when you are finished with it."

Mason pressed the "stop" button. Porter was looking intently at the blown-up detail of Emanuel Patos.

"I know him, at least by sight. He has been on the move in the jewelry world for a couple of years. He had some fence trying to sell me some inferior stuff in the store once and he was standing in the background."

"That must have been when his operation was smaller."

"Likely true. He won't remember. Besides, I can always look different. He won't know me."

Mason looked at the pictures as well. Patos was a handsome man. He had the soft look of someone who lives too well, though.

"You know what this means, right?"

Porter sighed. "Yes, it means that Sienna is going white-blonde.

I dislike her hair the most when it is that color."

Mason laughed. "That wasn't what I meant! The jet I have access to will only hold four people in addition to the crew. It is going to be a skeleton group."

"Oh. Well, if you are taking input..."

"Of course I am taking input. What do you think?"

Porter looked out the window for a minute or two. Finally, he looked back at Mason. "I think you should have Sienna, me, Michael, and that other girl for Michael. Plus, the women can help each other out if we get separated, which is my gut instinct."

Mason nodded slowly. "I like this idea. Let me think it through a bit. But, Porter, are you all right with this?"

Porter sighed. "I won't really know until I'm there, Mason. I know that is a cop-out answer, but it is true. I think I am okay, but I might not be. If you choose me, make sure there is some way to contact you that is both safe and secure so I can call you if this is too much."

Mason looked at him for a while in silence. Then he nodded. "All right. I will take that into consideration. I really appreciate that input, Porter. Give me a couple of days to get things arranged. I'll call you if I need you. Deal?"

Porter smiled slightly. "Deal." They shook across the table. "Now let's get this off the table before the food gets here. Did you order wine?"

"I think so."

"No, there is no 'think' on things this important. After that discussion, I need wine. Now go make sure you ordered some." Porter said firmly as he carefully put everything back in the envelope and stashed it in Mason's briefcase. He looked pointedly at Mason. "Haven't you left yet? The sooner we start with the wine, the better for both of us. And we can talk about nothing in particular for the rest of the time."

Mason laughed and got up to find the host.

Part I

Chapter 1

Michael wasn't feeling well the day Mason called him. He had been sick for a few days and he hadn't been able to do as much on his workouts as he had wanted. Now that he was over the sickness, he had pushed a little to regain his level. Then he had managed to get food poisoning the night before and that drained him.

Mentally, Michael was angry with the restaurant he had been at. His coworkers had also been sick. They had only gone to the restaurant to celebrate the end of the quarter at the tech company anyway. Michael didn't usually go out, especially not with coworkers, but it had been such a good quarter that they had rashly all gone in on the party. It had not been the typical team-building corporate exercise. It did give Michael an excellent excuse to take some time off work for whatever Mason wanted. Customer support was a good job; many of the customers were not terribly smart and when they saw Michael they often mistakenly thought he was more stupid than they. Michael took a malicious type of pleasure in disabusing them of that idea.

Mason would have good food and some good alcohol as well as several friends. Michael looked at the event for the evening as a haven in his life. If Porter and Juan were there, this would be even better. It was always better to hang out with people who understood him and didn't resent his obvious attributes.

Michael had always been muscular. He had entered weight-lifting competitions for several years and some in the sports shows had called him, rather grandiosely, the strongest man in the world. Michael knew that meant nothing as a title. It still sometimes cropped up and caused him some embarrassment. Michael had never been very comfortable in groups or social situations. He felt like an outsider, almost like he didn't ever understand the rules that the others were playing by. It made it awkward for him.

Porter, Juan, and Mason didn't care about his titles or trophies. They saw him as an equal and a friend. Michael hadn't had many of the first and fewer of the second. He always looked forward to parties at

Mason's house, even when they didn't involve an invitation to a side-job as a top-secret operative. Michael could really use a job to break the monotony right now.

When the evening arrived, Michael drove out to Mason's home. It was a nice house. The biggest room in the building was the kitchen. Mason often had parties where he and someone else made food for everyone else, sometimes even during the party itself. It was quite comfortable that way.

Porter and Sienna were already there. Michael was parking as they got to the front door, but they waited for him to get there before they rang. Michael liked that.

Sienna was one of those girls he had always been too shy to speak to. She smoothed it over by acting friendly without reservation, and it had helped him to feel comfortable. Now, he frequently found himself acting protective, much like a brother might.

Porter was an enigma. He always had been. The last mission they had been on together had brought about some startling and painful changes to him and as a result Michael had to confront some of his own prejudices. It had been difficult, but Michael found he relied on Porter's feel of a situation more than before. It was good to know someone had his back finally.

"Sienna, you are as beautiful as ever!" Michael smiled at the lovely woman as he gallantly bowed to her. She smiled at him with twinkling eyes. "And Porter, you are looking well." Michael shook Porter's hand.

"You, too, Michael. Although, forgive my observation, you look a bit out-of-sorts?"

"Got food poisoning the other day." Michael said shortly.

Porter winced in acknowledgement as Sienna rang the doorbell. "I hate food poisoning. It's the worst."

Michael nodded.

Mason swung the door open with a welcoming smile. "Welcome! Did you all car-pool up here? You should have brought Juan

16

too!"

Sienna laughed. "No, Mason, we just happened to meet up and decided to see if you wanted company."

"Oh. Well, yes, I did seem to make enough food for a large gathering. It is the oddest coincidence!"

Michael snorted. "Coincidence, my ass."

Porter nodded gravely. "I would not make any bets against your ass."

"Wise decision."

They all entered.

The house smelled like good food.

"Damn, Mason," Porter said as he removed his jacket and took Sienna's light coat, "What did you make? It smells positively delicious in here."

"I got a deal on some brisket that I just couldn't pass up."

"There's no chance it will be undercooked, right?" Porter asked suspiciously. Mason looked hurt. "No, it's cool, man. Just Michael here had a bout of bad food already. I thought I would make sure so that his delicate little tummy doesn't get hurt."

"Porter, I can take care of my own shit." Michael said firmly.

"Yes, I know, but I would rather take care of it before it becomes shit."

Mason and Sienna started laughing. Michael shook his head. He was trying to act indignant but Porter's outrageous statements were wearing his resolve down.

The doorbell saved him from having to pretend disgust. Sienna gently laid her hand on Michael's arm. "Would you escort me, Michael?"

"Of course!" He grinned over at Porter and winked. Porter faked a look of outrage and followed to the dining room area as Mason invited Juan in.

Juan was in high spirits which was no surprise to anyone. Juan was almost always in high spirits. He had an infectious optimism.

Michael especially liked Juan. They were good friends who understood each other well. Besides, Juan tended to be the energy of the party; that meant that everyone else followed his lead and kept up with his pace. In this group, it didn't matter as much, since they were all friends, but in other groups or with acquaintances it was much easier to relate when Juan was there to make everyone feel at east.

"Word, Mason!" Juan came in with his usual flair. "Who you got at this kickin' party, anyway?"

"Evening, Juan. I have invited the usual suspects, as it were."

"Awesome!" Juan and Mason came into the dining room. "Yes! This is going to be a kickin' party indeed! Mikey, my man! You looking good."

"Hello, Juan. I think you have been doing well, since you are more obnoxious than usual."

Juan shrugged easily. "I got to the next level in the down time at the IT department this morning. I am totally creaming Mitchell. He's only on level 50."

Michael laughed. "This explains why the calls kept going to the answering service then! Do you guys do any work at all?"

Juan grinned cheekily at him. "Not if we can help it, Mikey! You know it's only worth working if we can avoid actual work."

Porter laughed. "I have a similar attitude!"

"Of course you do. You never do anything by the book if you can wriggle around it."

"We all have our faults." Porter observed calmly.

Mason shook his head at them all. "How ever did I get into this mess with the likes of you?"

"Talent, Mason! You are just dripping with talent!" Juan responded with a straight face.

They all laughed and sat, chatting in a relaxed manner as Mason brought in the food. It was, of course, amazing.

"Mason, you are really getting good at this." Porter remarked as he cut into the brisket.

"Thanks, Porter. That's high praise coming from a chef like you."

"That's a low insult. You know I could never be a chef."

"Oh, I think you could be." Mason responded calmly, "But you might be miserable doing it."

"Same thing."

Sienna shook her head gently at Porter. "Let it go, my dear. You know it isn't worth it."

Porter saluted with his knife. "As my lady commands!"

Michael had the sense that there was something here, something that Porter was trying to work out within himself. Everyone in the room knew that Porter was in therapy; Michael believed it was one of the best things for Porter after their last joint mission had wrecked such havoc on them all. He had himself been in to see his own counselor. It made him come to terms with his own feelings and problems. Counseling never made the problems go away but it sure made the world more livable.

Porter was a little more volatile than he had been before. Michael knew he should pay attention to that, since it seemed like this might be another mission for them. He therefore watched Porter a little more closely.

No one else seemed overly concerned about it, and Michael wasn't going to embarrass his friend in front of other people. That wasn't something he approved of.

The dinner continued without incident. When Mason stood up formally at the end of dessert, they all grew quiet, except the irrepressible Juan who made a loud shushing noise that was totally unnecessary. There were some snorted laughs after that.

Mason smiled in acknowledgement. "Yes, Johnny boy, you are right. There is a business proposition to be discussed now. Would any interested parties please adjourn to my study for further discussion?"

"And further drinking?" Juan added, quickly.

Porter stood. "That was implied."

Michael laughed. "If it wasn't said outright, then it might not happen, Porter! You know Mason is stingy with his alcohol."

Porter smiled. "True, that."

They all walked to the study. Michael grabbed two chairs as he went, just to make sure there were enough. Porter helped him with one.

"Listen, muscles, just because you are buff beyond belief doesn't mean you have to show it off all the time." Porter admonished. "It's okay to ask for help still."

"You should talk," Michael retorted. "When do you ask for help? Like never."

Porter didn't smile right away. It was too close.

Michael immediately regretted it. "Sorry, man. I didn't mean to put you on the spot like that."

Porter sighed. "I know you didn't, Michael. It just happens to be true."

No one else had heard the exchange; they were all in the study.

Michael put his hand on Porter's shoulder. "Really, man, I want you to feel comfortable asking for help if you need it. I am always here for you. Always."

Porter smiled at Michael. He reached over and tousled Michael's hair playfully. "I know it, and I appreciate it beyond what I can say. I promise to ask for help more often. Now, are we going in or are we going to have a male-bonding moment out here?"

Michael laughed. "Can't we do both?"

Porter also laughed. "Sure! Let's do it!"

Mason was looking towards the door questioningly. When they came in he nodded in a knowing sort of way and glanced back at his notes. Michael thought he might be giving Porter time to adjust himself.

They all sat and made themselves comfortable. Porter sat nearer Sienna and Michael sat in the middle of the room. Juan was to his left. He leaned over with a huge grin.

20

"Hey, Mikey boy, what you wanna bet we going all eastern? I just got feeling this is farther there than here."

Michael shrugged. "Whatever Juan, I don't care where we go."

Juan snickered. "No, you stand out no matter where. I would love to see you in a Mandarin jacket though, with little pink flowers all over it…"

Michael looked at Juan for a second. "You fucking asking for trouble, boy?"

Porter laughed softly. "Of course he is. Juan lives on the edge."

"He's gonna be on the edge all right. Especially if he keeps this shit up."

Juan shrugged airily. "Life ain't fun if it ain't lived, Mikey!"

Mason smiled. "Are you finished?"

Michael smiled back. "I am. I can arrange for Juan to be finished, should that be a problem." He looked at Juan with a raised eyebrow. "Want to be annoying, Johnny? I will throw you in a headlock faster than you can blink."

Juan backed away. "No, thanks, Mikey. The last one you put me in gave me a fucking neck cramp for two fucking days."

"Then shut the hell up."

"Sir, yes, sir!" Juan threw a mock salute and shut his lips with an exaggerated gesture.

Michael grinned at him. "Thank you, sir!"

Mason inclined his head at them both. "Thank you both. Now, this is, in fact, an Eastern assignment." Juan wriggled in his seat. He was always excited to be right. "It is Hong Kong."

"Yes!" Juan shouted, then immediately sat down again and was quiet.

Mason nodded. He handed around the pictures he had received in the envelope earlier in the week. "This is Emanuel Patos. He is who we need."

"Uh, doesn't 'patos' mean 'duck' in Spanish?" Juan asked.

Mason shrugged. "I don't know, but it doesn't matter. You

know that names are as easy to assume and discard as a coat. He has probably changed his several times."

Juan nodded. "It just seemed odd is all. Continue."

Mason nodded again. "Anyone fancy a drink before we get started on the details?" He gestured to a tastefully laid set of crystal glasses on the side board. The glass-fronted cupboard above held an assortment of alcohols.

Juan stood up. "Michael? I can pour you a scotch." He offered as he went to the side.

"Thanks, Juan. Maybe half."

"Porter?"

Porter seemed to hesitate. That was a new thing, since Porter usually drank at any occasion. "Uh, maybe just half a scotch for me. I have been trying to cut back."

Juan looked at Porter very hard. There was no hint of his usual humor when he asked, "Why, Porter? I wouldn't ask this if I didn't think we need to know, you know."

Porter nodded soberly. "I know, Juan. The thing is... Well, let's see. After the last time, and with Cinna and all that went there, I have been trying to accept the person I am more. I know I have been difficult to be around. I appreciate all your being patient with me. I have been a fucking idiot and I am trying to accept that. One thing I am trying to do less of is get drunk, since that's just an escape for me. Of course, that means you all might have to remind me of that, because frankly it is one of the suckiest promises I have made yet. That explain it, Johnny? You need any more?" Even though he said the last bit with a smile and a light tone, it was obvious to Michael that this was a sensitive subject.

Fortunately, Juan seemed to notice as well, or perhaps he had no other questions, and he shook his head. He carefully poured out the drinks, then he handed one to Porter. Before he let go, he looked straight into Porter's eyes. "Porter, I respect you a lot, man, but I am not trying to fuck you over. Please don't fucking bite my head off? You're my friend. I ask hard shit of my friends." Then he let go of the glass and brought Michael's over as if nothing had happened.

"Sienna, my lovely, may I pour you something?" Juan asked lightly. He did not mention anything in regards to how Porter's hands were shaking so much he almost spilled the drink.

Sienna had an unreadable expression. "Why, thank you, Juan. I would appreciate some scotch as well."

"Of course, beautiful lady!" Juan poured and looked at Mason questioningly. "Mason?"

"No, thanks, Juan."

"Your loss, man." Juan shrugged and put the bottle away. He handed Sienna her glass and took his own back to his chair.

Mason glanced at Porter, who seemed receptive, even though Michael noticed that he was still rigid. Sienna calmly reached over and put her hand on his leg. Michael looked away quickly.

Mason flipped through his notes again. "Okay, let's get this figured out. First off, only four are going to Hong Kong. Juan, you and I are staying here to monitor and provide support."

Juan looked a bit downcast. "Ah, fuck. I wanted to go."

"I know. I did, too. The thing is we have a private jet that only sits four. There are going to be two couples going. Porter and Sienna, you are an acting couple. Michael, you are going to have a love-interest named Beatrice. She is already an insider with Patos' group. You'll meet her in New York at the annual diamond gala. Porter, I believe that you have an open invitation to that very exclusive event?"

Porter nodded. "Yes, I do. I hardly ever go. I am not as interested in diamond sellers as I am stones. I care less who they come from. I do have some contacts there though, and they always invite me. I can send several 'representatives' to it."

"The reason I asked Porter about that is because Patos has not left behind his own jewelry initial excursions into forgery. He has fenced gems in false settings that look like the real thing before. The diamonds and gold are real, but they are modern fakes, not the older models he purports them to be. He still keeps tabs on the markets for that. He has recently branched into forgery of art and literature, and he has allegedly masterminded or been involved with several art robberies. He then copies the stolen pieces and puts the copies on the market."

Michael had raised his hand. Mason looked at him. "Mason, who is this Beatrice? I gotta know before I can act appropriately."

Porter nodded. "Same, Mason. I don't like surprises."

"She is an agent for the NSA. She has been embedded in the Hong Kong department for five years now. Here's her picture and bio." He passed a picture and sheet to Juan.

"Why the fuck you giving it to me?" Juan protested even as he looked at the picture and read the short bio sheet.

"Because, Juan, you are the fucking key to keeping everything running. You need all the information too."

"Yeah, okay." Juan frowned at the bio sheet. "She's pretty enough, but this thing says that she's only had two assignments. How did she get pulled for this high-level operation?"

Mason shrugged. "I don't know, but that's who we have to use this time. It was a stipulation from the higher-ups. She is supposed to be good and discreet. If she isn't or she fails, I fully expect my team to operate independently and in concert. This is a unique situation and I have no intention of trusting this woman completely." He looked very seriously at them all. "We have to use her, but we do *not* trust her. Is that clear?"

Sienna nodded gravely. "Yes, Mason. She is an unknown and should be treated that way."

"Exactly. I will have a disposable phone and number that any of you should use to contact me. It will need to be an emergency to use; I can't guarantee safety there."

"We understand, Mason." Michael said softly. "I can tell that you are not happy with this setup. That gives me an indication of the level of trust you have put on us. We'll try our hardest to stay safe there."

Mason nodded. "Thank you. I do not want to lose friends."

Michael looked at the picture. It was a pretty woman with somewhat unnatural-looking blonde hair and dark eyes. She had a roundish face. The bio listed her first assignment within the Pentagon and then her current assignment in Hong Kong. He passed them to Porter and looked at Mason. "What are we supposed to do, then?"

"You need to get Patos alone, without his entourage, to the embassy along with proof of his involvement in the forgery ring at whatever level he is involved. And if possible, within a week. The longer it takes, the worse it will be."

Michael was a little surprised. "That's a hell of an order, Mason."

"I know, and it gets worse. I have learned that Patos keeps the women he is interested away from his other interests. That means that the two groups are going to be operating individually. You will be allowed to communicate, since it would be hostile to keep you from that and he wants to cultivate a veneer of civility, but you will be apart physically quite a bit. He also goes for platinum blondes, especially dyed ones."

Porter sighed and covered his face. "There is absolutely no accounting for taste, is there?"

Sienna smiled but tried to hide it. "I will get it lightened. It will take two or three visits to get it that blonde."

Porter groaned from behind his hands. "Two or three visits too many! I don't like you as a blonde."

"Well, you will just have to pretend you do. We are, after all, supposed to be a couple."

Porter looked up at her sharply. "We *are* a couple, Sienna."

Sienna looked startled. Then she blushed and looked down. Porter seemed a little confused, but he did not recant.

No one spoke for a moment. One of the trademarks of this group of friends was that they let some things work out in silence. Finally, Sienna looked back at Porter. She took his hand. "Are you serious, my dear? Really serious this time?"

25

Porter looked haunted. The moment stretched between them. He nodded once, and two tears ran down his face. "I hope so, Sienna." He said gently.

Sienna's eyes widened, then she blushed again.

"Yes!" Juan yelled again.

Michael laughed and reached over and roughly grasped Porter's shoulder. "You lucky fuck!" He said delightedly. Mason also was laughing. It was turning into one of the best nights.

When they had all calmed down, Michael looked at Sienna and then at Porter. "You are a lucky bastard; she's even more beautiful now than she was before."

Sienna blushed deeply, but Porter nodded gravely. "I am the luckiest bastard ever, Michael." Then he smiled and Michael knew that he wasn't upset. "I still wish she didn't have to go blonde though."

"Agreed." Michael didn't like dye jobs himself. Maybe that's what was throwing him sour on this Beatrice. He looked back at Mason. "Is there anything else we should discuss before the serious congratulatory drinking starts?"

Mason laughed. "Let me look!" He quickly ran his eye down the paper on his desk. "Michael, you and Porter are going to be some jewelers. You are going to be interested in fencing some of his creations. You are looking to make sure he can keep up your standards. He is going to keep you around because of that, and for the forbidden jewel that Porter just claimed." Mason smiled at Sienna but quickly grew serious. "Sienna, he has personally killed at least three of his conquests. You must be careful. You will be essentially alone, and this is dangerous. Michael and Porter will kill many people if he hurts you. You may not have much chance to talk to them without being overheard. You must keep the true man in front of your mind. You are seducing a very dangerous man who has no scruples. None."

Sienna had gone pale, but she nodded. "I will keep myself safe, Mason."

"I know you will. I want us all to be very clear on this guy."

26

Michael felt a sudden clenching in his stomach. He was the type of man who was a defender. He had been Sienna's defender on a number of missions. Now she was going to be unreachable. It was a stressful thought. He looked at Porter and saw that he also looked upset. They were going to have to keep each other strong in this one. Porter looked at him and Michael nodded to his silent question.

Porter looked more sure and determined after that.

Mason continued. "I want you, Porter, and you, Michael, to also change your hair. It will make your women look blonder if you are darker, Michael. Go dark brunette or black. Porter, grow yours out a bit and let it curl more. You are supposed to be a little bit of a wild spirit. Kind of like Juan's."

Porter looked at Juan's shaggy mane in mock horror. Juan rolled his eyes.

"Clothes?" Michael asked.

"I will have them made. Get measured at Cynthia's Cuts. She has an order in already, but she needs you all to get measured. Anything else?" Mason looked around. No one seemed to have any more questions.

"All right. Then we're done here. Who wants to play cards?"

"Whooo!" Juan practically catapulted out of his chair.

Porter held up one hand as Michael and Mason both moved towards the door. "One moment, gentlemen, please." He stood, then knelt in front of Sienna and held a shaky hand out to her. "Sienna, my dearest love, will you marry me?" He put his left hand into his pocket and gently put a ring in her hand.

Sienna gave a little scream, covered her mouth with her hand, blushed, and then started crying. "Of course I will! Oh my God! Yes!" She threw her arms around Porter and kissed him full on the mouth. None of them had ever seen her that unguarded before. Michael felt a little choked up, himself. His eyes misted up and he rushed to congratulate the couple.

Mason, Juan and Michael crowded around them and cheered.

It was most definitely a great day.

"May I see this ring to make sure it meets our expectations?" Mason grinned at Sienna. She proudly held out her left hand. The ring had a diamond, of course. It wasn't a huge diamond and the gold and platinum band delicately swirled like a fairy mist. Porter had obviously labored over it for a long time.

"Porter, you are a fucking genius!" Michael marveled as he examined the ring. "This must have taken forever."

"Uh, I suppose so. I don't really pay attention to shit like that."

Juan was also looking it over. "Damn, man! If I ever get married, would you make my rings for me?"

"Juan, you don't even have to ask that. I would be honored." Porter said simply.

Mason grinned at Porter. "Is this an extension of those talks we had about getting anchored?"

"Of course, Mason. It hasn't changed, you know."

"No, I suppose not."

"You still need someone."

Mason rolled his eyes and sighed.

Sienna smiled at them both but didn't say anything.

Michael cleared his throat. "Who is up for some poker?"

Chapter 2

Michael took a leave of absence. It wasn't too hard to arrange, since there were always several contractors around who wanted the work. There were even some entry level kids who didn't mind the experience. Personally, Michael had no problem handing the job over to them. They could have it if they wanted. He didn't have to work at all. He just hated to have down time. He was geared to act, not sit.

He had no idea where to get his hair done. That was a problem. He contemplated many ways to get an answer to his question, and he finally went into The Diamond Nest and asked Sienna, his face beet-red. She had already been in to get her hair lightened once in the two weeks since the meeting; she'd have a good recommendation. Porter held his poker face firmly in place. Michael appreciated that.

Sienna had been beautiful before; she was radiant now. There was no other way to describe it. She positively glowed. As she went to get a business card for her own stylist, Michael watched her a bit wistfully.

"You are the luckiest fuck I have ever seen." He said to Porter.

Porter also looked after Sienna. He looked at Michael again. There was a deep understanding in his eyes. "Michael, you are getting close to the edge yourself. You know what I am talking about. You're almost there. You are going to go over sooner or later without an anchor. For some people, it is friendships, but you have always been a bit of an outsider. I don't mean to tell you what to do, man, but I feel you slipping away. Everybody keeps looking out for me. I really like that and appreciate it, but it means we are forgetting to look out for you." Porter reached across the jewelry case and put his hand on Michael's shoulder. "It took me losing one beautiful woman to realize what I had. It almost tore me apart. It hasn't been a long time since I held a gun to my head. We're not the contemplative type. We need to act, to fight, to do something. But without someone to do it for, we're just spinning wheels. It took me many years to figure that out. Don't do what I did."

29

Michael nodded dumbly. He hadn't realized how close Porter had been to suicide and he was fairly sure no one else knew it, either. The things Porter was saying were far closer to the truth than he had expected.

"So, Porter, why didn't you pull the trigger?" It seemed really important to know.

Porter glanced around to see that Sienna wasn't back yet. "I don't really know, Michael. I felt like I was the weakest, most disgusting, despicable thing because I couldn't do it. But then it was like I heard *her* voice again, and she laughed at me and told me that I was beautiful and I needed to live... and... ah, fuck." He wiped his eyes quickly. "Damn it, I didn't really want to be crying at work today."

"Sorry, man, I shouldn't have asked."

"Michael," Porter said with surprising dignity, "Not everything is your fault. The fact that I cannot hold my fucking shit together is not something you need to fucking feel bad about. Now look, we are going to be together for a while in the upcoming weeks. Quit fucking apologizing for all the shit that isn't your fault and I will try to not lose my shit every three seconds. Understand?"

"Yeah, man." Michael mumbled.

Porter sighed. "Look, Michael, you've been the outsider for a long time. I don't mean to pick on you. Here's the thing: I can usually fuck myself over pretty well. You are not the reason that I am the way I am, and while I appreciate the fact that you feel for me, I do not want to diminish your feelings by taking them and not reciprocating. You asked a question, I should be able to answer and you should not feel embarrassed because I have to pause, okay? I will get it together, eventually. If I can't, then it's still my shit to be worked through, got it?"

Michael nodded. He was embarrassed. Porter seemed to read him right through.

There was a small silence. Porter cleared his throat. "Anyway, who the hell knows why I didn't pull the trigger? I had a talk with Father Greg down at St Thomas' and he took the gun away. He said he would get rid of it for me. I still have knives, but well, you know that. I can trust myself with those."

"Good. Because I have a feeling you will need them."

"Me, too. Don't tell Sienna though. She is already a little stressed about this."

"No, I won't. Not until there is something solid to base it on."

Porter nodded. Sienna came back with the business card. Her face was blandly expressionless. "Here you are, Michael. She does a good, quick job." She looked at Porter then. "Are you finished with the heavy conversation and have you assured each other that I will be all right now?"

Porter smiled gently at her. "Yes, my dear, I think we are done making our man-pact to rip off any arms that get in your way."

Michael grinned. "And feed them to the owner. Don't forget that part."

Sienna gave a mock shudder. "You gentlemen and your brutal side!"

"It's for your own good, Sienna."

"Whatever, Michael, just go." She smiled at him then. "You are a very good man, you know."

That phrase jolted through him. It seemed that he was back in Tergistan and it was someone else saying it. Somehow, he could not argue.

Porter reached across the case again and shook his hand with an understanding look. "I know. Every once in a while, it happens. It almost kills me every time."

Sienna looked between them curiously. "What, my dear?"

Porter smiled at her again. "You being yourself. It is sometimes hard for us to reconcile, since you speak the truth to us and we have trouble believing it."

"Well, he is a good man. So are you."

"Perhaps." Porter said. "It is hard to accept, sometimes. Good bye, Michael. I'll see you again soon."

Michael kissed Sienna's hand and waved to Porter. When he stepped out onto the sidewalk, he looked at the business card and noticed his hands were trembling. What the fucking hell was wrong with him?

Michael called the stylist from the park down the street from Porter's store.

"Stylist Corner Salon, Stacey speaking." The young woman on the other line answered professionally.

"Yes, Stacey, my name is Michael. I was recommended your place by a friend?"

"May I ask who recommended us, sir?"

"Her name is Sienna."

"Oh, yes, Sienna. She has an appointment later today. She usually sees Emma. Would you like to see her, too?"

"Yes, please. Do you have an opening today?"

"That depends. What do you need as a service?"

"Well, I would like a dye job, if you have a time open."

There was a pause as the secretary checked her schedule. "Let me see. She has a dye slot open in about fifteen minutes. One of her regulars cancelled. Will that work for you?"

"Absolutely, thank you very much."

"We'll see you then, sir!"

Michael noted the address and got into his car. It would take about fifteen minutes to get there, unless the traffic was bad. He started driving. Sienna's comment was still shaking him up.

Parking was surprisingly easy to find outside the salon. Michael pulled into a two hour slot and hoped it wouldn't take nearly that long to get his hair dyed. He already dreaded this part.

The door binged pleasantly as he walked in. There were plants attractively arranged around the client seating area and displays of beauty products available for purchase. The smell of chemicals was bitter but not overwhelming. Music played softly in the background. It wasn't the usual slow jazz but contemporary hits. Michael liked that, for some reason.

The secretary had looked up when the bell sounded. She smiled at him. "Yes, sir?"

"My name is Michael."

"Oh, yes! Let me get Emma for you. She is available right now to take you." She turned her head and raised her voice slightly. "Emma?"

Another young woman with red curly hair came out from the back area. She smiled at Michael. "Oh, you must be Sienna's friend." She raised one eyebrow. "I didn't realize she had such attractive friends! Maybe I need to ask her to send me more of you!"

Michael blushed. Emma laughed gently. "I am only teasing. Well, only a little. You are quite attractive, you know. Anyway." She turned professional and motioned for him to follow her. "We'll be in the room to the right. The left is for facials and all that jazz."

Michael was glad when they got to the other room. There were four chairs and cutting stations arranged with a minimum screening of plants between them. It made the area feel more private and comfortable than the standard barber shop. Emma led him to the farthest chair and got him seated.

"Now, what are we doing to your hair today?" She asked, carefully running her fingers through it to get a feel for it.

"I need it a shade or two darker, please. But I want it to look natural. I don't like dye jobs. Uh, not usually." He really hoped he hadn't just offended his stylist. She didn't seem to mind.

"Hmm. Well, I think we can do two shades without it being obvious. I am the master of that, as Sienna can probably attest."

"Yes, she always looks good."

"That's God's own truth." Emma laughed. "You have very nice hair. I think this is going to be a fun job!"

"Thank you." Michael said shyly. He wasn't good with girls, especially not girls who complimented him.

Emma spun his chair and considered his hair for a moment or

two. "You know, this might not be my business to say, but usually Sienna wants a complete change; hair color, cut, all of it. She usually lets us do a promo shot or two of her when we are done. Free modeling and all. Now, I am not trying to convince you to be a model for us, but I am guessing that you also want to look different than what you do now. Am I right?"

Michael nodded.

Emma smiled in a satisfied sort of way. "I thought so. Would you object to a cut, just to make it a bit different?"

Michael thought about that. He knew Porter was supposed to be a bit of a free spirit. If he were in the same group, he would have to be one, too, logically. People tend to work with people like themselves. "Okay, I think that I can agree to that. Can you do something that is popular with the college-age crowd? I know my hair isn't real long."

Emma waved that aside. "It will be no problem, gorgeous! And if it turns out well, maybe you will take off your shirt and pose for us. Is that a deal?"

Michael blushed furiously. "Well, uh, if that is what you want, I guess."

Emma looked at him curiously. "Honey, I think every woman in this town would want that from you. Probably some men, too."

She spun him back to face the mirror and put a plastic cape on him. She was humming to herself in time with the music. "I don't have any other clients today until Sienna gets here. Would you mind if I turn up the music? I like to rock out."

"No. You do what makes you happy."

"I am definitely asking Sienna to get all her friends to come here!" Emma turned up the volume a little more and went to get her dyes.

She washed Michael's hair first. Then she carefully dyed it. It seemed like it took a long time, but then the last time he'd had it done the girl had made him look terrible so Michael wasn't complaining.

"Okay, this has to set for at least half an hour. I'll check it then, and we will decide for longer or not." Emma checked her watch. "Sienna is due here in a few minutes. I will have you both in here at the same time. That won't bother you, will it?"

"No, not at all. It's your shop; you do what you need to."

"Sugar, you are about the best thing that has happened to this place in a long time." Emma went to ready another station. Michael wasn't sure if Emma was always this outgoing or if she was being genuine. It didn't much matter, he decided.

"Emma!" Stacey called from the front. "Sienna's here!"

"You all right?" Emma asked Michael. "I will be right back. Will you need anything? Water? Beer?"

"You have beer here?" Michael was a little surprised.

"Of course, honey. We want men to be just as comfortable as women. Ale, regular, what?"

"Do you have any stout?"

Emma smiled at him. "I knew it would pay off! Yes, I scored some Brooklyn Brewery Black Ops this year."

Michael was surprised. "You did? I would love one!"

"Coming right up, sugar!"

Emma was back quickly with Sienna and a bottle of the special stout. Sienna smiled at Michael in greeting.

Emma handed the bottle to Michael and said to Sienna, "You absolutely must send all your friends here if they are half as charming and hot as this one."

Michael blushed again. This was getting to be a habit. Sienna laughed. "Oh, Emma, you are outrageous! You should know that all my friends are hot and charming!"

Emma nodded. "Oh, I kind of had an inkling that way. Anyway, for reals, girl, thanks for sending him here. I appreciate it."

Sienna shrugged. "You're the best. Why would I send him anywhere else?"

"True. Thanks all the same. And now, you are at station two and you said you want to lighten, eventually to platinum? Why, you going all Playboy Bunny on me?"

"No, I am quite happy where I am, but that is definitely the level of blonde I want."

Emma spun Sienna around and considered her hair with the same scrutiny as she had Michael's. "Yeah, we can do that. It is going to take at least two more visits though. I know your hair accepts bleach pretty well, but sometimes going that light can give hair an initial greenish sheen. We don't want that. I think some honey lowlights will add some subtle warmth and depth too. You cool with that?"

Sienna smiled and nodded. "You are the master, woman! Do what you do! Work your magic!"

"That's what I like to hear!" Emma spun Sienna back, then she seemed to think of something. "You know, you have done some promos for us before. I was wondering something. If it would be possible, could I get a shot or two of the both of you when you are done here today? It'll be just a quick shot, nothing too hard."

Sienna looked at Michael. "Well, Michael? It is up to you. I have no problem modeling, as you know."

"Because you are a fucking pro." Michael sighed. "Okay, I will do it if you help me out. I don't have a clue what to do."

Emma grinned at him. "You are going to be *perfect*!"

Michael watched as she quickly got Sienna's hair started bleaching. It smelled a bit stronger than what she had put in his hair. Michael had to admit that, while he didn't like having his hair messed with, Emma at least made it the most bearable of anyone he had been to yet. He rather thought he would be coming back here sometime.

She came back over to him. "All right, sugar, let's see what this looks like." She unwrapped his hair and looked at it critically. "Hmm. What do you think?" She handed him a mirror. Michael looked at his hair.

"Uh, whatever you think. I don't really have an opinion."

Emma smiled. "Okay, I just don't want you upset by it is all."

"No, it's fine."

"Then I think we will wash the dye out and do a quick cut. Come on over to the sink for me."

Emma was very good at cutting. She didn't hesitate or pause and she was done in a very short time.

Then she dried his hair and Michael looked at himself in the mirror. His hair was much darker, but there were some hints of red or other colors in there, too. It looked natural. She had given him an uneven razor cut, and it looked good enough. He wasn't much of a judge.

"It looks really good. Thanks."

Emma spun him and said, "Sienna, what do you think?"

Sienna considered him gravely. "Yes, that looks amazing. You are truly the best there is, Emma. You have got it exactly right."

Emma smiled. "Aw, thanks, Sienna. I think this is one of my better jobs." She looked at Michael again. "Yes, I like this one a lot. If you are serious about modeling, honey, you'll have to wait for about another half an hour until Sienna is done."

Michael shrugged. "I have nothing to do today. I can wait."

"Awesome!" Emma looked at his hair one more time. "Yes, definitely one of the best."

Emma was done with Sienna within the half hour. Sienna wasn't white blonde yet, but she was at least honey blonde and had an asymmetrical cut that was longer at the front. There was probably some name for it that Michael didn't know. It didn't look bad on her, but then, she didn't look bad anytime. Michael still liked her natural color best.

Emma called Stacey, the secretary, in. "Stace, these two are going to do a promo or two for us. Would you grab Manuel from the other room real quick?"

Stacey nodded. "Of course!" She looked at Sienna and Michael appraisingly. "Honestly, Emma, you get better every time. Those are some of your best work yet!"

"I thought so, too."

Manuel came in. He considered the two of them for a few minutes. "Okay, let's shoot it in the dark facial room. It has a nice industrial feel to it. Besides, the flash will work best in there." He considered them a few seconds longer. "Are you as stacked as you look?" He asked Michael.

Michael flushed. Sienna stepped in. "Yes, he is. I can vouch for that."

"Fabulous. Would you be averse to taking off your shirt, yes?"

Michael sighed softly. "No, I suppose not."

"Okay, so here is what I want. Sienna, you have experience in this. I want you to stand holding each other. Sienna, I want you to full-on seduce the camera. Michael, you just stand there looking muscular and beautiful. The feel is that this beautiful woman has just got this beautiful man and is looking around for her next one. We can do this, yes?"

They both nodded. Michael was getting much more nervous.

"To the room!" Manuel led the way, with Emma and Stacy following.

Sienna walked beside Michael. "Don't worry, Michael." She said calmly. "It doesn't really hurt to model."

"I know, Sienna. I am just not used to it is all."

"Michael, you have one of the most beautiful bodies I have ever seen. You should learn to be comfortable with who you are."

Michael didn't respond to that. This was a situation he had never been in before. No one had ever wanted him to model anything.

Manuel positioned Michael, and then he asked him to take off his shirt. "No comments, please." Michael said and took it off.

"Oh. My. God." Stacey whispered, staring.

"This is the best day of work. Ever." Emma breathed.

Michael wished they would leave.

Manuel nodded critically. "Yes, very beautiful. Love it. You are beautiful. You should do this for a living."

Michael shook his head. "No way."

38

"Too bad. Okay. Sienna, do you have an undershirt or something on under that?"

Sienna glanced down at her professional attire. "No, but it won't much matter. I have a sleeveless on. This is 'Illusion'."

"Great. You know what to do." Manuel frowned slightly. "We are gonna need a box or something to get you up higher. Emma, do we still have that old stool?"

"Yep. Cupboard to the right on the bottom."

Manuel put the box in front of Michael. "Stand on this, Sienna. Michael, put your gorgeous arms around her waist. Little lower. Yes, perfect. Sienna, make this camera want you, Baby!"

Michael was terribly uncomfortable holding one of his best friends' fiancé. He was sorry he had agreed to do this.

"And, one! And one more! Perfect! Thanks so much!" Manuel took two or three pictures rapidly, the flash blinding Michael.

As Michael pulled his shirt back on, Manuel stepped over to him. "Look, man, I know you are not comfortable with it right now, but you could do modeling on the side of whatever you are doing now and make some seriously good money. You have a natural body, and that is pretty rare in the field these days. I won't say anymore, but if you feel like it, give me a call. Me and Emma, we fix you up right."

"Thanks, Manuel. I will think about it." In about a million years.

Sienna laid her hand lightly on Michael's arm. "Would you join Porter and me for dinner, Michael? Just the three of us?"

"Of course. I have no plans."

She smiled at him. "Porter is in the waiting area. Shall we go?"

Chapter 3

When they got to the waiting area, Porter stood up to greet them. Manuel had followed them to look at his pictures in better light. He stared at Porter. He turned back to Sienna. "Girl, *that's* your man?!"

Sienna smiled and nodded.

Manuel looked between Porter and Michael. "You have all the luck, girl! All this gorgeous manliness in one room...! And you just drip sexuality! So hot. Someday, I am going to get all of you in one sitting. That will be the best picture of my career."

Porter smiled a half-smile at Michael. "I assume there is a story here. I will wait for it."

Michael winced. He was regretting this whole thing.

Manuel walked over and showed the pictures to Porter, who nodded appreciatively. "Very good. I like the feel you have." Porter was an artist and he knew what artists consider complimentary. Manuel smiled widely in appreciation.

While Sienna paid, Porter looked at Michael with one eyebrow raised and a twinkle in his eyes. Michael was fairly sure he was trying not to laugh at him. He flushed a little. This had been a horrible day for him on that front.

He hurried to pay. Stacey gave him a slip of paper with the amount on it. It was blank.

Michael looked up. "There must be a mistake. There isn't a price here."

Emma smiled at him. "Honey, we don't charge our models. Even if we did, all your hotness deserves to be paid for, not charged."

"Oh." Michael left a large tip then and turned to go.

"Just remember what I said." Manuel said as they left.

"God but that was awful!" Michael announced when they were outside the salon. "Please do not ever let me fucking do that again!"

Sienna looked at him seriously. "Michael, my dear, I wasn't lying when I said that you have a beautiful body. You don't see what other people do. You only see the problems you have. Well, I can tell

40

you that no one sees those things. No one."

"Sienna, I am not saying you are lying, but come on. I have scars everywhere and bruises from lifting and working out. They aren't gonna wanna see that shit."

Porter smiled at them both. "He isn't ready for it, Sienna. Please just let it rest for now."

She made a face at him. "Since when are you the expert?"

"I'm not, but trust me, he isn't ready."

"Very well." She sighed. She looked earnestly up at Michael. "I really wish I could make you see what I see when I look at you. Both of you." She added, looking at Porter, too. "Neither of you knows what you have. It is an endearing trait, I suppose, but it is also misleading."

"Possibly." Porter said smoothly. "Now, I would like to change the subject. Is there some reason we are all walking together right now?"

Sienna laughed at him. "Yes, my dear, I invited Michael to come to dinner with us." Michael had a distinct feeling that Sienna was not happy about having the subject changed.

"Oh. What are we doing for dinner, Michael?"

Michael was still embarrassed from the whole salon experience. "I don't give a flying fuck." He growled.

"Now, now, there is no need to be surly. How about pizza and beer? I like that combo on days when I feel a bit shitty on the world."

"Yeah, that sounds good. Where at?"

"Hmmm." Porter considered for a moment. "Would All American be acceptable?"

"Isn't that the college haunt?"

Porter shrugged. "I don't know. Nor do I care. They have good pizza and a variety of beer."

"It works for me, Porter." Sienna said. "I did have to get sharp with one of the waitresses there, though. She was getting handsy. Pissed me off. I don't do that shit."

Michael stared at her for a second. "You're serious?"

"Yes, my dear, I am afraid so. Women are sometimes even more obnoxious than men, especially when they are tipsy."

"You had a tipsy waitress who hit on you?"

"Yes. I spoke quite firmly to the management about that."

Porter smiled slightly. "I bet he didn't hear a word you said."

Sienna sighed. "I know. It is hard to take attractive women seriously, I think. We must be too fucking stupid to understand anything, the way people act."

"Well, you will have Michael and me there to fend off any and all comers."

"Good. Maybe I will do a saucy little table dance, just to give you something to do."

"God, no! Don't tempt me like that, Sienna!" Porter was half joking. Only half, though.

"Same here, Sienna. Please don't do it. I still remember the one you did." Michael begged.

"I won't. It is good to know the power I have though. It is a nice feeling, somehow."

"You are an evil, evil woman." Porter accused.

"Yes, I know. And you love me." She replied calmly.

Porter looked at her helplessly. "With all my being." He said simply.

Sienna blushed slightly and didn't respond.

Michael realized that he had never heard Porter say anything quite like that to Sienna before. It must be painful for him to be so open.

All American Pizza was a happening place. There were quite a few customers milling about. The tables weren't all full though, and the bar had some empty stools. They opted for a side booth after Porter noted that the tables were probably not big enough for both himself and Michael together.

As they made their way to the booth, Sienna's face grew stiff and disapproving. "She's there still."

Porter turned casually and looked at the young woman weaving through the people on the dance floor with drinks in her hands. Michael looked, too. Then they exchanged a glance and nodded. Sienna was going to not worry about being harassed tonight.

"This crowd is noisy." Michael observed as they sat down.

"Friday nights are like that." Porter said wisely. "Who wants something to start with?"

"What's good?"

"The IPA is palatable. I prefer the wheat beer, though."

"I already had Black Ops stout at the salon. I think I will go with the IPA."

"Really? They had a Black Ops?" Porter was impressed. "Hmm, maybe I need to look into this modeling thing more..."

"Trust me, man, you don't wanna go there."

Porter looked at him for a full minute. He didn't say anything, but he seemed to understand something that Michael did not.

Their waitress came to the table for their order. It was not the same one as Sienna had trouble with. Porter ordered two specialty pizzas and they each ordered a drink.

Sienna looked around. "I used to go to places like this all the time. I like dancing. But then I had to stop."

Michael found that curious. "Uh, why would you stop doing something you like?"

Sienna smiled at him. "I got tired of fending off people, Michael. I am not very big, and it just got to be too much."

"Perhaps we can help you with that tonight." Porter said. He looked at Michael. "Have you been in for measurements yet?"

"Yes. It was as bad as the salon. I can't be that unique, but these ladies keep making comments and stuff. It was uncomfortable in the extreme. She said I could come back after the weekend for the clothes."

Porter nodded. "Same here. On the time frame, that is. I didn't pay attention to the other stuff."

Sienna shook her head in mock despair at the two of them. "You two! You're driving me crazy! Anyway, I have to go to the bathroom. Will you excuse me?"

"Of course."

She stood and walked into the crowd.

Porter leaned over towards Michael. "Are you sure you are okay? You seem a little touchy today."

"I think I am just nervous about this upcoming mission. At least, I hope that is what it is."

"I hope so, too, but I don't think it is. You seem very unsure of yourself, for some reason. It isn't like you. Or, actually, maybe it is like you. Maybe that is why you always take big risks in fights and shit like that. Maybe you have to prove something to yourself."

"Fuck, man. What the hell?" Michael was a bit irritated and he wasn't sure why.

Porter was still looking him right in the eye. "If it isn't true, then why are you so fucking upset with me right now?"

Michael couldn't answer that. Finally he said, "What the hell you want me to say, Porter?"

Porter shook his head. "Nothing, man. I want you to think about it and we can talk about it later. Preferably when Sienna isn't here. I think it will involve shit that she doesn't need to hear or see from either of us. I don't want to scare her."

"Whatever, man. I think she is stronger than you think and you are fucking scared to reveal too much to her."

"Of course. I am fucking terrified of who I am. Why the fuck you think I hid it so long? Just think on it. We can meet up tomorrow night, maybe at Mason's? That work for you?"

Michael looked at his calendar. "Yeah, that works. Bring the cards."

"Of course."

There was a loud commotion happening on the other side of the room. Michael glanced at it. "Oh, hell no. Porter, we have to go

44

and rescue her."

Porter jerked his head around. A group of younger men had gathered around Sienna and were cat-calling and otherwise making complete assholes of themselves. She looked agitated.

Michael and Porter stood up and sauntered over. Michael calmly picked up two of them and set them aside. They were probably drunk and wouldn't really notice, but he didn't care.

"May we escort you?" Porter asked Sienna as he casually elbowed a young man in the face.

"Yes, allow us." Michael added as he used one arm to hold off three men and extended his other to Sienna. She took his arm and took Porter's arm on the other side.

They walked back to the booth amid a hostile silence. None of the young men followed.

"Thank you, gentlemen. I appreciate that, but I fear that the proprietor is going to come and speak to you."

"Let him." Porter said with an ominous edge in his voice.

"Be nice, Porter."

"Yes, you be nice, Porter," Michael said encouragingly, "And I can tell him where to go and who to fuck there."

Porter laughed.

Sure enough, an official-looking man was talking to the young men and they were pointing over at their table. "Here it comes." Porter said lightly. He was obviously enjoying this. "You wanna intimidate him, or should I?"

"Let's just wing it." Michael suggested.

Porter grinned. "You know I like that idea."

The older man came over. "I apologize for any inconvenience, sirs, but there appears to have been a misunderstanding." He suggested.

Porter took another drink of his ale, then looked up slowly at the manager. "Yes, I believe there was. You see, those fuck-offs assumed that my friend and I would allow them to harass a young lady."

Michael nodded. "We don't like bullying, as I am sure you can understand." He said it evenly, but he knew that people were intimidated when he said things vaguely threatening.

Porter took another drink. "We naturally assumed that you would frown upon such behaviors in your establishment."

The manager was nervous now. "Well, yes, of course we do..."

"Then I fail to see any problem." Porter cut him off coldly. "My fiancé has had problems with your staff and with your customers before. I do not like having her worried about her personal safety every time she wishes to stand up. Either adopt a better culture or be prepared to ignore our own attempts to keep her safe."

The manager actually stepped back before he realized it. Michael liked this tough-guy attitude Porter was using. He was going to remember it for later.

He also took a drink of his IPA. "Look, we don't want to have to take steps. You need to either tell those young assholes to go somewhere else or else cut off their alcohol. They've had too much to be good customers tonight anyway. They are just going to scare off all the women, then they will go out looking for where the girls have gone. Your choice, sir. We're staying here, and we won't cause trouble unless we have to." Michael paused for effect before looking the manager straight in the eyes. "And if I have to start trouble, you will know it."

"Now, now, gentlemen," Sienna said smoothly, "I'm sure he understands the situation. Don't you?" She added to the anxious manager. "I would so hate for there to be a fight tonight."

"No! No fights! I.... It's just... There was a complaint and..."

"You have followed it up." Michael said ominously. "Now fuck off."

The manager stepped back, then turned and hurried away.

"That might have been a bit abrupt." Sienna suggested.

"I don't fucking care. Little men with imagined power piss me off. They are some of the worst bullies there are."

Porter nodded. "We'll just see what happens. I am not leaving until after I eat."

"Of course, Porter." She agreed.

They talked together after that quite comfortably. The atmosphere got a little louder as more people came in. The pizzas came and they ordered another round of drinks. Michael liked hanging out with his friends. They didn't expect anything out of him.

Porter was being outrageous and Sienna was egging him on. Michael enjoyed being part of the evening with them.

The music had gotten a bit louder as more people came in interested in partying. The DJ put on one of those sappy power ballads from the eighties. Sienna laughed. "I used to have this daydream that Prince Charming would come and sweep me up and we would kiss to this exact song. Talk about your after-school specials! How lame was that? And what a terrible soundtrack!" She laughed again.

Porter got a very wicked twinkle in his eyes and a grin.

Sienna saw it. "No, Porter! Don't you dare!" She protested, still giggling.

That was just the dare Porter wanted. He stood up, pulled Sienna's chair back and picked her up. Then he carried her onto the dance floor and kissed her quite thoroughly. Michael was smiling. They were such a good couple. He was a little jealous. Not of Sienna, but of what they had together. He took a drink of his IPA as he watched them dance. Sienna was saying something with a smile and Porter was smiling back. They didn't seem to notice anyone around them.

Michael scanned the crowd out of habit. He was used to being in places he had to be aware of. He noticed that some of the young men were still there, and that they were looking at Porter and Sienna with very unfriendly looks. Michael paid more attention when three of them moved together and stood, glowering with arms crossed and muttering to each other.

The song wound down, there were screams of approval from the dance floor, and the DJ spun up another power ballad. Porter and Sienna were still there, seemingly lost in whatever they were talking about. Michael pushed his glass away. If he was going to have to act, he didn't want to pause.

The three young men had been joined by another two. This could be serious. Michael knew he could take them all without too much trouble. He didn't want to hurt anyone tonight.

He stood up and moved out from the table. The group across the dance floor seemed to remember he was there. Several of them shrank back visibly. They all looked very worried. Michael found that rather satisfying. He crossed his arms and stood there, just watching them. They exchanged some comments and slunk back into the crowd.

Porter and Sienna came back to the table.

"What's up, Mike?" Porter asked softly. He could tell something was not right.

"Those young punks were trying to start something. I think they remembered something to do somewhere else."

Sienna looked at him steadily. "And yet, you think you are not worth noticing..." She said quietly.

Porter gently took her hand. "Later, love. We should probably leave. This is a little more serious and I don't want to fight tonight."

They paid and left quickly.

As they walked down the crowded sidewalk, Porter looked casually over at Michael. "Did you get to look at those pictures that Manuel guy took?"

Michael flushed a bit. "No, and I don't want to."

"They're actually quite good. Did he ask you to pose for him again?"

"Yes. He said I could make lots of money."

Porter nodded. "You can." He said quietly. "He has a good eye and you looked really good in them. Very natural."

"Porter, you are just saying that to make me feel better."

Porter stepped in front of Michael to force him to stop. Sienna stepped back slightly. Michael was 6'2 but Porter was at least three inches taller. Michael had to look up at him when they were this close.

48

"Michael, I seem to recall once when I said that to you and you told me to fuck the hell off. Now it is my turn. I don't fucking say shit just to make you feel good. What I said is what I truly think, whether you want it to be or not. Don't tell me what to fucking say or what to fucking think."

Michael stared at him. This was not at all what he had expected. "Fuck off, Porter. Those things are always doctored up and lighted and shit."

Porter just stared at him. Michael glared back. He didn't really know why he was upset. It didn't make any sense.

"What the hell is up with you, Michael?" Porter asked softly. "This isn't like you at all. What are you so pissed at?"

Michael turned aside. "I don't fucking know. Can we fucking drop this now?"

"Like hell." Porter reached out and jerked Michael around so they were looking at each other again. "What the fuck is wrong with you?" Michael knew that Porter was worried about him. He wished he could say something to make Porter leave him alone.

Sienna reached out and touched both of them gently on the arms. "Gentlemen, might I ask we take this somewhere other than the sidewalk?" She said firmly.

Porter and Michael stared at each other for a few seconds longer before Porter nodded. "Of course. This is not over, Michael. We are going to discuss this, in depth, and now. Tomorrow is too fucking long to wait."

He reached into his sport coat and pulled out his phone. "Mason?... Hey, you busy? No?... Michael and I are coming out, now, if that is cool with you... Awesome. Have something to drink.... Oh and cards... No, nothing like that... Thanks, man. I owe you. Later."

Porter turned to Sienna. "My love, I am afraid that I am going to be a terrible date and ditch you. I know you had some other engagement tonight with your girls, so I do not feel as badly as I would have. Will you please excuse us?"

49

Sienna nodded. "Don't hurt each other too much, boys. I will see you tomorrow at the store, Porter?"

"It might depend on how tonight goes."

She nodded again, stood on her tiptoes, and pulled Porter's head down to kiss him. Then she looked up at Michael and did the same thing. "You two must figure this shit out, and soon. You are both at some sort of limit, and I can't help you with it. I was serious when I said you were both driving me crazy." She said seriously. Porter handed his key to Sienna and she waved. She did not smile.

"She is absolutely right, you know." Porter said calmly. "We are both at a limit or two. Let's go explore those fucking limits. And I won't take 'no' as an answer."

Michael sighed. "This day has been one of the worst fucking days I can remember."

"Hopefully it will get better. It'll probably get worse first though. You're driving. Let's go."

Chapter 4

Michael was tense the whole drive out to Mason's house. Porter didn't say anything.

Mason answered the door immediately. He had a serious look on his face. "What the hell is going on, Porter?" He asked after the door was shut.

Porter shrugged out of his sport coat. "Michael and I have some shit to work through. Wanna join us?"

Mason considered the two of them for a minute. "Hmm. This is pretty serious. I am a little surprised that you are leading this charge, Porter."

Porter shrugged. "I am trying to pay more attention to my feelings, Mason. Plus, I feel bull-headed and pissed off tonight, so I would at least like a reason."

Mason still considered them. Michael felt very confused and surly about this whole thing.

Finally, Mason said, "Is this going to be a fight, gentlemen?"

"That really depends on Michael. I am fully willing to go a few rounds with him, if that is what he needs." Porter said simply.

"Fuck you, Porter! I wouldn't fight with you, bastard!"

Porter grew very pale for a moment. His eyes were suddenly very bright. Then he sighed and let go of his anger. "You're probably right to call me that, Michael, even though you didn't mean it to be. I could very well be a bastard. I wouldn't fucking know."

Michael was a little shocked. "No, I didn't mean... Oh, fuck, I am sorry..."

Porter slapped him across the face. It wasn't very hard, but Michael could tell he was really angry now.

"Shut the fuck up! I told you not to do that!"

Michael stepped back in alarm. Mason quickly stepped forward. "Porter! Enough of that! If you want to fight then fight, but no sucker punches!" He snapped.

Porter stepped up to Michael, bulling into him. "Wanna fight, big man? Let's fight! You have been on edge for days now. Fucking throw down, right now! You can't hurt me!"

Michael backed again, half instinctively raising his hands to fend off an attack. "Porter, no, I don't want to fight..."

"Well, what do you want, boy?" Porter roared at him and threw a left jab. It was experimental, gauging. Michael dodged it with ease. Porter was feeling him out.

"I don't fucking know, Porter!" Michael shouted back. "I already told you that!" He backed away from Porter again.

"Find out! Fucking hit me! You keep dancing away! Hit me, bitch!"

"Fuck off!"

"No!" Porter moved in again and feinted with his left. Then he hit him with a right hook to the ribs. Michael hadn't expected it and it hurt a bit. Porter had reach on him.

"Porter, leave me the fuck alone! I don't want to fight you."

"Too fucking bad!" Porter feinted again and hit him again. It was the same combo. Michael couldn't dodge it. He knew Porter was a good boxer and could change his method in a second. Unless he fought back, he was probably going to hurt.

Porter was still angry. His face was set and furious, but calculating. Michael figured he was going to keep going for body shots, so he crouched a bit more and circled away.

"Porter, please don't."

"Michael, go to hell. This ends now." Porter said from between clenched teeth. "You are not going to fucking lose your shit on me in Hong Kong; I will beat it out of you now if you don't act so let's go. Now!" He again feinted and hit the ribs. Michael winced unconsciously. Three hard blows to the same spot were hurting him. Porter feinted again, but this time, Michael countered with his own left jab.

Porter took it and hit him anyway. Michael was going to have to protect that rib shot.

He threw a cross to the body on Porter. Porter shifted his

weight and the punch went a bit wide. Michael hadn't fought someone with real talent in a long time. He was going to have to work for this.

They traded blows for a few minutes. Suddenly, Porter stepped back and held up his hands, breathing a little harder. "Feel better now?"

Michael pulled up short, also breathing hard. "What?"

"I said, do you feel better now? Are you ready to talk, or you just gonna piss about how sorry you are?"

"Go to fucking hell."

"Good. Let's go get a drink. Although the fight option is still open."

Mason exhaled loudly. "You two assholes had better be done. You can't just come in here and have a fucking fight without warning me. Fucking gave me a heart attack." He turned and led the way to his study.

Michael glared at Porter. "What the fuck was that all about?" He demanded.

Porter glared back. "You been pissy all day. Best way to get out of that frame of mind is to fight about it. We done that, now we can talk about it. You have to be angry to want to talk about the shit in your life."

Michael shrugged and winced. "You fucking bastard. You could have broken a rib."

"Too fucking bad."

"Why the hell are you doing this?"

"Because I am pissed and fighting makes me feel better. Also, I am pissed at you and hitting you makes me feel better. But mostly, I am trying to make you angry enough to hit back, jackass. You are acting all afraid of everything. Fuck that. You are hiding from something. Fucking face it already. We are going to be here until you do. Fuck therapy. You are going to work it out, and if I have to beat the hell out of you until you respond, fucking bring it."

Michael opened his mouth to protest, but Porter put his hand over it. "No, fucking listen. This has to end, Michael. You need to fucking face who you are. Who you really are. You think I like who I am? I fucking suck, man. But at least I know that I have to accept that now. Can't do it yet, but I know I have to. You haven't even fucking accepted that you have to. Why you think taking pictures bugs you? Why you think Sienna complimenting you makes you blush like a school girl? Who the hell are you, anyway? We're here, and we are staying here, until you start to look at you, got it? Sienna knows that's what you need. We have discussed it before, and that is why she let me come here with you. "

"You fucking talk about me?" For some reason, that hurt.

"Fuck, what do you think, idiot? Of course we talked about this! My God, you are pretty out of it if you think we don't."

Mason had cleared his desk.

"What, you talk about me too, Mason?" Michael demanded. It had hurt a lot more than he thought it had to hear that.

"Michael, what the hell do you think? Yes, I see you going nuts, of course I ask my team, your friends, if something might be wrong."

Porter shoved Michael into a chair and leaned over to get in his face again. "Dammit Michael, do you really think you are the only one who protects people in this fucking group? We all protect each other. You are pissed because we watch your back?"

Michael shook his head. "No, but... this seems different."

"Well, it isn't. Now, what is pissing you off? Besides me. I already know about that." Porter sat down near him. Michael had the distinct feeling that Porter was there to smack him around again if he needed it.

"Shit, man! Let me think about it! It's not like I planned to fucking clear my conscience here!" Porter waved that aside. He and Mason waited. Michael knew they wouldn't let him leave until he came clean, really came clean.

"Well, let's see." He thought about it. What did he fear the most? What did he not like about himself the most? "I guess what I am

54

pissed about the most is that I still feel like an outsider. Like I am not really your friend, or something. That's why it hurt that you are talking about me."

Porter nodded. "Okay, so how do we convince you otherwise?"

"Dammit, Porter, I don't fucking know!"

"Then we'll work on that. There was only one thing that really convinced me, but I can't do it for you."

"What worked for you?"

"You, asshole. You did. You made me realize that every damn thing Cinna said about me was true, and that everything Sienna said about me was true, even though I didn't want it to be. I wanted to be shit, because then I wouldn't have to like me or get to know me. I'm not, and that sucks."

Michael nodded slowly. "So, when Sienna says something, you believe her?"

"No, I don't. That's something I have to work on, probably forever."

"Damn. I was hoping it would get fixed and then be okay."

Porter laughed at him, but there was no humor in it. Michael knew he wasn't being made fun of. "Look, you think I can just start loving myself? I have been hiding for the last thirty-seven years! I don't even know what my last name is!"

"You don't?"

"Who the hell is going to tell me? The orphanage didn't record that shit and I don't have any relatives."

"Damn. Look, I am sorry." Michael held up a hand. "No, I really am this time. I feel for you, Porter. Really."

Porter smiled. "Good. That's a first step. If you can feel for someone outside of yourself, really feel for them, I have read in my books that you are taking a good step."

Mason nodded. "You are. Anytime the focus is away from the self, it helps to put the true self into perspective. That's what both you fucking idiots lack. Neither of you has any perspective yet."

Michael suddenly felt overwhelmed. "You guys... you are really doing this for me, right? This isn't some big plan for the team?"

Mason shook his head. "No, we are here for you. Just like you are always looking out for us. We saw a problem, and we are here for you."

"Why? Why would you want to do that? I mean, really, why? I am just..."

"Shut the fuck up." Porter growled. "Do not finish that. We are here because you need us, you are worth us being here, and we are going to fucking be here because we fucking love you, idiot. You are worthy of being loved. Fuck whatever you think."

It was like he was drowning. The blood was pounding in his ears and his vision seemed to be going fuzzy. What the fucking hell?

Mason stood up in alarm. "He's going, Porter!"

Porter was beside him instantly. "Get me that water, Mason." He said quickly.

Michael was staring at Porter but he didn't see him clearly. The roaring grew louder and his vision dimmed more. Then everything refocused with painful clarity. He was still sitting in the same chair. Porter was bracing him with his hands on his shoulders. Michael was clutching Porter's arms so hard his knuckles hurt.

Porter was looking at him grimly. Then, when he saw Michael focus on him, he smiled. "Are you back?"

Michael nodded. "What the hell just happened?"

"Who knows? You didn't pass out or anything fun like that."

Michael shook his head, trying to clear it.

"Do you think you could let go now?" Porter asked. "You're going to break my fucking arm."

"Oh! Shit, yes! Sorry, man." Michael let go quickly.

Porter smiled and rubbed his arm. "It is paybacks for the ribs."

Michael smiled. It felt good to smile. "Damn straight. I always knew you cheated when you fought."

Porter laughed.

Mason looked at them both. "Are you two better now?"

Michael shrugged. "I don't know. I feel... a little looser or freer inside."

"I think you had a reaction." Mason said. "Maybe you had to physically rid yourself of something, some internal block. You look the same, but something in your eyes is different."

Porter nodded. "Absolutely. You look, I don't know, softer there or something."

Michael thought about that for a moment or two. "I feel a little less tight inside. Like some knot went away or some such shit. There's still something tight, but less." He looked right at Porter then. "You really don't know your last name?"

Porter shook his head. There were tears in his eyes. "No. I really don't. Cinna used to joke about it and called me 'Porter-with-no-last-name'. It's funny, but we put so much fucking importance on names. I don't even have one."

Michael nodded thoughtfully. "Well, if it makes you feel better, I don't know what my real name is either. I got baptized when I was three and the name on my certificate is what I am called now, but I don't know if that was it before. My father just went through the motions and then he split. It was just me and my little sister. We looked after each other."

Mason looked at him, a deep, searching look. "You don't have a little sister anymore, do you?"

Michael shook his head. Now it was his turn to tear up. "No, she got pneumonia and she went quick. I think she was seven or eight. It was awful. There ain't no way to fight that." Now he was crying. It felt awful but he couldn't stop. "She just died, man! I had to watch her! All this fucking muscle and I couldn't do fucking shit for her!"

He hadn't thought about Emily for years. He wanted to hit the wall, break a table, something.

Porter seemed to know that. "You can't hurt the pain away." He said softly.

"How do you get it out?" Michael shouted. "What makes the pain go away?"

"Sharing it." Porter said just as softly. "Why the hell you think I told you to get somebody to anchor you? Love is the one thing that makes the pain livable."

Michael put his face in his hands. This was horrible. He felt twisted up and nauseous.

"Friends help, too." Mason said simply. "We do love you, Michael. Nobody sits here and listens to shit like this for fun."

"No, no one does." Michael managed to gasp out. He wiped at his face. "God damn this whole fucking world."

Porter nodded. "That about sums it up."

Michael took some deep breaths. "Fuck. This sucks. Who the hell wants to love someone who can't do shit for someone they love?"

Mason looked at him sternly. "I do."

Porter raised his hand. "I do, too."

It sent Michael off again. He knew they weren't lying; he couldn't accept it, not yet. He sobbed for a few minutes. Mason handed him a box of tissues. Porter went and got some drinks for them all.

"Fuck. I hope I stop sucking soon. I can't operate at this level for much longer." Michael said in a choked voice when he was a bit calmer.

"No, but you won't be at this level again." Mason said gently. "It will be less, because we already know and have accepted you here, at this place in your life. You don't have to come back to this place ever again."

"Is it gone?"

"More like the door can be closed inside you and never reopened, if you choose."

"Good."

"That's one of the reasons we were all so worried about you. You hadn't faced the dark part, so you couldn't close the door."

Porter sat down again. "Michael, the dark can eat you alive. That's why I tried to kill myself. I couldn't handle the dark inside me. No one can handle it alone."

Mason looked sharply at Porter. "The fuck you talking about?"

"You fucking heard me, Mason. You think this has all been roses and honey?"

"You fucking bastard!"

"I'm sorry, Mason. I was weak. I won't do it again."

"You had better fucking not! Trying to hide that shit from me!" Mason was very angry. He looked at Michael. "You either. God, you two! Both of you! Argh!"

Michael started laughing. He couldn't help it. He knew he was going to make Mason angrier. All the emotion, the wonder of experiencing true friendship, the loosening of whatever he had held pent up, he couldn't stop.

Porter was laughing too. Mason stood up rigidly. "This is not fucking funny. You two walk in here, have a fucking fight in the front hall, fucking try to beat the hell out of each other, fucking cry and yell, then you tell me you tried to kill yourself? And you probably fucking hid it and just slipped up! This better not happen again, or I will kill you both! Damn you both! Damn you both to hell!"

Porter and Michael laughed harder. Mason stalked out of the room. He turned in the doorway. "When you two idiots are finished, I will be in the kitchen. Come there if you ever fucking get it back together." Then he left and slammed the door.

"God, I hope this mission isn't this bad." Michael finally managed to say. He had laughed so hard that he was crying. It felt good. Porter had partially regained himself.

"Oh, I don't know. We can always have another fight, if we need to."

"Fuck that! You cheat!"

Porter shrugged, smiling. "I never promised to be fair, Michael."

Michael laughed again. He felt like he hadn't really ever laughed before. There had always been something holding him back a little, a need to appear some way or other. The knowledge that Porter and Mason accepted him, fully and unconditionally made that ridiculous. The fact that Porter and Mason also demanded he change for the better made him feel valued. It was a challenge, and he wanted to win it.

"Porter, man, really, thanks. You have made me feel like I should get better because you want me to be the best. I haven't had a challenge like that before. I'm a little scared of it, to be honest."

Porter smiled again. He looked out the window at the night scene. "I don't think any of us wants to change, Michael, but none of us are perfect. Besides, what kind of friend would I be if I couldn't ask you to get better? Everyone keeps me in line, and I guess that's what friends do." He glanced over at Michael. "It's not like I have tons of experience in that either, you know."

"No. So let's just do what we think friends do and not tell anyone if we are doing it wrong."

Porter grinned. "I can handle that. Besides, you know I like the idea of sneaking around the rules!"

Michael laughed. "So do I!"

There was a knock at the door. Mason opened it. It was obvious that he was still not happy with them. He was holding his cell phone. "Porter, Sienna called. She is extremely worried about you two idiots. She is starting to freak. Would it be all right if I tell her she can come out and see you?"

Porter winced. "Oh, fuck, I forgot she would be upset. Yes, tell her to come. It's cool now. We are almost ready for some cards."

Mason nodded. "All right. I have some food ready in the kitchen. Perhaps we can play at the bar in there? It is less formal."

Michael stood up. "Yeah, that'd be great. Mason, thanks so much. Not many people would be willing to host a fight, two jerks being jerks, and male-bonding all in one night."

Mason looked at him for a moment, oddly. "Michael, that's what friends do. Don't you get it yet?" He turned, dialing as he did.

Michael looked at Porter, who shrugged. "Hey, don't look at me! I got no fucking idea what he is talking about."

"Good. I'm hungry. You definitely bruised me up on the side here, bitch. I outta sucker-punch you a good one."

Porter nodded solemnly. "And yet, you won't. Because I am that fucking awesome."

"Whatever, man."

Mason had laid out a nice little appetizer selection.

"Were you planning on this or something?" Michael asked curiously.

"We did plan to get together tomorrow, remember?"

"Oh. No, I forgot that."

"Clearly." Mason was not smiling. "Now, listen, both of you. Sit down and shut the hell up. I am pissed at you both. Not because you're fighting or sniping at each other. I am pissed because you both have some serious issues and you aren't fucking working them out. I am about this close to calling the mission off."

Porter sat up straight. "What? Like hell you are!"

"Porter, you fucking shut up! You aren't better! You are almost as bad as you were. Fucking don't lie to me again!" Mason turned to Michael, his face furious. "And you! Fucking come in here and drop shit like that! You two don't even know what your little combined temper tantrums have done to your friends! I haven't been sleeping for a fucking week, bitches! This ends. Now. Either commit to getting your shit together, or you two are done. I can't fucking keep this up; you two have to get fucking better on your own damn terms. What is it gonna be?"

Porter winced and slumped in his chair.

Michael also grimaced. He hadn't considered that he might be influencing people around him. "Fuck, Mason, I am sorry. I guess I thought my shit was private. It isn't. If you think I should be off, then I

61

will respect that."

Mason's face hadn't changed. "Do either of you idiots think you should be pulled?"

Porter looked at Michael. Michael looked back at Porter. He shrugged slightly. He had no idea.

Porter sighed. "Mason, if you think we should go, we will. It is your choice. We will follow your lead."

"Good." Mason slapped his hand on the cutting board hard. Michael jumped slightly. "You fucking idiots had better not be lying to me again. I don't like it when I have to guess what you are thinking. You are killing us all off, fucking idiots. All right. You are still on, but no more lies, bitches. No more hiding. No more tantrums or sulking."

Porter and Michael nodded. Michael had never seen Mason so angry before.

The door bell sounded softly. "Oh, and one more thing, assholes. You are going to tell all this to Sienna. Now. She deserves to hear it all." Mason leaned forward and glared at Porter. "Fucking got it?"

Porter looked miserable but he nodded.

Mason turned his glare on Michael. "And you?"

Michael swallowed hard. "Yes, Mason." He whispered.

Mason glared a few seconds more. He went to answer the door.

"Fuck, Porter, this sucks worse than anything else tonight."

Porter had gone very pale. "God, I hope she forgives me." He whispered to no one in particular.

They heard Mason talking and a woman's voice answering, both too low to make anything out. Porter's hands were shaking and he was still terribly pale. Michael found he was sweating and shaking himself. Mason was certainly putting to them a hard assignment.

Mason came in with Sienna beside him. He pulled one of his bar stools around so that she was facing Michael and Porter. Then he pulled another around for himself. Nothing like feeling he was on trial,

Michael thought desperately.

Sienna was pale and her face was set. "Let's get this started, gentlemen." She said crisply. "Mason told me some of the shit you two pulled. Now, you two have something to say, is that it?"

Porter couldn't look at her. This was a terrible struggle for him. The silence stretched uncomfortably. Finally he gave up and started talking. "Look, Sienna, I am sorry. I didn't want you to get to see the real me. I tried to keep it away, tried to be the man I thought you needed. I can't, babe. You need more than I can ever be. I am so sorry."

Sienna went even paler. She didn't say anything. Porter still couldn't look at her, so he didn't see the tears start in her eyes. "Three weeks ago," Porter went on, softly, "I tried to kill myself. I put a pistol to my head but I couldn't do it. I didn't want you to know how weak I was, am. I got rid of it. I didn't tell anyone, because I am so ashamed of it. I can't...I am sorry. I wish I could ask you to forgive me, but I can't. You probably hate me now. I can't blame you if you do."

It was nearly unbearable. Michael wanted to rescue his friend, so he cleared his throat. "And, Sienna, I have been trying to fake a strong exterior so that you would rely on me. I wanted to be strong enough on the outside to keep all my hurt on the inside from coming out. I couldn't keep it down and I didn't realize that it was hurting you, too. I am so very sorry to have put you and Mason and Juan and Porter through all that I have. I am so sorry." He looked at Mason, too. He was starting to get an idea of how one person could affect others. It was a little scary.

Sienna didn't say anything for a while. She was holding her hands clenched tightly together in front of her. Finally, she looked up at the ceiling. "God damn you both." She said softly. "Michael, you are a good man, but god damn you anyway. You have fucking put us all right to the edge, trying to fucking guess when you will lose it or start some random fight because you are upset. And Porter..." Porter closed his eyes and braced. "What the fuck did you think I would do? People don't run out on people they love. What the fuck? Of course I don't hate you. You both had better start accepting that, too. I love you, Porter. I love you, Michael. Start accepting it."

Michael didn't feel much better about this. Somehow, it seemed even harder, now that Sienna didn't hate them and wasn't pissed. It was like she expected them to do what they didn't want to do. Damn.

Michael nodded. Porter was apparently not listening. He had his eyes tightly closed. Sienna came over to him.

Slowly, Porter opened his eyes and looked at her. Gently, he reached up and wiped all her tears away. "I am not worth even the tears that fall from your eyes." He whispered.

"Fuck that! You are worth more than my entire life, Porter! If you die, then I die." Porter closed his eyes again, as if what she said hurt him. She kept on speaking though, relentlessly. "You think you are the only ones who feel ashamed? You think you are the only ones who feel weak? Fuck you both! I don't need you to act all strong all the time! I need you to be weak so that I can help you! Fucking talk to me, you two assholes! I don't like being torn in half by this shit. You two need to figure out who you are so I don't have to race around picking up the fucking pieces every time you two fucking fly apart!"

That hurt. It hurt a lot. Michael hadn't realized how much Sienna cared about him.

Mason looked at them both grimly. "This is what it means to be friends. You either work on your shit, together, with all of us, or you are out."

Michael nodded dumbly. He glanced uneasily at Porter. He was still shut up inside himself.

They waited. Eventually, Porter gave a huge sigh. "Fuck. I hate myself sometimes. Fuck fuck FUCK! Why do I suck so much? Why? Why do I hurt you all so much?"

Mason slapped the cutting board again. They all jumped. "Porter, shut that kind of talk up. We don't fucking care. We love you anyway. Fucking accept it."

Porter jerked back. He finally nodded. "Yes, I will try."

Sienna started sobbing then. She buried her head in Porter's lap and sobbed. He looked very surprised. He looked up at Mason, questioningly.

"She fucking loves you, you idiot. You don't show love by hiding who you are. That just drags us all through the mud. Haven't either of you fucking noticed that she's been losing weight? What the fuck did you think it was from, anyway?"

Two tears rolled down Porter's face. He bowed his head and put a very unsteady hand on Sienna's hair.

Michael found that he was crying again. He didn't think he was even capable of this much emotion. Mason pulled out some towels and gave one to Michael. He handed two to Porter.

"No more of this shit. Not from anybody."

Michael and Porter shook their heads.

Sienna got control of herself and stood up. She was still beautiful, even with a blotchy face and runny eyes. She didn't say anything more to Porter; she just kissed him on the mouth, hard.

"You don't hate me?" Porter whispered, still disbelieving.

Sienna shook her head. She went back to her seat.

Michael couldn't believe it, himself. This whole friend/love thing was going to take a lot of work.

Chapter 5

Nobody said anything for quite a while. Mason turned to Sienna. "I have some things that you might need for the mission in my study. Let's go get them and give these two a chance to talk it out a little."

Sienna nodded. She looked at Porter and Michael. "No more hitting, boys."

They both shook their heads. Sienna stood up and walked with Mason out of the room.

Michael sighed. "That was even worse than I thought it would be."

Porter was still pale. Michael was a bit worried about him. "Hey, are you okay?"

"No. I am not okay, but I am good enough." Porter took a deep breath. He closed his eyes. "I hope this stops sucking soon."

"Same here." They were both silent for a little bit. Michael kind of smiled as something somewhat silly occurred to him. "Although, to be honest with you, I am glad you were there with me for it. I couldn't imagine going through hell like that with anyone else. I mean, I love Juan and all, but... damn..."

Porter snorted. "Oh, God, that would have been awful."

Michael looked at Porter tentatively. "Seriously, man, are you okay?"

Porter sighed. He picked up a piece of celery and toyed with it. "I suppose. I just can't quite bring myself to believe her, not yet. I know it hurts her, and that hurts. I don't want her to hurt."

"No, but we don't choose how others hurt."

"No, we don't."

"If it helps, she chooses to hurt with us. And, dammit all, I choose to hurt with you. Unless it is that wicked hook of yours. That thing was money."

Porter smiled slightly. "It was a signature move, once upon a time."

66

"Back when Porter was state champion."

Porter looked over at Michael. "How did you know that?"

"Really, Porter? When I heard you were a boxer, I looked it up. Research, you know."

Porter shook his head. "That was a long time ago."

"In a galaxy far, far away, when we were different people."

"Yeah, pretty much." Porter snapped the celery. "I can't take much more heavy shit tonight. Did you realize it's only eleven o'clock?"

Michael blinked and looked at his watch. It was true. "Whoa. I thought it was later than that."

"If I am going to feel this shitty, I would really rather be drinking at the same time."

Michael nodded. "Same. When is the diamond exchange?"

"Next Saturday evening is the opening soiree. I have an invite. I always have one, but I have only gone twice, and never to the opening shit. Buncha people dressing up and trying to impress each other. Lame."

"We're going to have to go this time. We should catch this Patos' eye and hold his attention as soon as possible."

"You're probably right. You got a tux that fits?"

"Uhhh... Maybe?"

Porter smiled again. "Nope, wrong answer. If we are up to it tomorrow, I will take you to get one."

"I can get my own damn tux, Porter."

Porter turned his head very slowly. His eyebrow rose menacingly. "No, you can't. I am taking you to get a tux, and I am going to get mine at the same time and you can fucking suck it."

Michael flushed slowly. "Why the fuck are you doing that?"

"Because, I am going to help you see yourself. You are going to do the same for me. I meant it when I said I was going to try harder."

"Oh...." Michael looked away in confusion. "I guess that is okay."

Porter reached over and put his arm around Michael's

67

shoulders. "Look, Michael, we are two very fucked-up guys. We have to help each other. I need you to watch my back. You need me to watch yours. Let's try to do the best job we can to help out our friends and ourselves."

"Okay, Porter. I get it. You just surprised me is all."

Mason and Sienna were coming back, from the sound of their voices.

"No more heavy stuff tonight." Michael warned Porter.

"No." Porter agreed.

Mason came back into the kitchen. Porter held up his other hand, since he still had one on Michael's shoulders. "No more heavy tonight, Mason. I can't take it. I will work on it, but not now."

Mason looked at them both very hard. Then he nodded. "Fine, but you better remember this time."

"I will. Do you have any vodka?"

"I thought you were cutting back."

"Not tonight."

Sienna sat down across from them again. Mason nodded. "Yes, I have some, but I don't have a lot."

"Ha." Porter said softly. "You're lying, but we will take what you have."

Mason assumed a look of exaggerated innocence. "Lying? Me?"

Porter snorted. "Definitely."

Michael nodded vigorously.

Mason smiled slyly. "You'll never fucking know, now will you?"

Sienna smiled at that. "You are a very mean person, Mason."

"I know, Sienna. They have given me hell for days now. I am only reciprocating." He left to get the vodka.

Porter was looking at Sienna. She glanced at him curiously. "What is it, Porter?"

He sighed. "Nothing. I just like to look at you. But now I think I am really seeing you for the first time, and I am sad that I have missed it

68

for so long."

Sienna blushed and looked down.

Porter gave Michael's shoulder a squeeze and let go.

Mason came back with half a bottle and pulled some glasses down. "Who wants some?" He asked.

"Me." Porter and Michael said together. Mason smiled and poured two glasses.

"And I would like a finger, Mason." Sienna said.

"Rocks?"

"Yes, please."

He poured two drinks with ice and passed her one. "Cards, gentlemen?"

Porter tossed his vodka down. "Of course. Give me the deck. And another shot."

Mason did both.

Michael also drank his quickly. Mason refilled his glass.

Porter shuffled and cut, then shuffled again. "We were talking about the diamond exchange while you and Sienna were in back." He said as he began to deal. "We should probably go to the opening gala and grand ball next Saturday night."

"You have the tickets then?" Mason asked.

"Always. It is the formal event of the year, very high end and fancy. Sienna, you will be stunning, I guarantee it. The women all drip diamonds, of course. I think you will outshine them all."

Sienna assumed a very regal tilt to her head. "But of course, my love!"

"That is exactly the right attitude. I have some experimental pieces that I think you should wear."

Mason coughed slightly. "Not to disrespect your work, Porter, but perhaps she should have a different ring."

"I thought of that. I think that my persona this time will be more flamboyant and would have given his woman a showier, less beautiful ring. Anyway, I have one that I think will work. It might be a little big in the band size, though. I will get that done tomorrow after the fittings. Michael, you better come, too. We'll need to pick out some things for this Beatrice to have. "

Michael looked at his hand. It sucked. He was just going to have shitty luck all night long. "Mason," he said absently, "Have you talked to this girl yet? I don't think I wanna act engaged to her, not this time. But I think we should get to know her a little first."

Mason was also looking at his cards. "Yes. She will be in Friday to brief you guys."

Michael looked up, surprised. "Not you?"

Mason shook his head seriously. "No, I think I don't want her to know what I look like. I don't trust her much, for some reason. Something feels wrong about this whole deal."

"Okay. Well. Where are we meeting her?"

Mason smiled slightly. "You meet her here, of course! She'll think it is Porter's house. I don't mind being the chef or butler or whatever."

Porter rearranged his cards. "I think that will work out well, Mason. Maybe you can be chauffeur and drive her here. That way, she won't be able to map it out."

"I like that idea, Porter." Mason frowned and folded. "I like that a lot. That is a good way to keep everyone safe."

Porter inclined his head mockingly. "All my ideas are good."

Michael laughed. "Like hell they are." He also folded.

Sienna folded as well. Porter smiled. "Just like it was a great idea to hold a ten, an eight, one five, one four, and a two." He picked up the pot and reshuffled.

"You did not!" Mason protested.

"Oh, but you'll never know, now will you?" Porter said with a smile and wink.

Mason laughed at him. "You are impossible!"

"I know. That is why you love me."

"No, that is why I can't stay angry with you though."

Porter shrugged. "Same thing."

He dealt the next hand. Michael had shit again. "Porter," he said, not even bothering to draw anything before he folded, "have you figured out names and all that yet?"

"Um." Porter said, looking at his own cards. He frowned slightly. "Um, not totally. We will do that tomorrow. Speaking of which, Sienna, do you have a gown?"

"Wedding or otherwise?" She asked casually.

Porter hadn't been very focused on what she might say, so she caught him off-guard. "*What* did you say?! Oh. Oh, you played that perfectly. No, a ball gown."

Sienna laughed softly, mockingly. "I have a deep purple ball gown, but it will simply not work with platinum blonde hair. I will need another."

Porter nodded gravely. "I will get you one."

"What, you? But you don't know my size!"

"Oh, but I do." Porter looked her up and down very slowly and deliberately with a suggestive smile. Sienna blushed brightly. "I know it well enough to get you a dress. I want you to stop all conversation for fifty yards in any direction."

"Very well. Will you be able to keep your hands off me though?"

"That's the fun part. I don't have to."

She smiled at him. "Are you going to be making sure this dress fits? Because, you know, sometimes things like zippers get caught. I might need...help...."

"I certainly hope so!"

Mason laughed. "You two! Can't this wait until you are alone?"

Porter smiled. "But you are stuck with us all night, Mason. You can help, if you want. That might be fun, too."

"Uh, no, thanks."

"Just offering."

They played poker until quite late. Michael did abysmally. He didn't much care. They never played for any stakes that might be worthwhile anyway. At the end, he had lost maybe two dollars in four hours.

Mason looked at the clock. "Okay, it is three-thirty. I gotta get some sleep. You are all welcome to sleep here, you know. Just don't be too loud getting up if I am not up yet."

"I think I would like that, thank you, Mason." Sienna said, stretching. "I don't want to drive home right now."

Porter put the cards away. "I am too tipsy to drive." He looked at Michael. "You?"

"Yeah, same here."

"Then I will get you all some pillows and blankets." Mason offered.

Michael stood up. "I call big black couch!"

Porter made a face. "Damn. Then I call recliner."

Sienna stood up as well. "And I call... Porter."

He looked up at her quickly. "Are... are you sure?" He obviously still couldn't quite trust himself to believe that she had forgiven him.

"Oh, I think so. Get used to it, my love."

Porter looked down in confusion. Then he looked up again, almost shyly. "I think I will like that."

"Hey, you said no more heavy shit." Michael reminded him.

"I did. Well, I apologize. So there."

Michael laughed.

Chapter 6

Michael woke up and it took him a few seconds to remember anything that had happened and why he was currently on a couch in Mason's living room. It was at least eight o'clock in the morning. He rarely slept this late.

He stretched and yawned. His side was awfully fucking tight. Looking around he saw Porter in the recliner with Sienna snuggled into him. Then Michael remembered everything that had happened the night before. Surprisingly, he didn't feel a sense of shame, but resolve to make sure he never had to deal with hurting someone like that again.

Porter wasn't asleep; he opened his eyes when Michael shifted.

"Morning, asshole." Michael said softly.

Porter smiled slightly. "Same to you." He said, just as quietly. "We should probably map out our day. We have a bunch to get done."

Michael nodded. "Yeah, we do. Man but I am hungry. It feels like I worked out all night."

Porter's smile widened ironically. "We did, idiot. Remember?"

"Oh. I suppose so." Michael wanted to change the subject. "What's for breakfast?"

"I don't know. I bet Mason has some good stuff though. You wanna make it or do you want me to?"

"Well, you are a much better cook. But then, you are stuck in that chair."

Porter laughed softly. "Damn, I guess that answers that! Seriously, though, she should wake up pretty soon. Nobody in this group ever sleeps all that much."

Michael nodded. "I don't want to get up, either."

Sienna stirred and opened her eyes. "Mm. I think I could get used to this."

"Same." Porter kissed her forehead gently. "However much I would like to lie here all day, I have to get up and make the breakfast or else it will fall to Michael to do it."

"Oh, please God no." Sienna said with great drama.

73

Michael laughed. "You are as wise as you are beautiful."

Sienna smiled at him. She sat up and stretched. "Ah, well, if that is the way it is. Porter, what are you making?"

Porter stood up. "Eggs. And whatever else I feel like."

"That sounds heavenly."

Michael also stood up. "I think I might even need some coffee this morning."

Porter moved towards the kitchen. "I think Mason has some tea, if you would prefer that. Less caffeine."

Michael considered as he folded the blankets he had used. "Tea actually sounds great. Thanks, man."

"Hey, I can always offer other people's shit."

"And I can always take it."

Porter was rummaging around in the refrigerator. Michael began to assemble the coffee and tea supplies. "I guess I had better make a pot for Mason, huh? It is his house, and he did let us fight in the hallway and bitch all over his study."

Porter was cracking eggs. "You certainly have a way with words, Mikey." He said without looking up. "That is a phenomenal mental picture."

"You got a better way to say it?"

"No."

"Then fuck off."

After they had all finished for breakfast, Michael refilled his tea cup. "Mason, we appreciate you letting us use your house for our shit."

Mason smiled. "You are welcome. But no more fucking shit like that. I am serious when I say I worried about you two for weeks."

Michael raised his cup in approval. "Absolutely not, great leader! Now, we probably have to get going soon. Porter has some great scheme to get us all duded out and shit like that."

Porter choked on his own tea. "Excuse me? Great scheme?"

"Isn't it? You always have some scheme going."

"Perhaps, but that sounds so... sneaky or something."

"Whatever, man. Where are we going?"

Porter drank his tea slowly. "Stan's, first. Then if we need to, Marx's. Then, if they don't have what I want, we will wing it. Then we will have to go to the store. I have the pieces there that I want to look at, and I want your opinion, too. Then we will go ball gown shopping. Sienna, do you want to come with us for that?"

Sienna smiled. "I would love to, but I am working the counter all day today. James has the day off, and Muriel is sick. I asked Nadine to work, but she is only set to cover my hair appointment time, since she had other plans."

"Damn. Oh well. We'll do it without you then. What size shoes do you wear?"

"Seven."

"Very good. Sound like a plan, Michael?"

Michael shrugged. "You're the master manipulator. I will follow your lead."

"Then that's the plan. Mason, do you want to come?"

"No, Porter, I have things I need to get done, as well. I think I will just have to trust you."

Porter nodded and stood up. "Michael, shall we go, then?"

Michael sighed. "I am not looking forward to this." He warned.

"Too fucking bad."

"You just like saying that to me, don't you?" Michael accused as they walked out to his car.

"Of course." Porter squinted up at the sun. "Okay, here's the next part of the plan. I need a shower. Wanna go to my place or yours? I have two bathrooms at mine."

"I only have one shower. Let's hit yours, but let me get some clothes from mine. It is on the way to."

"Fair enough. You won't mind if I come in and get some water while you are getting clothes, will you?"

"Nah, man, my house is yours."

"Good. I am really thirsty today."

It only took fifteen minutes to get to Michael's condo. Porter had been there before, of course. While Michael dug through his clothes, Porter got himself some water and looked around in the other room.

"Michael, how come you have only shit in this house?" He yelled from the living room.

"What the hell you mean?" Michael called back. He was looking for some socks that wouldn't be embarrassing to take his shoes off with at a store.

"You have no pictures or anything, man!"

"It never occurred to me." Michael came out with a bag of clothes. "What the fuck does it matter?"

Porter turned. "Because a living space is supposed to reflect the person who lives there. I only notice because my house is the same way. Shall we go?"

Michael looked involuntarily at his walls as he closed the door to his condo. Porter was right; there wasn't much there in the way of decoration. He hadn't noticed before, but maybe that was why he didn't like inviting people over. His house was uncomfortable for him to show off. That was probably some profound psychological commentary on his interior self. Or some such shit.

After they had showered and shaved, Michael felt much better. His outlook on the day had risen considerably.

"Ready?" He asked Porter.

"Well, aren't you all fucking bright-eyed and bushy-tailed now?" Porter observed laconically.

"It's probably your sweet and sunny disposition rubbing off on me." Michael grinned.

Porter laughed softly. "That's it. I knew it was something like that." He felt various pockets to make sure he had everything he wanted. Then he absently pushed his longer hair out of his face, still thinking. "Let's go."

Stan's was a very high-end men's wear store. Michael had

never been to it before. He stared at it apprehensively. "Uh, help me out here; who are we and what are we doing?"

"You are going to be Sean Connor and I will be Thomas O'Flynn. That is who we will be for the rest of the mission. I think that we can be anyone we want, but the Gala is in New York City; there is a significant population there descended from the Irish. Plus, those names are so generic that they won't be traceable."

Michael smiled. "I like that idea. You have passports and all that?"

"Not yet. I am working on it. Oh, Sienna is going to be Marie Flanders. Also, terribly generic. We'll get the paperwork done today or tomorrow. I might need some help with that."

"Juan and I are available to help, just let us know when and where."

Porter nodded. "Let's get this going." He got out of the car. Michael sighed. He wasn't quite sure what to expect.

Porter walked into the store like he owned it. He didn't as much as look for help; it was almost as if he expected it to appear. Michael liked this attitude. He knew he should study Porter to get his own persona right. "Sean" was the same type of guy as "Thomas"; they should act similarly.

Help appeared within seconds, in the form of a young man with a sweater vest and horn-rimmed glasses. "Sirs? May I help you?"

Porter glanced over from the jackets he was looking through. "Yes. We have a gala to attend next Saturday. We need some tuxes, because, frankly, I am sick of my current selection. I want something trendy, understated, well-made." He turned back to the rack. "Oh, one more thing."

"Yes, sir?" The attendant asked, respectfully.

"Money is no objection. We want the best and we pay for it when we get it."

The young man nodded firmly. "I will give you only the best, sir. May I ask you both to try on some jackets to get your sizes estimated?

Then I might be better able to help."

Michael nodded. "Of course. I should warn you that I tend to be hard to fit."

The young man looked him over professionally. His eyes widened slightly. "I can imagine, sir! All right, a challenge." He rubbed his hands together. "This I like. Let's start here with you, sir." He handed two jackets to Porter. "And you, sir, let's try these." He handed two to Michael. "While you put on those, I will call for some back up help. If you will excuse me." He stepped around the rack and headed somewhere.

Michael carefully put on a jacket. It wasn't bad, considering. It could use at least one more inch through the shoulders though. And maybe a bit through the arms. Porter's jacket was not a great cut for him. "Yeah, I don't like that on you, Thomas. Something about it is wrong."

"That's why we are here. They are experts."

The young man returned with another, older man. "Thank you, gentlemen! My name, by the way, is Aaron. This is another attendant, Samuel. He has agreed to assist me."

Samuel stopped when he saw Michael and Porter. "I thought they had an appointment. Why are you asking for help for two like that?" He complained.

Aaron froze and turned very slowly. "I'm sorry," He said softly, "I seem to have not heard anything you just said." The tone he used was dripping with sarcasm.

Samuel caught it right away. "Uh, I, it's, uh, nothing. Just, um…"

Porter looked at him coolly. "If you have any questions about our ability, I shall go so far as to ease your mind by assuring you we only pay cash." Samuel still looked very upset. He clearly didn't want to help people he thought weren't worth it.

Aaron looked at him for a full minute. "Very well. Since you cannot give our customers the level of attention that this store prides

78

itself on, you may go to the back room and sort. You may also stay there. If you cannot improve your attitude, you will be dismissed. Go." He turned his back on the furious Samuel, effectively shutting him out.

Samuel left, fuming.

Aaron came over. "I do so apologize. That is not the level of customer care we provide."

Porter was looking in the mirror. "Apology accepted. The fit of this is fine, but I am not sure of the cut."

Aaron looked at him. "No, sir, I do not like this. I think you should emphasize both your slender physique and your height. A closer cut will do that well. Please allow me to get another jacket. And you, sir? Have you looked in the mirror?"

Michael shook his head and stepped over. The jacket fit okay, he guessed.

Aaron, however, shook his head, dissatisfied. "No, this is all wrong! Shoulders this broad need to be shown off! Plus, this is not the correct size. We'll get it nailed down, gentlemen! Just give me time and I will have you both so arrayed that no one will be able to look away!" He whisked off to find some other jackets.

Porter raised his eyebrow at Michael. "Well, Sean? Look at yourself. No, really look at yourself. What do you see? You don't have to tell me, but you better fucking do it." He stepped away from the mirror and motioned for Michael to step up.

Michael sighed. "All right. I promised I would try."

"That's right. You did."

Michael looked in the mirror. He saw what he usually did. He needed to comb his hair better. He had a bruise on his right cheek. Porter must have hit him there. His hands were scarred on the backs. He'd split a knuckle on Porter's ribs last night, too.

Porter laughed from right behind him. "I know what you are looking at. Stop. I want you to look and try and pretend it's someone else. Some random stranger. What would you see then?"

Michael turned his head and stared at Porter. What the fuck?

But he had promised to try. He turned back to the mirror. If he were a stranger, what would he notice? How he moved, probably. Michael was very light on his feet. His balance was good and he was ready for action. He always noticed that in other people, even Porter. He had known Porter was an athlete even before he knew he was a fighter because of the way he moved.

Aaron came back with a stack of things.

"Now, I assumed that you gentlemen might like to start black, as that is the traditional color and all, but I think I might be able to interest you in something a bit more contemporary. However, if that doesn't work for you, black is always a nice option." He looked at Porter specifically. "You I would love to get into a very sexy deep blue. Maybe even velvet, although that might be a bit much."

Porter looked a tad nervous, but then he smiled. "Blue. Yes, I had not considered that. I might like that. Let's see the black first, and if it isn't right, then we can go more exotic."

Aaron smiled. "Of course! You, sir, if you would sit for a moment, I am afraid I had better focus on one at a time." He motioned apologetically to Michael.

Michael nodded graciously. "Thank you. I understand your method."

Aaron inclined his head. "I am so glad that you two have come in today. Real gentlemen are so hard to find."

Porter smiled. Michael nodded again. It was not as hard to accept compliments when he knew he had to.

The fitting continued. Porter did go with the dark blue, although not velvet. Michael had to admit that it made him look very mysteriously elegant. Michael went black, but with a subtle pinstripe through in satin and a cut that brought out his broad shoulders. He found he liked it and it surprised him. Porter had a cream vest, cream tie, and white shirt. Michael had a dark gray leather vest, shockingly blue tie and a light blue shirt. Aaron was clearly very good at this sort of thing.

"Shoes, gentlemen?" He asked after about an hour of bringing them things to try.

Michael nodded. "Yes, I definitely need some shoes. Maybe a dark gray, to match the vest?"

Aaron clapped his hands. "Absolutely! I would not have thought that first, but let's try it."

Porter also was looking at himself in the full-length mirror. "Hmm. I have always been drawn to black and white saddle types."

Aaron nodded. He came back with several shoe boxes. The dark gray went pretty well, Michael thought. Porter also liked his shoe selection.

Porter nodded. "I think that really is it. You, sir, are the best. I have never experienced this level of care. I highly commend you."

Aaron smiled happily. After they had removed the suits and shoes, Michael realized he didn't have enough cash to cover his part.

Porter waved it aside. "You can pay me back someday." He said as he pulled a large wad from his pocket.

Aaron counted the amount. He held out some bills. "You gave me two hundred too much."

Porter smiled and shook his head. "It's a tip, from one artist to another."

They took their boxes and left.

The Diamond Nest had one customer looking at bracelets when they came in. Sienna smiled at them.

"When you have a moment, I would like to see you about something." Porter said in a quiet professional voice. Sienna nodded. Porter waved Michael to the back. "Let's go."

The back room wasn't very big. There was a large rough table with tools and projects all over it. Porter set his boxes on a side counter and went to a safe.

"The stuff I think we should use is in here." He came over to the table with several velvet rolls. He set them down rather casually and unrolled one. Michael gasped involuntarily. There were lots of very beautiful diamonds there.

"Pretty, huh?" Porter said negligently.

"You did all this, Porter?" Michael was amazed. He carefully held up a cuff that looked like chain mail, very sparkly and expensive chain mail.

"Yeah, this isn't my favorite line, which is why I won't mind if something happens to it. I think you should probably not have too much jewelry. Me, neither. Sienna is going to carry it for us. I have these, though." He held up two diamond tie-tacks. One was very industrial looking, the other set to look as if it were floating. "Here. This one is for you." He handed the industrial one over. "Oh, and this watch." Porter went to another safe and came back with a watch that had a cut-away face.

"Did you do this?"

"Nah, James, my apprentice, did. He does a lot of steam-punk stuff. He will be a first-rate jeweler. He has the vision. Anyway, you can wear it. If you break it, oh well."

They looked through the jewelry some more. Sienna came back after about ten minutes.

"How did suit shopping go?" She asked, closing the curtain behind her.

"Awesome. We did a great job. Wait until you see it." Michael smiled at her.

"Really?"

"Really."

Porter looked up. "Sienna, my beautiful, would you come over here? Let's see if this fits." He slipped a ring on her finger. It was some sort of knotted thing with a large diamond in the center. "It was my first try. I don't think it was quite right, but I like the idea so I made some other pieces." He held up a bracelet, also a knotted piece with diamonds set in each knot, a clip of stylized flowers and a necklace. The necklace was big. Porter put it carefully on Sienna, along with the clip and bracelet. Then he and Michael stood back to admire the effect.

82

Sienna smiled and posed regally. Porter smiled at Michael. "Garish, isn't it? But the theme of diamond events is 'go big or go home', and we need her to dazzle everybody."

"She will do that, for sure." Michael agreed.

"My love, is there anything you want in a dress?" Porter asked as Sienna took the jewels off.

"No, my dear. I should say that twenty pounds might be the most I can wear all night, dancing and such. I have not regained all my energy yet." Michael felt a bit guilty over that. He hadn't noticed that Sienna was losing weight over them.

"Noted." Porter said softly. Michael thought he felt the same way.

"Then have fun, boys!" She waved and went back through the curtain.

"Let's go dress shopping, Mikey!" Porter said with feigned enthusiasm. "It'll be fun!"

"Fuck off."

Porter laughed.

They went to Marx first. It was bigger than Stan's, mostly because there were women's high end things, too.

Porter stood for a minute getting a feel for what was available. "What do you think?"

Michael seriously considered it. "Well, you are in blue. She shouldn't be too close to you, because that can look weird. And she's blonde now. So…" Something caught his eye. "How about this?" He held up a diaphanous creation in pink.

Porter nodded slowly. "Hmm. It has potential. Or perhaps this?" He held up a sea green gown covered in subtle rhinestones and swathes of fabric. They fanned out and held various others up. Michael drifted to a section labeled "custom designs". Porter held up an off-white dress that looked way too much like a wedding dress to Michael, although he didn't say anything about that.

"That might work." Michael looked around again. "Oh,

Thomas, I think I have it."

"Really? Where?"

Michael held up a sapphire blue gown. It was cut low in the back and had interesting origami-type folds. There was a golden sheen to it that glowed when it caught the light.

"Just imagine her in this, with those blue eyes and that gold necklace."

Porter was staring at it. "This, yes. Good job, Sean. How heavy is it?"

"Not too bad. It is silk, so it is not as heavy as some of those others."

"Hmm." Porter came over and looked it over. "It is going to fit close on her, too. Show off that sexy little waist. She is going to be delicious."

Michael blushed suddenly. "Man, do not do that to me. She is yours and I feel awful when I have those kinds of thoughts about your fiancé."

Porter looked at him curiously. "Well, okay, Sean. I will stop. I didn't mean to make you uncomfortable."

"Thanks, Thomas." Michael cleared his throat. "How about shoes?"

"What do you think?"

"She's going to be dancing, right?"

"So are we."

"Maybe not too high of heels, then."

They walked over to look at the shoes. Porter glanced at several. "I kind of like this gold sandal here." It was strappy and not too high.

Michael nodded. "That'll be good, I think. Don't want to distract from her diamonds."

Porter looked at the shoes and the dress together. "Yes, I like this. What size is that dress?"

"Uh, six?"

Porter shook his head. "Nope, she's a four at most."

They got the right size and went to pay.

"Let me get this for her." Michael said quietly. "I really want to make it up to her." Porter nodded.

"Now we'll just have to make sure it all works together. We might need to get the dress fitted by an expert. Bring all your stuff on Friday, to Mason's?" Porter said as they drove back to the store.

"Yeah, that works. See you then."

Chapter 7

Friday found Michael again at Mason's house. He was meeting Porter and Sienna there. It was early still since Beatrice wasn't due in for another two or three hours depending on her flights. However, Michael wanted to get everything ready.

"Honey, I'm home!" He announced after he opened the door.

"Too bad, precious." Mason shouted form the back room. He came out from a storage area, shut the door, and firmly locked it. "This door does not exist."

"Noted. What's in there?"

"My personal shit with names or pictures or such on it."

"Smart, Mason."

"Thanks." Mason looked at his watch. "You're a tad early. Her plane got held up a little."

Michael shrugged. "I didn't have anything else to do, and I thought maybe I could help you."

Mason nodded. "Yep, you can. Grab that box over there."

Porter and Sienna showed up about half an hour later.

Porter shook hands with Mason, then Michael. "Did you bring the clothes?"

"Yeah, they're in the car. I suppose I had better go and get them, huh?"

Porter smiled at him. "Can't have your lady not knowing what you are wearing. That would be bad form."

Sienna rolled her eyes. "Which is why you haven't showed me, right, Porter?"

"No, that was to be a total ass. I know it drives you crazy." Porter replied calmly. "But we did make sure her dress fits. A few alterations and it is perfect. No one is going to see anyone else. I bet you make this NSA chick green with envy, my dear. Positively green."

"I hope not. It always upsets missions when there is jealousy involved."

Michael laughed. He went out to his car and removed his

clothes boxes. "And, before you ask, yes I did take them out and have them cleaned, Porter." He said as he came in.

"I wasn't going to ask."

"Really? Aren't you feeling well?"

Mason laughed. "Let's see these suits you have."

Michael pulled it out and draped it over the back of the sofa. Mason raised his eyebrows and whistled. "This is an excellent choice for you. And yours, Porter?"

Porter draped his out as well. Mason smiled at them both. "I would never have thought either of you would go this far off the standard line."

Porter shrugged. "We're trying to get better, Mason. That includes listening to others, you know."

Mason nodded. "All right, let me see this knock-out bombshell gown."

Porter held it up. "You know, to get the proper feel for it, you really have to see it on her. It is impossible to look away."

Mason stared at it. "Good God! Who chose this?"

"Uh, me." Michael said, a bit embarrassed. "Is there something wrong with it?"

"Wrong? Hell no. It is perfectly right! No one will ever forget her!"

Porter nodded. "That's the idea."

Mason shook his head admiringly. "My dear, you will melt them all."

Sienna smiled wickedly. "I know. Patos won't know what hit him."

Mason looked at his watch. "Well, Simon here needs to get over to the airport. I'll text you to let you know what is up."

Porter nodded. "Drive safe."

"Naturally."

Mason left and Porter began to make something to eat in the kitchen. "Shouldn't let her think I am a poor host." He said.

Michael nodded. "Need any help?"

"Yes, go get some alcohol from Mason's study. High end stuff, and some glasses. Nothing too heavy though. I don't want to get too drunk to be alert."

Michael nodded.

When Porter got the text, he announced, "She's in. He's bringing her now."

Sienna had stretched out in the recliner. "Oh, too bad. I just got comfortable. Although not as comfortable as the other night."

Porter blushed slightly but said nothing.

Michael laughed. "Is that the first time you slept with her? Well, not slept with, but slept with?"

"Yes." Porter sounded a bit tense about it. "And what?"

"Nothing. I just wondered."

Porter smiled at him. "Well, I doubt you can really be bragging about your own sex life, Sean."

Michael flushed. He let it slide though. Porter was right. "I know, Thomas, but you don't have to rub it in."

There was the sound of an engine outside. A car door slammed. The front door opened. "Right this way, madam." Mason said respectfully.

The young lady swept into the room like she owned it. Michael rose to greet her. She had a hard look in her eyes, like she didn't quite expect to be among friends.

"Your guest, Master Thomas." Mason said obsequiously, touching his hat.

"Thank you, Simon. You may go." Porter said grandly.

"Simon? Thomas? I thought I was going to meet with a Mason." Beatrice said, perhaps a bit sharply.

Porter came out from behind the bar. "There's been a slight change of plans. Mason had a work commitment." He lied smoothly. "He asked us to make you comfortable in his absence. If he can make it later, he will drop in. In the meantime, we don't really need him to be here; he is merely a contact for us. We are the team who will be performing the mission this time. My name is Thomas. This is Sean, and the lady who will be assuming the part of the other love interest is named Marie." He gestured to Sienna, who stood gracefully and nodded.

Beatrice nodded stiffly back. She apparently didn't adapt to upset well. That, Michael thought, was not a good sign.

Porter continued as if he noticed nothing. "Sean here will be your partner for the Diamond Grand Gala tomorrow night. We have taken the liberty, great as it was, to procuring our evening wear already. We have it here for your perusal." He again gestured and Beatrice took in the clothes. She nodded again.

"Also, a close, personal friend has loaned me some of his extensive diamond line. We are able to borrow several pieces for you ladies to wear. If you will step this way, I have them in this case here and you may choose what pleases you."

Beatrice shot a curious look at Sienna. Sienna was as calm and graceful as ever. The two women stepped over to where Porter had his special briefcase open. Inside were the pieces he had already shown Michael and Sienna, as well as a formidable cuff and some others. Beatrice drew in a deep breath when she saw the jewelry.

"Who did you say you got these from?" She asked.

"I didn't say." Porter replied blandly. "Suffice it to say that it is a friend. He would rather I did not go about hawking his name."

"Ah, yes, of course." Beatrice lifted the cuff out, as well as a chain-link necklace and tiara. She tried them on and studied her reflection in the mirror. "These are quite good. I wish I knew who your friend was. He deserves to be famous."

Sienna laughed. "Fame is in the eye of the beholder. He is quite well-known, in the circle he chooses to be known at all in." She also tried on some jewelry, not because she wanted to, but so that it would look more natural. She chose all the pieces that Porter had showed them before. Understated indeed, next to the heavy jewelry

Beatrice had chosen. Michael didn't really like this Beatrice very much. She seemed like she had a chip on her shoulder, or something. He made a mental note to speak to Mason about it.

After the jewels were distributed, Beatrice seemed to relax a bit more. They ate and talked lightly of what to expect from Patos. Michael was quieter than usual. He was watching. He drank no alcohol, and he noticed that Porter drank only water. When Beatrice excused herself to go to the bathroom, Michael looked meaningfully at Porter's glass. Porter winked at him.

Sienna had also risen. She was holding her dress up, admiring it. "You did a fabulous job, Sean." She mused. "I could not have chosen better myself."

Beatrice came back out. She stopped and stared at the gown. "That's what you are wearing?" She asked with a hard little note in her voice.

Sienna turned with a smile. "Why, yes, it is a custom make." She also was deliberately casual. Michael thought that Beatrice looked a bit downcast.

Porter had watched this exchange with a shrewd look. He stood up. "Shall we adjourn to the study? We have more to plan out before I call my driver for you."

Sienna nodded and set the gown back down. "Will you escort me, Sean?" She asked politely.

"But of course." Michael hastily stood and offered his arm. Porter offered his to Beatrice and led the way to the study.

Mason had carefully cleared it of anything of note and Porter had brought a few things that changed the character of the room somewhat, like books and a laptop.

They sat, except Porter, who leaned against the desk. "Now then, the Gala opens at nine o'clock, but no one who is anyone ever gets there at nine. We should be no later than nine forty-five. That way we can hit all the principal players early and cement the attraction of Marie and Beatrice with Emanuel Patos. Does that sound fair?"

90

They all nodded.

"This is a grand ball, so there is dancing. It is formal dancing. Waltzes, foxtrots, that sort of thing. Everyone is all right with that, correct?"

Again, everyone nodded.

"You seem to know a good deal about this ball; have you been before?" Beatrice offered.

"Yes, and I have been personally invited. Several times, in fact. The invitation always gives instruction on what to expect." Porter replied calmly.

"Who invited you?" Beatrice pressed.

"It is of no moment. I have connections beyond this little excursion into the diamond world." Porter said smoothly. "The point is that I have the invitation. I merely want to make sure that we are all in understanding of what is expected of us."

"Oh, of course." Beatrice backed off hastily.

"I will be escorting the lovely Marie, and the equally lovely Sean will escort you, Beatrice. We have worked together before, and it will be more natural for Marie and me to act as a couple. Sean is, I assure you, a perfect gentleman in every way."

Beatrice looked at Michael for a moment. Then she shrugged. "As you wish." She said without emotion.

"Sean, is there anything I am forgetting?" Porter asked, turning to Michael.

"Oh, I don't know. Let me think." Michael ran through the list in his memory. "I seem to recall that you covered the ball expectations quite well. I do believe you may have been a bit quick on transportation though. We have a private jet to take us to New York, and then to Hong Kong once Marie and Beatrice are firmly in the good graces of Mr. Patos."

"I am already in his good graces." Beatrice said.

"Ah, my apologies." Michael inclined his head in her direction. "I did not mean to imply that you were not. I shall modify my statement

91

to when Marie is in Mr. Patos' good graces, we may then fly to Hong Kong. Thomas and I have a safe place there, and we will act from that base. If necessary, we can house you ladies as well, although our preliminary data collection indicated that it was more likely that Mr. Patos would like to keep you ladies closer to his household."

Beatrice nodded. "That is correct. I have been imbedded for a year now, and he keeps a couple of women around him to act as secretaries, social gatherers, and other interests."

"Thank you for the confirmation." Porter said to her. "It helps to know what we are walking into."

Beatrice smiled a bit sourly. "It does, especially when you are not professionals like I am."

Sienna raised her eyebrows but said nothing. Porter smiled laconically. "Oh, but we are. You think because we do not draw a government salary that we cannot operate at the same level?"

Beatrice was still smiling the acid smile. Michael found that irritating. He suddenly laughed. He thought he understood something. Beatrice looked at him. "Ah, please excuse me. I think I understand. Many who work with us believe that we cannot be as discreet or professional, to use your term, as they can. That is your choice to believe, but you have to work with us on this assignment. I suggest you observe how we operate tomorrow night before you make any other judgments as to our abilities."

"Very well." Beatrice said stiffly. "I make no secret of the fact that I opposed outside interference in my own circle. I have been ordered to work with you people to get confirmation of the alleged counterfeiting ring and art theft that drives it. I am a professional and I will act as I have been ordered."

Porter inclined his head again. "Thank you. That is all we require. Now, if there is nothing else to discuss, I can call Simon to drive you to your hotel."

No one had anything more, and Beatrice left with Mason.

Michael shook his head. "She's a firecracker."

"Yes." Porter agreed. "We're going to have to make sure she doesn't go off on us. Anyway, tomorrow, we fly to New York City for this Gala thing and the weekend Diamond Event. Then we're off to Hong Kong. Sienna, make sure you are captivating."

Sienna gave him a wicked look. "But of course. I'll just have to practice on you."

"That's what I am talking about. Exactly that. We have to have an invite to Hong Kong as soon as you can get it."

"Done, Porter." She shrugged.

"All right. Tomorrow, then."

Michael was pretty nervous as they flew into New York. He kept checking his phone. Porter was antsy too. Together, they were driving Sienna crazy. Michael was pretty sure she would have thrown them off the plane if she could have managed it.

Finally, they landed. "All right," Porter said. "Let's get ready and go."

The rooms they had were spacious. Porter and Michael got ready quickly.

Michael looked dubiously at the large diamond tie-tack. "You really think I need that?"

Porter nodded. "Yes, Michael. I know it is huge and dreadfully ugly, but no one will believe that you are a serious contender in the diamond world if you don't have at least one on. Very tacky."

Michael sighed. He didn't like standing out, and the tack had to have at least half a carat on it.

There was a discreet knock at the door. Porter crossed and peered through the peephole. "It's the ladies."

"Wow, they got ready fast."

"Sienna isn't wearing much makeup or anything, just her eyes. Word on the street is that he goes for straight hair, so that's covered, too." Porter opened the door for the ladies.

Sienna and Beatrice came in. Beatrice did not look happy. Sienna appeared to be ignoring her companion's expression. She swept in like a queen. Michael stared. He had seen her often enough, but she had the ability to command all eyes when she wanted to. The fit was perfection and the color stupendous.

"Don't stare, my dear; it's not polite." Sienna chided gently.

"I can't help it, Marie; you are gorgeous."

"You like?" She smiled slightly and turned for them to admire. Beatrice definitely looked sour. She was wearing a black velvet asymmetrical gown and the jewels Porter had supplied. "You clean up pretty damn nicely yourselves. The two of you are almost good enough to eat."

"We'd probably disagree with your stomach." Porter said blandly.

"Oh, I don't know. Let's find out, shall we?"

Michael blushed slightly but smiled. "Some other time, perhaps. We need to get going."

Sienna sighed. "Spoilsport."

Porter bowed and held out his arm. Sienna took it and they led the way, Michael escorting Beatrice.

The entrance to the Gala was lighted and carpeted. It was clearly the place to be for anyone who thought they were anyone in the area. Porter had removed a very ornate invitation from his vest pocket. He glanced at it.

"Here's our ticket in. Remember, we need the attention of Mr. Patos and his personal invitation to Hong Kong. Marie, gorgeous, are you ready?"

Sienna smiled at him. "Watch, baby. Watch and learn."

The door was opened for them. Sienna and Porter swept in like they owned the floor. Michael and Beatrice followed, Michael also acting like he was perfectly at home and expected others to recognize him for it.

The room was politely chatty. Michael noticed that the sound gradually died out as people turned to gawk at them.

Porter loftily ignored it all. Sienna smiled her wicked smile, challenging the entire room.

The lighting was a type that naturally played up diamonds, and they flashed everywhere. It looked like little flashes of cameras going off all the time.

Porter looked over at Michael and then glanced towards the dance floor.

Michael turned to Beatrice. "Would you like this dance?" He asked formally. It was a waltz. She nodded a bit rigidly.

After they took a turn on the dance floor, Beatrice asked Michael to get her some champagne. Michael escorted her to a table conveniently close to Patos, who had two blonde women with him.

Porter and Sienna were out on the floor still. Michael figured Patos hadn't seen them yet.

He snagged two flutes from a waiter and gave one to Beatrice. He stood looking casual, glancing at Patos from time to time. He therefore could pinpoint exactly when he saw Sienna.

It was during a tango, which had cleared the dance floor significantly. Patos literally dropped his champagne flute. It shattered on the ground and one of his attendant women jumped back with a little protest. He didn't hear at all.

Michael smiled and raised his eyebrows appreciably. "They are good dancers, aren't they?" He said casually.

Patos looked at him quickly. "Yes…. Heavenly…"

"Oh, I apologize, sir. Your glass caught my attention. My partner and I are attending this event. He has brought his fiancé, as you can see." He nodded towards Porter and Sienna.

"Charming. I would be interested in a meeting with you both, later, perhaps? My name is Emanuel Patos." He gestured for one of his women to hand a card over.

Michael bowed slightly. "I would think that would be beneficial for both of us. We have heard your name from reputable sources. I did not think to see you here, however. My name is Sean Connor. My partner is Thomas O'Flynn. This is Beatrice Germaine, and the other woman is Marie Flanders."

Patos nodded. He seemed alight with curiosity. "Perhaps we can meet tomorrow for lunch?"

Michael consulted his small pocket book. "We should be able to make that meeting. One o'clock?"

"Absolutely, at the deli on 3rd."

"We shall be there." Michael bowed again slightly.

Patos again stared at Sienna. "Do you think you partner would mind if I were to ask the lady for a dance?"

Michael pretended to consider it. "No, I think that would be quite permissible."

The tango had ended to applause and Porter escorted Sienna off the floor.

"Thomas." Michael extended his hand. "You are as good as ever at that."

"It's the Latin in me, Sean. It responds to the music." Porter winked as he shook Michael's hand.

"Ah, that explains it. By the way, I have been having a lovely chat with Mr. Emanuel Patos, here. He would like to entertain us at lunch tomorrow."

"Charmed." Porter also bowed to Patos.

"If I may be so bold," Patos stood up then, "May I escort this intoxicating lady for the next dance?"

Sienna smiled at him. "Of course, sir! Any friend of Sean is a friend of mine!"

He took her arm.

Porter watched them dance clinically. "Money shot. We are so fucking in. That was a smooth invite, Sean."

Beatrice was staring at them both with a grudging respect. "I didn't think that would work as well as it has." She whispered.

Porter shrugged. "Sometimes it is easier than others." He said offhandedly.

Sienna was, of course, a very good dancer. Porter escorted

Beatrice in the next waltz. Patos brought Sienna back at the end of it. He glanced curiously at Beatrice.

"Ah, I know you, don't I? Yes, yes, you are Beatrice! And these are your friends then?" He said, although Michael was sure he knew who she was.

Beatrice smiled and nodded. "Yes, I am. And, yes, these are my friends."

"Charming. Well, I can see that there will be no impediment to our doing business together, gentlemen." While he said it, his eyes drifted unconsciously to Sienna.

Porter smiled. "No, I don't perceive there will be. Let us discuss it tomorrow. Tonight, we party!"

Patos laughed appreciably. "But of course! With all these lovely ladies, let us have a night to remember indeed!"

Although he could dance well, Michael didn't really enjoy it too much usually. He smiled and went through the motions anyway. He escorted several ladies to the floor, especially two or three who asked him if he would dance. After the third time, he came back to the table to see Sienna smiling at him knowingly.

"Would you escort me, please, Sean?"

Michael bowed floridly. "Of course, beautiful lady!"

When they faced each other for the dance, Michael realized belatedly how low the back of her dress was cut. All sorts of lovely creamy skin was there and he had to put his hand on her. He got a little flustered.

Sienna smiled distantly. "Yes, distracting, isn't it? I got quite a rise from Thomas earlier. And from Mr. Patos, of course."

"I just bet you did. And I bet you enjoyed every minute of it."

"Well, I won't deny I enjoyed Thomas." She looked at him gently. "Sean, my dear, you are very handsome tonight. If you don't want to believe me, believe the ladies who are all just dying to dance with you. Thomas, too, has had his share. Women don't ask strange men to dance just because they are bored."

97

Michael thought about it for a moment. "No, you're probably right. It still seems odd. I don't think I am at all unique, still."

She nodded.

They danced and partied until two in the morning. Sienna was the center of the men's attention, but Michael noticed that he and Porter were being asked to escort ladies much more than other men seemed to be. Maybe there was something in it, after all. He even started to enjoy the attention a little. It didn't feel as hard to blend in when he thought that the people around saw him as someone to be aware of. That didn't make any sense, but it was true all the same.

At two, the party began to close down. It was mainly a place to see and be seen and make connections. Porter, Michael, and Sienna had made the connection they wanted.

It had been highly successful.

Chapter 8

The lunch meeting the next day also went smoothly. Porter and Michael held their own and presented a believably united front. Patos tried fishing for information but Porter evaded giving concrete names. Michael had it slightly easier since he didn't know any concrete names.

At the end of the two hours, Patos smiled. "I would love to further our acquaintance. I think I might be able to provide you gentlemen with some samples of our own work."

Michael nodded, trying to think of a way to get an invite from him. "That would be good, but mightn't it be better if we were to come out and see your production mechanism? That way, you know we are serious buyers, and we know you have the level of integrity we demand."

Patos considered it, casually smoking a very offensive cigar. "Hmm, yes, this idea appeals to me. I am centered in Hong Kong. Will there be any problem for you to get there?" He threw it out casually but his eyes were suddenly shrewd and calculating.

Porter smiled. "Of course not. We have methods of transportation. When will be best to come?"

"I am flying back myself tomorrow morning."

"We were going to leave the Event tonight. Will it be a problem to contact us if we are there before you?"

"No, no problem. Here is my address and phone number." Patos scribbled it on one of his cards.

Porter took it and glanced at it. "Also, my fiancé has expressed interest in going other places. Would it be all right if we bring her along? I am afraid she would find our business dealings boring, but you might know of people who could entertain her?"

Patos smiled knowingly. "Of course! She is most welcome. I can provide a suite for her, should you wish to concentrate on business matters."

"That is most kind. I think that, so long as I pay attention to her at breakfast and perhaps dinner, she would be quite glad to accept your
99

generosity."

Patos nodded. "Then when I return, I shall expect to hear from you gentlemen. Thank you for the opportunity to get to know you both."

Michael stood and shook hands with Patos. "The pleasure has been ours."

Porter also shook hands and they left.

Michael smiled. "Poor Sienna. I hate the smell of cigars."

Porter nodded. "They turn my stomach, but she is a good enough actress to realize what she has to do."

"Why do you think he was so interested in us having our own ride?"

"I bet it was to prove that we are the real deal and not just mooching off him. He seems pretty sneaky and shit."

"Oh, yeah, that makes sense. You were damn smooth though."

"Thanks. We are going to have to give you a crash-course in jewelry soon though. We both need to be experts."

"Whatever, man. I am not an expert in anything." As soon as he said it he knew it was a mistake.

Porter looked at him, one eyebrow raised. "Really, Michael? You want to fucking start that here? I will slap you shitless."

"Just forget I said anything."

"Like hell. You need to stop putting yourself down."

"Whatever man, like you are any sort of expert."

"No, I'm not. Fucking call me on it. But you quit."

Michael flushed up. "Okay, I will. Can we fucking drop it now?"

"Only because we have a fucking job to do."

They returned to the hotel.

Porter knocked respectfully. Sienna opened the door.

"Ah, Marie, you are looking fabulous. Are you busy just now?"

Sienna shook her head. "No, my dear Thomas. Please, come in."

"We have our invitation, ladies. We should leave as soon as

100

possible for Hong Kong. The flights are long and brutal."

Beatrice nodded. "I have a commitment. I will fly separately this time."

"As you wish. Will you need us to take anything for you?"

"No, I have made arrangements. Thank you."

"How may we reach you, to make contact again?"

Beatrice wrote her name and an address. Also a phone number. Michael took it.

He touched Porter's arm. "We need to get packed, Thomas. If you will excuse us, ladies."

When they were packing, Michael turned to Porter. "I don't like this idea of her flying separate. It seems wrong." He said quietly.

"Same here, but we can't do anything about it. If she raises a cry about it, she can blow the whole thing."

"I know."

They were packed and to the jet within forty minutes.

Porter had sent his jewels back to his store and they had nothing out of the ordinary on them.

"Porter, you are not going to be absolutely fucking annoying," Sienna told them both firmly, "or I will fly on my own."

"Yes, I know. I will try to be calmer. I was worried about the Gala."

She snorted softly. "Bullshit. You hate flying."

"I don't deny that, Sienna, but I will be better."

"If he isn't," Michael broke in, "I will take care of it."

Porter looked at him quickly. "How?"

"Oh… you never know, Porter…" Michael grinned at him. "I might just make it up as I go like you always do."

Porter looked disgusted. In fact, he was much better on the flight. They all chatted rather intimately the whole time about nothing in particular. Porter fidgeted with his business card case a little, and he played with a pen absently, but other than those nervous habits, he was very calm, for Porter. Michael didn't have to do anything to him at all.

101

They were both glad.

Hong Kong had the feel of a happening city. There was a pulse to it and the noise was almost deafening.

"Where are we going?" Michael asked Porter.

"There." Porter pointed to a young man holding a sign with their aliases on it. "He is our handler here. He'll drive us around and keep us out of trouble."

"Really? No one can keep you out of fucking trouble."

"Well, he'll at least keep us from getting caught."

"That's more like it."

The apartment wasn't small, but it wasn't large, either. The air was humid and felt a bit sticky. There were two rooms off a combined front room and dining area. The kitchen was small but serviceable. There was one bathroom. The whole place was sparsely furnished.

Sienna looked around. "I will sleep in the front room." She cut off all their protests. "No, I am going to be at Patos' place. I can make it one night here."

"Very well." Michael sighed. He didn't like making a woman take a hardship when he could help her avoid it. He was old-school like that.

They went about arranging the rooms. Porter had some little jammers that Juan had made for them. They would cut any audio transmissions from the apartment aside from cell phones. Michael had a detector for surveillance objects, also made by Juan. They put up the jammers. Porter seemed to relax a bit after that.

They sat around adapting to the time change and playing cards together. Although they would be involved in some high-stress maneuvers, Michael still enjoyed being with his friends and enjoying their company. They were so much fun to be with. He found himself more relaxed than before, somehow.

Sienna was laughing at something outrageous Porter had said, when she suddenly stopped and looked at them both searchingly.

"You two are so much more intimate tonight. You are really

present, here, now, and I am absolutely loving it."

Porter frowned as he thought about it and shuffled. He looked up after a moment. "I guess I feel like you already have seen the worst. I don't have to try to hide it."

Michael nodded. "You already accepted us, so we can accept ourselves a bit more. Not totally, but more."

"However," Porter said, dealing, "you are never going to accept how much I trounce you in this hand."

"Whatever, man. Talk is fucking cheap."

"Ah, but this hand is going to be damn expensive."

They quit the games around eight o'clock at night and went to bed. The time change was going to be challenging.

When his alarm went off at seven-thirty, Michael jerked up, a bit confused. Then he remembered where he was and what they were there for. Yawning, he pulled on some clothes and left his room.

Porter was up, of course. Porter was always up, it seemed. He was quietly making some hot cereal for breakfast.

"Porter." Michael greeted him softly.

"Michael." Porter replied just as softly.

"Do we have any tea and milk in this fucking apartment?"

"Of course I do. The tea is brewing there," he pointed to a ceramic tea pot, "and the milk is in the refrigerator."

"Thanks. I need it to face the day."

"Absolutely."

After they had all eaten, Porter pushed back his chair. "We're going to be at a disadvantage, being here early. It makes us the pursuers, but we do hold the trump card right now. There is no way Patos can resist Sienna. She has piqued his interest and is the key. Therefore, I say we sit tight for all today, at least until dinner time. He knows we are here, so if we call then, it will seem that we have been sightseeing or something. Does that sound good to everyone?"

Michael and Sienna nodded. Michael raised his hand. "Question. How are we going to call?"

Porter pulled out a cell phone. "On this."

"He might be able to track the number then?"

Porter shrugged. "It's possible, although I hope to use it only a few times, so by the time he thinks we are a threat he won't be able to track it by then. Sienna, you will be especially vulnerable. He won't let you call out on any phone he hasn't bugged. We'll be able to see you for arranged breakfasts, but that is all. We'll have to use the physical code to pass any information."

"I understand. It takes a while to pass information that way though."

"I know, but it is a guaranteed way to keep anyone from overhearing anything."

She nodded.

Michael looked out the window. "We need to play onto his innate phobias, I think. We need him to think that there is someone out to get him and that we offer the only protection. Work on that subtly, Sienna. If we can make him put his trust in us, then we can get him to the embassy without much trouble."

She smiled at him. "You are right, I think. I should be able to convince him that there is a mole in his group and that we can keep him from being found."

Porter nodded. "We also are going to need an address for his commercial exploits. We may not be able to get in to see them, so whoever goes in there is going in to raid it. It has to be the right place and there has to be no warning."

"I will do what I can."

"I know you will. We should be done with this within the week. Any longer is going to be too suspicious. We also need to protect Beatrice's embed. We can't compromise her position if we can avoid it."

They all nodded. Michael raised his hand again. "Are we all finished with this stuff now?"

Porter considered. "I think so, why?"

Michael stood up. "I think I need to go out and figure out where this address is and how to get there. Want to come along?"

"Of course! Let's go see the sights."

They spent an enjoyable afternoon walking through the overcrowded streets. There was so much traffic and noise happening all the time that Michael began to develop a headache by the end of two hours. He glanced over at Porter and noticed that he also looked a little strained.

"Shall we return?" Michael suggested.

They made it back to the apartment with little trouble. Michael had a good memory for places and routes, and Porter was good at finding the shortcuts. Sienna seemed to be just enjoying herself and their company. She didn't need to know the routes all that well. She probably had a general idea of how to get there; that was enough.

Once they had settled a bit, Porter suggested they make the phone call.

"Okay, but you call. I'm hungry." Michael said, digging through the food.

"You're always hungry."

"So?"

Porter laughed and called the number Patos had written on the card.

Michael and Sienna came to the table quietly as Porter carefully set the phone down and put it on speaker.

"Hello?" A female voice answered.

"Yes, hello, my name is Thomas O'Flynn. I was given this number by Emanuel Patos."

"Oh! Yes, sir, Mr. Patos did say you would be calling. I'm afraid he is in a meeting right now, though. He asked me to extend his regards and to ask if you had plans for dinner yet?"

Porter glanced and Michael and Sienna. Michael glanced meaningfully at Sienna and then back to Porter. He nodded. Out loud, he said, "I'm afraid that my partner and I have things we absolutely must attend to this evening."

"Oh, I am so sorry to hear that."

"Yes, I am very sorry myself, as Mr. Patos is a wonderful host. However, we have business." He paused and said as if he had just thought of it, "My fiancé is available though. Would it be an acceptable substitution for us if we were to allow her to come in our place, with our sincerest apologies?"

The secretary hesitated for a moment, as if considering. "Uh, let me see if I can relay this information to him. Would you hold, please, Mr. O'Flynn?"

"Absolutely."

There was the quiet click that signaled the phone was on hold. Porter quickly pressed the mute button. He looked at Sienna very seriously. "We have to get you into that circle as soon as we can. You must be careful. You said you would die if I killed myself. I can only pray that I would die if you did, because a life without you would be the worst horror I could ever imagine."

Sienna looked at him just as seriously. "Porter, I have never had any intention of losing you in any way. I will be as safe as I can. I want to see you at breakfast, at least every other morning. I will arrange for it not tomorrow, but the next day, when I am more certain of how I can schedule things. Is that acceptable?"

Porter nodded. "Yes, I will be there. Michael will, too. We might need to provide a united front."

"You aren't fucking keeping me away, united or not, dammit." Michael said softly.

The phone made a little clicking noise. "Sir?"

Porter unmuted his phone. "Yes, I am here."

"Sir, Mr. Patos would be delighted to entertain your fiancé. He suggests that, if possible, you bring her to his address by 7:30. You have his address?"

"Allow me to check." Porter waited a few seconds. "Yes, we have it."

"And you will be able to drop her off? Mr. Patos would be willing to send a car for her."

I'll bet he just would, Michael thought grimly.

"We should be able to drop her off. Thank you ever so much for your assistance." Porter said. "We shall be at Mr. Patos' address by 7:30. Good bye."

"Good bye, Mr. O'Flynn."

Porter hung up. "That's done. Now, Michael, while Sienna is working her devilish charms on Patos, we are going to have to sniff around and see what we can find on our own. We will have to meet with Patos, probably tomorrow, to inspect his jewelry and his offerings on that front. I will coach you on that, so we can both be experts."

"Fine with me. I don't want to look stupid."

"You won't look stupid anyway. I just want you to be an expert." Porter turned to Sienna. "And you, my dear, you must get Patos to the embassy by the end of the week. All right, you are set with everything you need?"

Sienna nodded. "Don't worry about me. I will take care of myself, and I don't trust this Beatrice. I am going to act just like I think I have no friends there. I'm pretty sure I don't."

Michael looked at her for a long moment. "I think you are right. Do you know why you don't trust Beatrice, or is it just a feeling?"

Sienna waved her hand helplessly. "I don't know, Michael! Something just seems wrong with her. Of course, it could just be that she is acting hostile because she is jealous. I know she is that."

Porter looked at her with a smile. "Who the hell wouldn't be?"

"Now, Porter, be nice."

Michael looked at the two of them for a moment. He had a unique opportunity to repay them for all they had done for him over the years he'd been a part of the group. The opportunity might not come by again, and he wanted to show how much they meant. He nodded to himself and stood up. "All right, you two. Here's what's going to happen and you're not going to fucking argue with me about it. I am

107

going out, and you two will have some time by yourselves. I'll be back in two hours. No, no fucking discussion. I love you both. Bye."

Porter also stood. He shook Michael's hand. "Thank you." He said, simply.

Sienna stood beside Porter and gently hugged Michael. Then she stood on her tiptoes, pulled his head down and kissed him. Her eyes were very bright. "Thank you, Michael."

He blushed a bit. "You're welcome." Then he grinned at Porter. "You better not fucking waste it playing cards."

Porter grinned back. "Oh, I won't."

Sienna laughed. "You two are horrible."

Michael left and softly closed the door. He went out into the street. Their handler wasn't back yet; he wouldn't' show for at least another hour. Michael saw that he was close to a commercial area so he decided to go shopping. If there was a jewelry store or two, perhaps he could buy some pieces as examples for Porter to teach him about.

He set out for the shops. There were indeed two jewelry stores. Michael went in the first and just looked for about half an hour. He wanted to get a feel for what was available.

Then he went in the second and did the same. It seemed like he was starting to notice some things about the construction and quality, but he wasn't sure. He bought two rings, one bracelet, and two necklaces in the second shop. None were as striking as Porter's, but he liked the way they looked and felt. He bought three necklaces, two bracelets, and two very beautiful brooches in the first shop. Then, because he couldn't think of a good reason not to spend all his ready money, he bought a very interesting enamel and sapphire gold clip. He thought it might go in someone special's hair, if he should ever find her. Michael had never bought something for a girlfriend he didn't have. He had never even really had a steady girlfriend. He'd always been a little shy around girls, and a little afraid that they would reject him if they knew him better. He bought it because he thought he might like to have it for when he did have a girlfriend. Again, he was probably being a bit ridiculous; it seemed like the thing to do. He took his jewelry, tucked it very carefully up under his shirt, and left.

He knew he probably looked a bit odd with little bulges under his shirt but he didn't care. He wasn't about to sacrifice his stuff just to look cool to people he would never see again and wouldn't notice him anyway.

It was close to seven by the time he got back to the apartment. He thought about knocking before going in, but then, with a small smile, he very softly opened the door. Porter and Sienna weren't in the front room. Good. He hoped that they were doing something fun in the back room. He just as quietly shut the door and went to the table. He poured himself some tea and waited, sipping it and considering his bags. Almost everything he had done was out of character for him. Everything usually was carefully considered to maintain his appearance of being outgoing while keeping his real feelings hidden. He rarely acted impulsively, and he almost never did things that might let other people get to know him better.

After about ten minutes, Sienna came out. She looked a bit pink in the cheeks, but otherwise the same. She smiled at Michael. "Oh, hello, Michael. I didn't hear you come in."

"That was the idea. I didn't want to interrupt anything important happening."

Sienna sighed tragically. "Alas, not as important as I might have liked!"

Porter, who had come out as well, suddenly blushed furiously.

Sienna began to laugh at him. "My God, Porter! I have never seen you lose it that badly!"

Michael grinned at Porter, as well. "Fucking looks like a cherry, doesn't he?"

"Fucking shut up." Porter said, still quite red.

Sienna continued to laugh.

"Sienna, do you suppose we could wrap this up? We have to get you to dinner."

Sienna stopped laughing, although a lovely smile stayed on her face for quite a while and her eyes sparkled.

Michael raised his eyebrows at Porter suggestively. "Yes… dinner… since you've already done dessert…"

Porter flushed again and laughed. "Hell yes, Mikey. But that's all I will say about it."

There was a knock at the door. Michael moved to look through the peephole. "It's our handler. Let's get ready to go. Marie, do you have everything you might need for tonight?"

Sienna thought about it as she gathered her things. "Yes, I think so. Well, Thomas, let's get this going."

When they pulled up in front of Patos' complex, there was one of his inevitable blonde beauties waiting. She gestured for Sienna to go inside and addressed Porter and Michael. "Mr. Patos wished to thank you in person, but he is unavailable just now. He has a business commitment to attend to. He did express interest in seeing you two gentlemen tomorrow. Will you be available around two?"

Porter bowed slightly. "There should be no reason we cannot be here at two."

The young woman smiled slightly. "Then he would like to see you then.

Michael smiled back at her. "Of course. And will you be there, too?"

The young woman gave a slight start. "Uh, I probably will be. Mr. Patos uses me as a secretary. Of sorts." Her lips twisted slightly in an ironic grimace.

Michael looked at her deeply for a moment. He thought she looked a little sad or something. He smiled at her again and nodded. "Then this meeting will be that much more profitable. Might I be so bold as to ask your name?"

She again started and answered hesitantly, "Um. My name is… Karen."

Michael smiled and bowed to her. "Then I shall see you

110

tomorrow, Karen. I look forward to it."

She smiled back, this time with the harsh edge gone. "I will, too." She said, shyly. Then, as if remembering where she was, she stiffened and turned sharply to the door. Before she closed it, she glanced back at them and blushed slightly.

"Well done." Porter said softly.

"Shut the fuck up."

Back in the apartment, Porter and Michael made some food for themselves. When they were sitting at the table, Porter looked earnestly at Michael. "Michael, I was serious when I said 'well done'. You were completely natural for like the first time, minus fighting. You have made an ally in that house. We might need it. Plus," he said, cutting his spring rolls, "she seems pretty and not completely jaded yet. Something tells me she is an important add."

"I'm not sure what the hell happened. It just seemed like the right thing."

"Michael," Porter said gravely, "we both need to pay more attention to our feelings. You did that, and I think it was the perfect thing to do."

"Well, thanks, I think." Michael was still confused about the whole thing. Why had he decided to act that way, anyway? She was pretty, but he saw lots of pretty girls. Something about this one had struck him, somehow.

They finished their food in comfortable silence. After the dishes were washed, Porter said, "What the hell did you do while you were out, anyway?"

Michael smiled at him. "Oh, this and that. You tell me what you did and I will tell you what I did."

Porter flushed a little. "We talked. And other stuff."

Michael shook his head. "Not good enough."

Porter flushed more and then he laughed. "All right, we made out. Heavily. Good enough?"

"Yes, I think so. Look, I know it is private stuff, but you keep trying to keep everything you can secret. Just trying to keep you from hiding everything."

Porter nodded. "Yeah, I get it. What did you do?"

Michael smiled. "I went and looked at jewelry. Just to get a feel for it. And I bought some to show you what caught my eye. Now you can teach me about it."

Porter stared at him. "You looked at jewelry for an hour and a half?"

Michael nodded. "It just... I dunno, it seemed like something I should do. I thought it might help. Or something. Shit. I dunno why I did it."

"Holy hell. Well, that sort of dedication deserves an expert opinion. Give it to me and we'll go over it now." Porter pulled out two jeweler's loupes and handed one to Michael.

Michael handed Porter the two bags. Porter unwrapped all the pieces and laid them out. He looked at them intently for a few minutes. Then he nodded to himself. "All right, you tell me why you bought each specific one."

Michael found that he remembered exactly why each one had caught his attention. Porter was a good listener, nodding occasionally and not saying anything at all. Michael gestured to the sapphire clip last. "I just bought that because it caught my eye and I thought... well... um... I thought I should have it ready for a future thing. Or something." He blushed.

Porter nodded. "Yes, it is one of the most unique pieces I have seen in a while." He said neutrally. "She'll love it. Whenever you find her."

Michael was very grateful that Porter understood. "So teach me about the rest of these."

The rest of the evening, Michael was given a crash course in the art of jewelry. Porter was very knowledgeable and a good teacher and Michael was a good student. He showed how to identify poor gold work, shoddy crafting, loose stones and other setting flaws. He also showed Michael to identify the tricks used to make lower quality diamonds look better. It turned out that Michael had not done too badly.

"You know," Porter said, looking at the sapphire piece again, "this is the best you have done. The workmanship is quite good and the stones are quality. No melting of crystalline structure, the colors are close but not exact, which tends to show that only natural stones were used, the gold work is masterful. She is going to love it."

Michael found he really liked hearing that from Porter. "Thanks, man. I just need to meet her."

Porter smiled. "Yes, but when you do, you'll be ready. If you would like, once you do find her, I would love to make something to go with this. It has piqued my interest."

"Thanks, man. Really. You are a good teacher."

Porter smiled at him. "Well, you are a good student, to be honest with you. And I like showing off."

Michael laughed. "Oh good."

Porter looked at him searchingly. "Michael, serious question: have you ever bought anything for a woman before?"

Michael looked at his plate. "Nah, man, I never have beyond the usual throw-away crap."

"The reason I am asking is because you chose something very personal to you. That, beyond the quality of the piece, is more telling than anything else to your friends. You don't even have a painting or picture up in your condo, so this tells me more about you than anything else I have seen of yours."

"What does it tell you?" Michael asked warily. This was unexpected.

Porter smiled slightly. "Oh, knock the fuck off. I am not some random stranger you need to be scared of. It tells me that you have a good eye for symmetry, that you are attracted towards the types of items that are unique rather than functional, and that you are a bit of an idealist."

"All that from a fucking clip?"

"Well, the piece is unique, in that many women do not have one, nor would many ask for one when a more serviceable piece might be available. It is symmetrical in that the scrollwork compliments and flatters equally. And you are a fucking idealist because you bought it for a woman you have never met."

"You don't think it was stupid?"

"Well, it might seem stupid to an outsider, but not to me." Porter smiled at him again. "I did make Sienna a total of two engagement rings, you know. Think of how long that took? "

Michael thought about that as they gathered up the jewelry again. Porter carefully wrapped the sapphire clip. "I have a secure compartment specially designed to carry jewelry. Would you like me to hold this for you? And the rest, but this is more important."

Michael nodded. "Thank you, Porter. You are one of the best guys I know."

Porter flushed a little. He did not deny it though. Instead, he said, "Michael, have you ever had a girlfriend?"

"Nah, man. Girls scare me."

Porter laughed. "Well, that just stands to reason. Dames are poison, after all."

Michael grinned. "No, I never have. You told me once you were a virgin still. Well, so am I."

Porter nodded. "I kind of thought so. Anyway, the way you acted around that Karen was completely different from how you have acted in the past. I wanted to encourage you with her. Something about it feels right to me, somehow."

"Me, too. I am glad that you agree though. Maybe we can arrange some sort of double make-out session with you and Sienna later on."

Porter blushed again. "Dammit, Michael, you know I am not terribly comfortable with that yet."

"Good. I think Sienna would be upset if it were routine for

you."

"Hmm. Good point. Well, good night."

"Sweet dreams, you fucking thief."

Chapter 9

The meeting was at 2:00, so of course Michael and Porter were ready by 1:00 and being driven to Pato's complex.

Porter looked out the window at the hordes of people that seemed to ebb and flow all around. "My God I hate the city sometimes."

Michael nodded. "Fucking impossible."

Porter stopped staring at the crowds. "It was one of the biggest draws back in Tergistan for me. No fucking people around."

Michael didn't say anything. They got out of the car in front of Patos' suites. The driver wouldn't be back for at least two hours. Porter warned that they may not be ready for him then, even, and to wait without speaking more than casually to anyone. The driver nodded. Michael knew the guy was a professional but it never hurt anyone to be reminded.

As the car left, Porter looked at the front door, absently buttoning his light sport jacket. "I hate my hair this fucking long. Drives me crazy."

"Oh, that's your problem then! It looks damn good that way though. All wild and crazy..."

"Shut the fuck up."

They went to the front door and Porter pulled the elaborate bell pull. A gong sounded somewhere. Porter gave Michael a look that spoke volumes. Michael laughed.

"I think the entry sound is quite indicative of a certain lack of confidence in the person of the house, Sean."

"You're probably right, Thomas. No one needs a gong when they know they can command a bell, as it were. Over-compensation, perhaps."

The door opened. It was Karen again. She looked surprised for a moment. "Oh! I did not expect you yet!"

Michael bowed his head quickly. "We find that being early to meetings conveys the correct impression. Besides, I look forward to

116

seeing you more, without the added complication of doing business at the same time."

Karen blushed and smiled. Then she looked down confusedly, as if she were afraid of her reaction. Michael found that both unnatural and telling. He glanced at Porter. Porter's eyes had narrowed a little. He had seen it too.

"Please, do come in. Mr. Patos is not ready for you yet, but I can entertain you until such time as he is."

Michael again bowed his head.

They were lead to a room off the foyer that was smallish but not tiny. They sat, chatting with Karen about nothing in particular. Porter said little, allowing Michael to be attentive. It worked out quite well, and Michael found that he liked Karen, although she seemed somewhat reserved about something. He couldn't place it. Some of her comments seemed bitter, and she once glanced at the shut door as if afraid of being overheard after she made one of those observations.

At five minutes to two, she stood and, excusing herself, went to see if Patos' was ready for the meeting.

Porter waited until the door was shut, then glanced at Michael. "You did very well, Sean. Something about this is a bit off though." He gestured around the room meaningfully.

Michael nodded. "It is almost time, Thomas. Perhaps he keeps a very tight schedule." He gestured as well, trying to convey what he felt about the household. Porter nodded. He understood.

"Yes, you are probably right. We should have felt the situation out more thoroughly."

The door opened and Mr. Patos stepped in. Karen was standing behind him, her face a bit flushed and her eyes downcast.

"Gentlemen! Please, excuse my delay. I was unavoidably detained." He gestured back towards the open area. "Shall we?"

Porter and Michael rose and smilingly followed him. Michael looked at Karen as he passed. She glanced at him then looked away quickly, guiltily. Michael sighed softly. This guy frightened her about something. He must have quite a hold on her. That made Michael a little angry.

Patos lead them to an ornate study. Sculptures and paintings tastefully dotted the book-lined walls. Michael looked around curiously. It seemed over-done and almost plastic, staged to look impressive. He glanced at a curious marble sculpture, the only piece that seemed personally evocative.

"You like this piece?" Patos asked, gesturing to the sculpture.

Michael nodded. "Yes, it seems quite alive, for some reason."

Karen, delegated to a humiliating place behind Patos, looked at Michael with a curiously tragic expression.

Patos smiled and nodded but said nothing more.

Porter sat across from the desk, Michael taking the other chair. "Let us get to business, Mr. Patos. Your time is valuable, as is our own. We have at our disposal a network with which we can introduce some of your pieces, provided you have only the highest quality. We simply cannot be expected to try to pass anything but the best."

Patos smiled. "But of course, Mr. O'Flynn. I would expect nothing less. I have several of my own pieces here for you to examine. Please, gentlemen," He snapped his fingers and Karen came forward to hand him a velvet lined box. He opened the hinged lid and displayed several gold and diamond creations. "Feel free to examine and comment. I want only honest opinions."

Porter pulled his jeweler's loupe from his watch pocket. He selected a piece and began a meticulous job of looking at it. Michael also took out his loupe and took a ring at random. He noticed right away that it was too heavy for the filigree style it was imitating. He went through the motions of examining it anyway. The diamond was passable, but the gold work was graceless.

He set it back and selected another piece. Mr. Patos seemed pleased that they were taking so much interest. The examinations took a long time. It was, Michael noticed with a start, over two hours later when they had finished. Porter had finally set down the last piece, the

118

ring Michael had started with, and looked at Michael questioningly.

"Well, Thomas, I am satisfied. You?"

"Yes, Sean. I think so." Porter turned back to Mr. Patos. "Mr. Patos, we can distribute some of these lines. However, they are not universally up to our expectations."

"Really?" Patos' eyes grew a bit dangerous.

Michael nodded. He gently picked up the ring that he had rejected. "This piece is just too heavy. The filigree is not quite delicate enough, and it is too much for our clients."

Patos seemed to relax back. "Oh, yes, you are right. That was an early attempt, and the line has been discontinued for the very reasons you mention. Any others?"

The negotiations continued for perhaps forty-five minutes more and ended with a verbal agreement for Michael and Porter to fence some of the jewelry at a later date.

Patos stood and shook them each by hand.

"By the way," Porter said casually, "I would like to see Marie tomorrow morning, if that is all right. I miss her charming conversation. Would it be acceptable if we were to come at 8:00 in the morning?"

Patos nodded. "Of course! She is a heavenly woman!" Michael heard a note of irritation in his voice, however.

Porter smiled again. "Then thank you, Mr. Patos. I think we will have a beneficial relationship. We shall darken your door only for a few days longer. Now that we are here in Hong Kong, we might as well do some other business as well."

Patos nodded again and Karen showed them to the door. "Will you be in tomorrow, sirs?" She directed it to Michael, with an appealing expression.

"I believe so, yes." Michael took her hand and kissed it gently. He continued to hold her fingers.

She started again, but she did not pull her hand back. "Your…your driver had to leave. He said something about time constraints."

Porter nodded. "That is all right. We can reach him."

Michael saluted her slightly and they left.

The car was not there. They knew how to get back to the apartment, so they walked.

At the entrance to the alley that lead to their front door, Porter looked up the street towards the commercial district. "Sean, if it is all right with you, I would like to go and look around a bit. Sometimes, I get ideas from seeing things."

"Whatever you want, man. I am going to be in here for the rest of the day."

Porter nodded and walked off.

Michael thought he might like to read a bit, so he got his book out and made a pot of tea. He didn't like coffee, but tea he had a weak spot for. The apartment hummed gently with the noise of the street outside.

It was about two hours later when there was a soft knock on the door. Michael became instantly alert. No one should be there. He retrieved his small automatic pistol and went to the door, standing to the side and out of line of sight. "Yes? Who is it?" He called through the door.

"It's Karen, Sean. Open up, please!"

Michael was shocked. This was the last thing he had expected. He debated not responding, but something prompted him to open the door.

He gestured her in quickly, glancing out the door. There was no one else in the alley.

He shut the door and locked it, then turned to her.

"May I ask what the fucking hell you think you are doing?" Now that he had her in here, he was going to have to figure out what to do about his mess.

She looked strained and upset. "Please, Sean, or whatever your name is, don't send me away. Patos will kill me if he finds out."

Michael gestured her to the table. "Would you like some tea?"

He asked, pulling a chair out for her. It seemed like a good way to buy time and think about what to do. She hesitated slightly, then sat.

"Yes, tea would be very nice, thank you."

Michael poured her a cup and sat across from her. He put the automatic on the table, carefully pointed away from her. "Why the fuck are you here? You must know I am not who I am pretending now, so you also must know I can't let you go back."

She looked away, blushing furiously. "I had to leave him! He's...he is dangerous."

"We know that."

"I know you know. I thought that maybe, perhaps, you could protect me and help me get out from under his control."

Michael considered that for a little while. They sipped tea in silence. He sighed finally. "Look, Karen, I can't make you any promises; not without talking to my partner."

She nodded. "I expected that. Here's something else: Patos isn't willing to let your friend go. I mean Marie. He won't let her leave. Besides, Beatrice thinks she is a spy."

Michael sat up straight. "What the fuck? How do you know? Tell me everything."

"I saw her sneaking down to his private quarters last night, so I followed. I listened at the door. They said a lot of stuff, most of it I couldn't really hear, but one thing I did hear was Beatrice saying loudly that Marie was a plant and that she wanted her out. Patos laughed at her and said he didn't care, that he wanted her, that he was going to win Marie over and that Beatrice should know him better. But he also said something about Beatrice going up in his eyes and that she was winning his favorite. Then he said something like, 'If she is a spy, I'll deal with her. She'll just disappear, like the other one you let me know about.'"

Michael stared at her. This was horrible. Sienna was in terrible danger now. "Fuck! She said... goddamn it all!" He pulled at his hair distractedly. "Fucking fuck!"

Karen just looked at him. Michael found that he was getting angry. Not good.

He tried to bring his temper back under control again. "I apologize, it's just... I don't want a good friend hurt."

She nodded. "There is more to it, though, isn't there?"

Michael wasn't sure how he would have responded, because he suddenly heard Porter outside shouting, "Sean! Get your fucking ass out here! I need fucking help!"

Michael jumped to his feet. He glared at Karen. "You stay right there. Don't get up. If I find you gone, you will not like what happens."

She shrank back a little, but she nodded.

Michael ran to the door and opened it.

Porter had walked into a group of perhaps eight men, and he was fighting hard. Blood had soaked his right sleeve from a cut high on his arm. Michael was in the thick of it before he stopped to think. The fight was short and ugly. Porter had pulled two knives and cut up at least three of them, and Michael downed three more from his end. Porter buried the knife in the chest of one of the last two. He looked furiously at the remaining man. "Get the fuck out. Never come back. As far as you know, this never happened. Don't tell whoever told you to do this what happened. Now fuck off or I plant this other knife in you and leave you for the rats."

The man ran out of the alley.

Michael pulled the knife out of the dead man and they put the bodies over the fence into the next alley to be discovered there.

"Fuck, man, you're bleeding." Michael caught Porter as he swayed.

"Yeah, well, a couple of them had knives. I had to take care of them first. You're no beauty yourself right now." It was true; Michael had cuts himself. One was deep.

Michael helped Porter into the apartment. "Listen, man, we got a problem."

"Yeah, we have a huge fucking problem, Michael! How the fuck did they fucking find us?" Porter was clearly furious still. He caught sight of Karen, still sitting white-faced at the table. His eyes blazed with fury. "You! Did you have anything to do with this?" He roared at her.

"No! No! Please believe me!" She sounded hysterical

"If I find out that you did..." Porter didn't finish that thought, because he almost fell.

Michael picked him up bodily and carried him to the table. "You're fucking bleeding, man! Can I at least fucking take care of that before you go off again?"

Porter looked at his right arm almost curiously. His coat was slashed and his shoulder bleeding freely. "Ah, fuck, somebody got a goddamn lucky hit."

Michael helped him take off the coat and his shirt.

Karen, still very pale, came around the table. "I have a nursing degree. Will you let me help, Thomas, or whatever your name is?"

Porter looked at her hard and nodded.

It took a little more than fifteen minutes to get all the bleeding stopped and the various cuts attended to on them both. Karen was good at it. Michael noticed that her hands were very gentle.

"Now," Porter said grimly "What the hell are you doing here?"

Karen told him the same thing she had told Michael. Porter grew angrier as she talked. When she finished he slammed his hand on the table. "Fucking hell! They gave us a fucking turncoat for a fucking in? What were they fucking thinking? And why the hell are you here then?"

Karen hung her head. "Because," she whispered, "you two were nice to me and treated me like a real person. I had forgotten what that felt like. I was afraid that you would leave and I would not ever get out."

Michael stared at her. "What the hell do you mean?"

"Patos always gives names to his girls, like we are defined by that name. You already know I had been to college and stuff. Well, I was trying out modeling, just to see if it would be a good sideline, and he came to a shoot. He liked how I looked and he wined and dined me, but I was too willing to give it up to him and he never liked me after all."

Porter was still angry, but he had calmed somewhat. "What name did he call you?"

Karen flushed and looked terribly ashamed. "He called me Bubblegum, because he treated me like my head was full of air."

Michael shook his head. "What a fucking wanker."

Porter nodded.

Karen was still blushing. "There is more, though. After I heard Beatrice, who he calls queen bee, or queenie, I went and looked through his files. He only writes things on cards, never puts it into a computer. He used to make fun of me for wanting to use a spreadsheet. I stole a key to his cabinet a while ago. Anyway, I found this card in his file." She reached into her shirt and pulled out a small index card. It had their aliases on it and a description. "At least within five miles radius, probably Southeast. XO"

Michael and Porter looked at it. Suddenly, Michael straightened. "Fuck! I know this!" He pulled out the card Beatrice had given them with her contact info. The writing was the same.

Porter stared at the two cards. "She's been in it from the start."

Karen nodded. "I think she wants to be the favorite."

Porter stood up quickly. Michael grabbed his arm.

"Let me fucking go, Michael, I am not leaving Sienna in that fuck hole."

"Porter, you can't go in there; he'll kill her. Fucking think, man!"

"Fuck you. Let me go!" Porter tried to free his arm roughly.

Michael didn't let go, but he did reach up and gently rook hold of the little Catholic icon that Porter wore. Porter stared at him. "Porter, you can't. Fucking think for a second. He will kill her. What will you do then?" Michael asked quietly.

Porter suddenly grabbed Michael's arm and bowed his head. He was crying.

They stood like that for a while. Finally, Porter nodded. He took some deep breaths. "All right. She has a job. I will go see her tomorrow and pass this along. But we need some overhead." He looked back at Karen. "You have to stay here, Karen. We can't let you go back and tell anyone about this. Michael will stay with you. He is either going to keep you safe or be your jailer. I don't give much of a fuck either way. Since you are here, you should know what is happening. We are trying to get proof of Patos' involvement in art theft and counterfeiting."

"Oh! I know what you are talking about. Patos took me and his other secretary to the warehouse once."

Porter pulled away from Michael. He went back to the table. "Are you sure? Could you pinpoint it on a map?"

"Maybe, with some help."

Porter looked at her for a moment. "All right. Here's what we do then. We fucking call in help."

"What the fuck?" Michael protested.

Porter ignored him. He pulled out a cell phone, different from the one he had used to call Patos.

"Mason? Get here as fast as you fucking can. We have a goddamn leak and we need you. Go by the shop. Tell James that I told you the air smells sweet and the cherry blossoms are blooming. He'll know. Bring the case with you. Yes, it was Beatrice; now get here. Sienna is in there alone and all the rules just changed. All right." He hung up.

Michael nodded. "Excellent, Porter."

Porter shrugged. "I made sure I had a way to contact him if I went off the deep end again." He turned to Karen. "There's no way they knew our address. You must have some sort of tracker on you. Start stripping, girl. There are jamming devices in this apartment, so they couldn't pinpoint you. That's why they were outside and confused instead of in here and killing."

Karen flushed again. She stood up and started taking her clothes off. Porter looked at each one. He handed the shirt, jacket, skirt and shoes to Michael. Michael saw the little devices immediately. Karen was standing in her slip and undershirt. Porter held up his hand to stop her. Michael glanced her over quickly.

"No more, Porter, these are clean."

"Good. Get rid of those, preferably in a taxi or something."

Michael went out. There was a military type vehicle outside in traffic. He tossed the clothes in the back casually and it drove slowly off.

"This is serious, Porter." Michael said as he came back. "Patos has trackers on his women. He could have trackers on Sienna, too."

Porter shrugged. "I know that but there isn't a damn thing we can do about it until Mason gets here and has some sort of plan for us to follow. I will let Sienna know all this. She is on her own, and I hate that worse than anything. What the fuck choice do we have though?"

Michael shrugged. "We can't get her out. There's no way with someone embedded as deep as Beatrice is."

"No, and we have to get that fuck to the embassy, soon. Mason will help with that, and the case he is bringing will help even more." Porter shook his head and said softly to himself, "I picked a goddamn terrible time to go fucking dry. Fucking promises. Sometimes I fucking hate you, God."

Karen was shivering. "Um, can I get something to wear?"

Michael stood up quickly. "Oh, I am sorry. Here, I think I have something that might help." He went to his room and came back with an ornate silk robe. "It was in there when we got here. It's clean."

"Did you wash it or something?" She asked as she slipped it on.

Michael smiled. "Yes, I did, but I meant clean of bugs. That is more important to me."

She nodded slowly. "I didn't think of that."

"No, why should you?" He looked at Porter. "I'll sleep in the living room area on the chair. She can have my room."

Porter shrugged. "That would probably be best. We'll get you some clothes, Karen. Also, you are going to lose the blonde hair."

"I don't really like it anyway."

"What color was your hair to start with?"

"Uh…" she seemed to be having trouble remembering. "Auburn, I think."

Porter stood up. "All right. I hate fucking sitting and waiting. I am going out to get food, get some hair dye, and get clothes. I'll be back." He looked Karen over seriously. "What size are you?"

"About a four, I think."

Porter looked at Michael. "She's your responsibility now. We can't let her get out. Patos will be furious that she is gone and that she hasn't been recovered. He doesn't like being crossed and he is paranoid or else he wouldn't have bugged his own secretary. We can't afford to lose her. Plus, I fucking want to piss him off. Fucking bully who uses and discards women deserves it."

Michael grinned viciously at him. "Just wait til he learns that one of his women turned on him and another lead us straight to him. I would love to see that."

Porter grinned back. "Me too. All right, I am off. I think I will have to buy another jacket, too. That rip and that blood can't be fixed. I shouldn't be more than an hour, two at the maximum. If I am, you call Mason on that phone and you tell him. I could be dead."

Michael nodded seriously. "Got it, but you better fucking live. I am not telling Sienna we lost you in Hong Kong. And stay away from the bars. I need you, promises to God or not."

"Oh, I am going to try my hardest. Just for fucking paybacks on that bitch." He went back for a new shirt and his money clip.

Karen was staring at Michael. "You are really going to keep him away from me?" She whispered.

"Well, I don't want anything to happen to you, so, yes, I am. I almost hope he comes himself. I would love to beat his ass in for thinking he can do that type of thing to women just because he wants to. People are people and they deserve respect just because of that."

She glanced down at the table again, seemingly confused. Then she looked up at him shyly. "Thank you."

127

"You're welcome. May I offer you some more tea?"

"I would love some tea. But I don't want to take your room from you."

Michael shrugged as he got some water set to boil. "I don't care much and I can be closer to the door if there is trouble that way."

Porter came out, pulling his shirt on. Karen didn't see him, but she blushed very red and looked out the window. "Please, I'm afraid of the dark. Could I at least stay in the same room? I promise I won't be any bother. I'm terrified of being alone at night."

Porter suddenly sat down by her again, surprising her. "Look at me, Karen." He said gently. She did reluctantly. "Did Patos ever use the dark to punish you?"

She started crying desperately. "I never told him I was afraid, but he seems to know what weaknesses are! He used to lock me in my room at night when he was angry and turned the lights off and I was so afraid! The next morning he could do anything he wanted because I was so glad to not be in the dark anymore!"

Porter reached over and put his hand on her arm. "You have no reason to be afraid here. We will keep you safe."

Michael came over to the table. "Karen, you do whatever you need to do to feel like we are your friends and want you to be secure. If that means sleeping with the lights on, that is no problem. I can sleep with lights on. If that means you only whistle 'Dixie' and eat Cheerios, then that is what we will do for you."

Karen looked at them both. She was clearly having trouble believing them. Porter looked over at Michael. "I really have to get going, Michael."

"I understand. Stay safe, you old pirate."

Porter stood up. "Karen, is there anything you want to eat, specifically?"

She shook her head. She was very close to crying again. "No, thank you."

"Then stay with Michael. There is no one I would trust with my life more than he."

Michael gripped Porter's hand in gratitude. Then he sat at the table with Karen. Porter left. They sat quietly for a little while. The tea pot whistled and Michael poured the hot water into their cups. She didn't believe him. He could tell. He sighed and just decided to go with his gut instinct. "Is there anything I can do for you to convince you that I am serious about keeping you safe?"

Her eyes brimmed over again. "No, I just can't quite understand why you would want to."

"Oh." He felt horrible that she kept getting upset. Without really thinking about it, he reached over and put his arm gently around her shoulders. Karen started crying hard then, and he stood up and went to where she was. He gently picked her up and then sat with her on his lap, and she wrapped her arms around him and cried. It took her a long time to stop. She still held him, even when she had stopped crying. It was like she needed to know that he was real and really there for her.

Porter came back. It hadn't been an hour, but it had been close. He gave Michael an understanding look. Then he cleared his throat. "I have some things for you, Karen, if you want to try them on. If not, that is also fine with me." He put his bags down on the kitchen counters and began to take things out of them. Most were food, but there were some clothes. One was a new jacket for himself, and Michael noted that it was very similar to the one that had been destroyed in the fight. The others were for a woman. They were mostly dresses and skirts.

Karen finally stood up. "Thank you. Thank you both. I can't remember anyone being this nice to me ever."

Porter glanced at her quickly. "That's because you haven't met anyone worthy of knowing you yet."

Karen smiled bitterly. "I am not worth knowing."

Michael firmly put his hand over her mouth. "Okay, the one of the ground rules of hanging out with us is you are not allowed to spout shit like that. We will not let you. You are a very beautiful and very

129

worthwhile woman. You have heard that you are not worth anything by a man who uses people like they are garbage. Well, garbage only sees other garbage. We see you as you are. We will have to make you see yourself that way, too."

Porter smiled. "Not to insinuate that we are perfect, since we both have the exact same problems ourselves."

Michael nodded. "True, but we are trying to get better. So, none of that talk, Karen."

She stared at them from behind Michael's hand. Finally, she nodded.

Michael smiled at her. "All right, you can talk again. Did you want to try on the clothes? Then we can dye your hair back."

Karen managed a half smile. "Okay. I think I would like that."

Porter handed her the clothes and she went back to change. Porter glanced at Michael and smiled, his dark eyes twinkling. "Don't lose that sapphire clip, Michael," he said softly. "She would look amazing in it."

Chapter 10

Porter had made some delicious food. Michael was always impressed with how his friend could throw off a meal with very little effort. Karen was still a bit shy around them. Michael didn't blame her, since she had every reason to mistrust everyone. The type of mental abuse Patos used would take a while to break through.

Michael and Porter did their usual casual banter. Michael knew that Porter was still upset about the way this mission was turning out, and he was also glad that Mason would be coming to help them with it. Porter and he both got too exclusive to plan out the mission the way Mason could.

Porter glanced at Karen at one point during dinner. "Karen," he said gently. "We don't care if you talk with us, you know. We like hearing ourselves, but we want to hear you, because, frankly, Michael isn't the prettiest person in the room and I already know what he thinks."

"I don't have anything to say." She protested, staring at her plate.

"You're wrong, you know." Michael said calmly. "Everyone has something to say, even if it is just to tell us to shut the fuck up."

She laughed at that, but still stared at her plate.

Porter shrugged. "She isn't ready yet, Michael. Let her be."

Michael remembered something. "You know, the last time I heard you say that, you beat the hell out of me later than evening."

"Well, what can I say? You deserved it, you fucking moron. Fucking moping around like nothing was good enough and fucking not trying to fix it."

"You didn't have to fight me over it; I would have fucking listened."

"Like hell."

Karen looked up. "You beat each other up?" She asked, almost involuntarily.

Porter smiled. "He was being an idiot. I love him like a brother, so I might have hit him a few times."

Michael snorted. "You were being just as much of a fucking idiot, fucking acting like you could fucking bull through it all. And those were sucker punches."

"They are only sucker punches if you don't see them coming and can't keep them off."

Michael shook his head. Karen was looking at them both. "You weren't mad at each other? You didn't... I don't know, want to kill each other or anything?" She whispered.

Michael smiled at her gently. "No, I would never want to kill Porter. He is one of my best friends and almost like my bother. Our ties go much too deep for that."

"But you hurt each other!"

Porter shrugged. "Love hurts sometimes, Karen. The thing to remember is that love hurts only to help us grow, in the end. That's the only reason love hurts. What Patos did to you isn't love because he never helped you grow. He kept you from it, really."

Michael nodded. "We hurt each other to force each other to try and see the value we have. Porter was trying to make me see that I was being selfish by trying to keep all my fears inside. People who love me want to share my pain. They want to be a part of my life. It is selfish of me to not let them share it. I was telling him that all his concern mattered less than my desire to keep my perfect exterior up, that I knew better than he did what I needed. I was fucking wrong and he knew it. We about killed Sienna off between the two of us with our fucking idiocy though. I will feel fucking guilty about that for the rest of my life, I think."

"I know." Porter said sadly. "Me, too."

Karen shook her head slowly. "This makes no sense."

"No, it doesn't." Porter agreed. "It's true all the same. It is selfish for me to ask Michael to keep his shit to himself just because I might be uncomfortable with it."

They ate a little more in silence. Then Karen glanced at them both. "Are you trying to say that you might love me? Even a little?"

Michael nodded seriously. "Of course, Karen. You are a person, and you are worthy of being loved." He said simply.

After the dinner dishes were cleared, Michael read the directions of the box of dye that Porter had brought back. It didn't look too hard.

Porter grinned at him. "That is all you, Mikey. Two of us trying would be a disaster."

Michael sighed. "All right, let's see what we can do." He said grimly.

It didn't take too long, and there wasn't too much mess, considering. Karen sat with the plastic over her head for twenty minutes, and when they washed her hair out, the color was a nice rich auburn. It seemed to be more vibrant, somehow.

"I hope you don't mind that we don't have a curling iron or whatever you use." Michael said as she dried her hair with a towel.

Karen laughed softly. "I always straight-ironed it because Patos only likes straight hair. I think it used to be wavy. I always liked my hair before, I remember."

"That's because it is beautiful."

She blushed. "Thank you." She said, smiling shyly.

Porter nodded. "Patos shouldn't be able to identify you anymore. You'll look very different to someone as shallow as he is." He stood up. "I am tired. That fight earlier and my being angry afterwards have fucking drained my energy. Being angry always does it to me, especially when I don't get drunk enough to forget it. Being fucking dry sucks. I am going to bed, and I am going to go visit Sienna tomorrow morning. I think I will go early. Michael, you are staying here. If you go anywhere, you take her with you."

Michael nodded. "I know, Porter. I have done the drill and all."

"Just making sure, man."

"I know. You be careful in that hell-hole. He is going to be angry and he will be watching and listening for codes and messages. I don't

133

like this at all."

Porter smiled. "I know. I have one that he will never intercept. Me and Thomas Edison. We got a good one. Night."

"Night." Michael looked at Karen. "Would you like to go to sleep now, my Lady?" He said a bit grandiosely.

For moment, she looked afraid. "I would, but..."

Michael smiled at her. "Okay, you tell me what you need and I will make it happen."

Karen hesitated. At last she said, "Well, I am still afraid to be alone. Could I... well, could I sleep with you? Not like that!" She said very quickly.

Michael nodded. "I understand, Karen. You don't need to worry so much about offending me. I'm a big boy, I can take quite a bit."

"I know you are, it's just.... I didn't mean...." She trailed off helplessly.

"Look, Karen, only little men with no self-esteem need to be constantly built up by shallow, hollow flattery. I know what you meant, and I am not offended. If you need that, I will do it for you."

Karen looked away, still conflicted.

Michael stood up. "Will you come this way, then? Do you need the light on, anyway?"

She shook her head.

Karen lay under the blankets away from the door. Michael lay down on top of the blankets and beside her. That way, she wouldn't have to worry about touching him in the night and being frightened by it. She seemed to fall asleep fairly quickly, but she might have been faking it. Michael found he didn't mind. She smelled nice and she didn't snore. He was fairly sure he would be neither.

Sometime in the night, Michael woke up with a start. Karen was still asleep, but she was clearly having some sort of nightmare. He gently reached over and pulled her to his side. She clung to him, shivering and shaking. He smoothed her hair and held her gently but

134

firmly until she stopped shaking and breathed more slowly. Michael considered letting her go. Then he smiled to himself in the dark. He rather liked this. Very softly, he kissed her hair. He drifted back to sleep, thinking how he could get used to it. Maybe Porter was onto something, the fucking old charlatan.

When he woke up again, it was morning. He heard Porter in the kitchen area, so he carefully got out of bed and grabbed his clothes from where he had them hanging.

Once he had changed in the bathroom and splashed his face with water, he went into the kitchen after checking on Karen. She was still asleep.

"Morning, Porter." He said very quietly.

"Michael." Porter said just as quietly. He was making something on the stove. "I thought I would make you some food before I leave. Plus I need to be doing something. I am too keyed up today. I didn't sleep much and I am still trying to get over that upset from yesterday. Fucking pissed." His eyes were dangerous as he mixed some eggs harder than might have been necessary.

"You are going to have to calm down or they will notice at Patos' house."

Porter nodded. "I know. Keep saying it and I might start believing you soon enough."

Michael snorted softly. "Bullshit."

"Hey, I might. You never know for sure. What do you want on your eggs?"

"Cheese. Bacon. Maybe sausage. Whatever you have that is protein." Michael went and poured himself some hot water. He liked hot water. It made him wake up, even without caffeine in it. "Don't take this as criticism, but you don't' usually get this pissed for this long."

"I know. Part of it is because alcohol lets me run away from it. That's one of the reasons I had to stop. My fucking problems don't go away if I don't do something with them. Running away is just that: running away. I can't be a fucking coward anymore. Father Greg made

135

that fucking clear enough."

"Makes sense. Maybe I should go talk to him sometime."

Porter glanced at the back of apartment. "How's she doing?"

Michael sighed. "It is going to take a long time to undo the shit he piled on her, I am afraid."

"Well, when we get back, you should try to get her into therapy. My guy is pretty good."

"Yeah, you're probably right. I hope she can start to relax a bit here though. And we are taking her out." He said the last part quite firmly.

"Well, hell, Michael, of course we are. What the fuck?"

"Just making sure we all understand."

"Chill, man, I know you are her protector, but be careful; that can become a hindrance too. No one can keep all hurt away. No one should."

Michael nodded. "I know, and I know it has to be her choice, eventually. Until she can make a choice though I am going to keep her safe. I can do that, and I need to sort out what I am really thinking and feeling, too."

"That's probably the best way. Mason might have some suggestions."

"Oh yeah, he probably will. Not like he ever does for any of us."

"Ha! No! Never!" Porter finished what he was doing at the counter and washed his hands. "I have to get going. Be safe, Mikey."

"Same at you. And you better keep Sienna safe, or at least as safe as she can be."

"Of course." Porter pulled on his jacket and raked his hair back. "God, I hate this hair! It keeps getting in my eyes. I don't know how Juan does it."

"Can't help that. Juan is crazy anyway." Michael grinned at him. "It does look really good on you. I bet Sienna fucking loves it. All wild and sexy..."

Porter sighed dramatically. "It's my curse; I only hope all the

136

ladies stay off me today."

"Get going, you fucking idiot. Your adoring public awaits you." Michael laughed at him.

Porter waved and left.

Michael had decided to do some training while he had the time. He cleared some space in the room and began to do some circuits. He enjoyed working his body when he was stuck inside. It made him feel like he was getting something accomplished. It also helped him concentrate on some of his thinking. Like about Karen. He wanted to keep her safe, but was it because he was attracted to her, or because he wanted someone to look after? Did it really matter, even? What if she didn't reciprocate? He pondered the different scenarios in his head. When they got back to the States, she was free to go; he would have to be ready to let her go. He had to get himself prepared for that sort of idea now. Grimly, he began to look at his different options for his own emotional well-being.

Karen came out sometime after seven-thirty. She looked a bit more relaxed. Michael was glad to see that. She poured herself a cup of tea and sat at the table.

"Good morning." Michael said without stopping what he was doing. He had decided to just keep up what he thought he should do and see what happened. Mason might be able to help in this area, too.

She nodded at him and smiled shyly. "Good morning. Thank you for letting me share your room."

"It was my pleasure. You smell nice. I can only imagine that I made up for the two of us in that area."

She laughed. "No, you are being silly now."

Michael shrugged. He looked around for something to lift. The chairs were a bit bulky. He looked more closely at Karen. "How much do you weigh?"

"Uh. Maybe 120?"

"Come here, I need something to lift a few times."

She stared at him for a second or two. "Uh, okay. I don't think I have ever been a weight before. This might be interesting."

"Oh, probably not, but I need it anyway. I haven't been able to lift for days now and I am going to get antsy if I don't use some energy."

She came over and he picked her up easily. "Try to stay rigid; that will make it better for both of us." He did some reps. "Want to stay on my back so I can do some pushups?"

"Sure!" She laughed.

After that, he felt much better. "Okay, that is probably good for now." He stood and rolled his shoulders.

Karen came around in front and gazed at him. "You are amazing. Your body is amazing."

"Thanks. I don't think it is anything special."

She shook her head. "I would not have believed it if I wasn't looking at you."

Michael was starting to get embarrassed again. "Whatever, it's just my body."

She started to say something but stopped. Then she started over. "This is one of those things you were talking about, isn't it? You are not all sure of yourself, either, are you?"

Michael shook his head. "Nope, I'm not. I wish that I could tell you it would all be better once we get out of here, but I can't say that. It may take a long time and lots of work."

Karen looked at him. "I understand. But what do you mean about getting out of here?"

"You didn't think we would just leave you here, did you? You are coming with us. I am not about to leave you in a hell-hole to fend for yourself. I said I would protect you, and that means as long as you need me for. Or want me for." Silently, Michael swore at his tongue. He hadn't meant to say that last part.

Karen looked very surprised. "Are you serious?"

Michael sighed. "Yes, I am. I didn't mean to say it that way, exactly, but it is the truth. If you don't want me, then just let me know and I will back off. I think you are really pretty and special. Anyway, I am sorry if I offended you." Nothing like a little awkwardness to make everything that much worse. He gave up. "Porter made us some food. Are you hungry?"

Michael heated the eggs and made some toast while Karen got dressed and washed up. Michael realized that she had been completely accurate when she saw that his embarrassment was similar to her own ability to not accept her own self. Perhaps he should be back to his own counselor once they got back from this fucking mission. There were obviously things he needed to work on.

Karen came out. She looked good in the plain clothes that Porter had got for her. The only thing she was lacking was shoes. Michael smiled at her appreciably. "You look very nice."

She smiled in return. "Thank you. I haven't felt this free in a long time. I feel like, oh, I don't even know. Like I don't have to put on a mask."

"You don't. Not ever."

She laughed. "I know. I don't even have makeup to put on!"

"It's just another mask anyway. Start looking at what you really look like."

She raised her eyebrow at him. "Okay, after breakfast, I will, but you have to do it with me. You said you wanted to know if I want you to back off. I don't. I definitely don't. I want something more, but I am not sure what. I want you to help me find out what it is."

"Me? But…um, okay." He surrendered.

She smiled. "I like this idea." She said, not saying what she was referring to.

After they had eaten and washed the dishes, Michael allowed himself to be led by the hand to the room. There was a full length mirror there. Together, they stood in front of it and looked at themselves. Karen didn't say anything to him. They stood for a little while, Michael with his arm around her shoulders. There was a knock at the door. Michael carefully and quickly put Karen aside. He put a finger to his lips and she nodded, looking scared.

Michael noiselessly went into the front room, taking his automatic off the counter as he went. He looked through the peephole. There were two men standing outside, neither of whom he recognized. He noticed that they had suspicious bulges under their coats. They were talking to each other idly, but they also weren't leaving.

Michael softly turned the lock. He jerked the door open and hit them both so quickly that they didn't get a chance to see much of anything. He picked up the two limp forms and carried them a few blocks over. He set them in a doorway and left them there. No one seemed to notice.

Back in the apartment, he again locked the door. "Okay, Karen, you can come out. They are gone."

She came out, still frightened. "You didn't kill them, did you?"

"No, I just knocked them out. They'll have some pretty bad headaches, but that's their own problem."

"Did you know who they were?"

"No, but it doesn't really matter. They were here and they weren't leaving. I had to take steps. That's one of my jobs, and I will keep you safe until you don't need me to."

"Did they hurt you?" She sounded concerned.

He laughed. "There were only two of them. They never had a chance."

Karen shook her head. "You are amazing." She said again.

Michael shrugged. "It's what I do. I am afraid you might be a bit bored. We don't have lots of entertainment here."

She smiled. "Then let's talk. I haven't been able to talk to someone for a long time. No one talked to me in Patos' house. I wasn't worth talking to."

"You are to me." Michael found that he was looking forward to this and getting to know her. "What do you want to talk about?"

Part II

Chapter 11

Sienna had not been looking forward to the dinner with Patos. She rode in the car quietly, considering her many options for attracting a man she was not interested in. It shouldn't be a hard assignment for her. Easy or not, it was not an engrossing thought, and she was going to have to keep it up for days. She would have much preferred to investigate some of the physical boundaries she and Porter had been engaging in while Michael was out.

The car slowed and stopped outside Patos' massive house. Sienna smiled over at Michael. "Thank you, Michael. I really appreciated your generosity earlier."

He smiled and winked. Porter held the door for her and she stepped out of the car, mentally preparing herself for her job. She nodded slightly to Porter and he took her elbow. They went up to the door the secretary was standing to the side of. The young woman stood aside and said something about Patos' being detained. Sienna thought that meant that Patos wanted her to come to him. Psychologically dominating and making himself the master. She smiled to herself. He wasn't going to intimidate her that easily.

The entrance hall was large and tastefully apportioned. There were expensive art objects placed around, but to Sienna's trained eyes it looked forced and fake. There was nothing personal in it. It could have been a museum or any public building for all the warmth exuded. Beatrice was waiting, her eyes very hard. Sienna ignored her. She was the center of attention here.

Mentally, she adjusted her view and felt herself instantly assume the character of the femme fatale she was going to be. She glanced into a mirror to make sure her hair was not mussed and her dress in order. She noted that Porter had smeared her lipstick just slightly. She smiled and carefully cleaned it up. Beatrice looked even more coldly at her. Sienna's smile widened a little; this girl was seriously jealous. It would be good for her to see what a real woman could do. Sienna raised her eyebrow at Beatrice, challenging her to start something.

The door at the far end of the hall opened and Patos stood framed in the light. "Ah, my angel, you are here!"

Sienna smiled warmly at him and swept past Beatrice, her hand held graciously out. Patos bowed over it gallantly. He held it longer than necessary, gazing at her for a while. "Yes, you are truly beautiful, Angel." He murmured.

"Angel?" She asked.

"Oh, please excuse me. I have a terrible habit of giving people nicknames and then I can't help but use that name for the rest of the time! But, tell me, have you never been called an angel before?"

"Oh, but I have. I have also been called a demon. And, once in a while, even a wild tiger in certain... situations." She smiled at him again, letting him think whatever he wanted.

Patos' eyes burned and he involuntarily raised his hand, changing the motion into a reach of a cigar. "Would you like to come to dinner, Angel?"

"Of course! Thomas occasionally forgets to eat when he is working."

Patos took her hand on his arm and they went into a dining room that could have seated at least thirty people. Beatrice followed, simmering and angry. Sienna was seated facing Beatrice on one side of the large table with Patos at the head.

"I believe that you have met my Queen?" Patos said by way of introduction.

"Why, yes, I have. Sean escorted her to the Gala. I did not think to see her here, though." Sienna said calmly, looking at Beatrice across the table. Beatrice glared back.

"Oh, I had forgotten that! Yes, the Gala was magnificent this year! I was so glad to have my Queen back afterwards."

Sienna raised her eyebrow deliberately at Beatrice again. So she was the queen, was she? Too bad angels fly higher than queens ever could hope to.

An efficient waiter came and began to lay out an elaborate and extensive dinner. Sienna noted that much of the food was quite heavy. She refused to eat anything that might make her too full and therefore complacent. She also drank only water. She was going to have to be on her best game here, especially since she was fairly sure Beatrice was more than she had told the team. Something was rotten in this.

After about an hour of sparkling conversation and casual flirting, the dinner plates were cleared and dessert brought in. It was a cake swimming in cream. Sienna ate two bites and declared she was full. She had every intention of taking this man's food like she took his compliments: as small in dose as she could.

Once the dessert was cleared, Patos looked at Sienna again. She thought she had him hooked. She pulled out a small mirror and pretended to be looking at her face.

"Well, Angel, may I ask you to step into my study?"

She smiled quite graciously. "Of course!" It was probably just as overdone and impersonal as the entryway. However, she was going to have him alone, and she was an expert at holding a man's attention when she had him alone. He seemed very attracted to her suggestively sexual comments. Now she would back that up with some physical promise. Not too much, though. If he were hooked, she would have to play him out carefully. Too much and he would think he had her and look elsewhere. Too little, well, there probably wasn't too little, but she wanted to make sure she commanded his attention every time she was in the room.

She stood smoothly. Her experience modeling had given her the ability to capture every eye when she wanted it. She stretched slightly. "I am a bit stiff from sitting, I must admit. A change of pace will be most welcome."

Patos held out his hand to her and she took it with a smile. Beatrice was still sitting and looking sulky. Sienna smiled at her as she passed. It was a little immature, but she was like that sometimes.

The study was every bit as stuffy as she had thought it would be. Patos closed the heavy, solid door and Sienna looked about her. She noted the same attention to detail and lack of personality. Some of the art was quite good. Whoever had chosen it had a good eye and a good feel.

Patos poured two glasses of a white wine and she accepted one with a smile. "Thank you. You are a most gracious host."

He smiled at her and took a sip of his wine. "Do you enjoy art?" He asked, obviously noting her looking about.

"Oh, yes, I do. Some of your pieces are very interesting. I especially like this one." She stepped over to a modern marble sculpture that was curving and evocative. "Would you be terribly offended if I were to touch it?"

Patos came up behind her. "No, my angel, touch anything you like." He said with a soft innuendo in the phrase.

Sienna smiled to herself. She had him tight. She reached out very gently and touched the smooth cold marble with her fingertips. She ran her fingers over the outside of one of the curves slowly, then she ran her fingers much more slowly over the inside curve. She closed her eyes and took a deep breath in through her mouth. She let it out slowly. "Oh, this piece has such life, such vitality. It speaks to me, somewhere deep inside. There is such energy in it." She whispered.

Patos moved closer, brushing her back. She heard his breath increase. "Yes, it is a marvelous piece." He whispered, brushing her neck with his fingers, gently pulling her hair aside. She let her head tilt slightly towards him.

There was knock at the door. She pulled back slightly, as if startled. "Oh! I do apologize! I am so impulsive sometimes. Please do forgive me!"

Patos also pulled back, his irritation obvious in his face. "Yes!" He said loudly, crossly. The door opened and a butler entered.

"I apologize, sir, you asked to be called at this time. You have an engagement. The lady's room is ready."

Patos went back to his desk. "Yes, that is very well."

Sienna sat on one of the chairs, crossing her ankles and making sure that her skirt rose several inches. Patos stared at her legs, and she pretended to only just notice her skirt. She pulled it down, leaving her fingers on her hem for perhaps ten seconds. Patos continued to stare at her legs, then he slowly raised his eyes to her face. She let a hint of promise into her eyes and raised her wine glass. She took a slow, very tiny sip. Patos again reached his hand out. He redirected the motion to his tie.

"Yes, the lady's room. Yes, very good." He said hoarsely. "I must ask you to excuse me, Angel."

She stood slowly, set her glass on the desk, and smiled at him. "I understand. I shall see you tomorrow, then, Mr. Patos?"

He nodded, still staring. She smiled at him again and turned to go. Let him think on that all night long.

The suite was very nice, but Sienna had expected nothing less. She washed her face and put on lotion, humming softly to herself. She knew the room was bugged. It had to be.

There was a knock at the door and it opened without her saying anything. Beatrice, her face clearly angry, stormed in. "What the hell do you think you are doing?" She snapped.

Sienna looked at her coolly. "Why, I believe that I am spending time with an attractive man in a nice house. I enjoy being the center of attention, and Thomas cannot give me that attention right now. Do you have a fucking problem with that?"

Beatrice glared. "You just watch yourself. This is my domain."

Sienna laughed. "Fuck off, girl. You are jealous of me. You must realize that I have dealt with that my entire life. You should have known better than to challenge a woman on her own turf when you are hardly more than a little girl. Get out of here. And don't let the door slap you in the ass as you go." She turned dismissively.

Beatrice grabbed her shoulder to force her around and continue the conversation. Sienna had been well-trained by Porter, Michael, Mason, and Juan. She spun with her elbow up and ready, hitting

148

Beatrice in the side of the head. She staggered back and fell against the wall.

Sienna stood over her, coldly now. "Get the fuck out of here, bitch."

Beatrice, her face flaming with indignation, scrambled to her feet and stormed out.

"Shut the fucking door behind you!" Sienna called after her. Beatrice, completely humiliated, slammed the door. While she was not overly worried about the episode, Sienna knew that she had made a very dangerous enemy. Anyone with power was dangerous, and doubly so when they were unsure of that power. Beatrice had Patos' ear, and she was still insecure in that. Sienna would have to use that inseurity and Patos' own paranoia to get him to trust her. She began to comb her hair as she thought it over.

There was something here she didn't quite grasp. Beatrice was acting more than angry; she was flat-out hostile. And what had that phrase about this being her domain meant? Porter and Michael needed to know this. It was a bit unfortunate that she wouldn't be seeing them until the day after tomorrow. However, that gave her about half a day to get her hold on Patos solidified. He had a meeting with Porter and Michael at 2:00. She would work on him all morning. She had to have him under her sway or else this wouldn't be possible. He had to get to the embassy, preferably his own idea. Or at least, under the impression that she was helping him.

She laid her comb down and began to get ready for bed. Again, she was conscious of the fact that her room was undoubtedly bugged. This was going to be a challenge.

The next morning, she went down for breakfast around 7:30. She was not one to sleep in usually, and especially not in a hostile house. There was some nice fruit, as well as toast and tea available. She spurned anything heavy. She rarely ate heavy food at breakfast, except when Porter made her. Besides, she wanted to be alert, and if possible, get a snack in with Patos later. That would help her

149

monopolize him.

He didn't show up until almost ten. Evidently he was one of those who stayed up late and got up late, as well. Sienna was reading a newspaper and doing the crossword to pass the time.

"Good morning, Angel." Patos stopped beside her table.

She smiled up at him. She did not rise, but she did hold out her hand to him. "Won't you sit, sir?"

He kissed her fingers gently. She thought his hands were quite warm. He didn't let go of her fingers right away, but he did sit. Gently, she pulled her hand away, acting like she didn't notice that he didn't want her to.

"How did you sleep, Angel?" He asked as he gestured for coffee.

"Very well, thank you. I could make no complaints about my room. Thank you very much for your generosity."

He nodded. "Would you excuse me if I ask you a question about your fiancé and his partner?"

Sienna was wary, but she smiled cordially. "Of course not! What would you like to know?"

"How long have you known Mr. O'Flynn and Mr. Connor?"

She paused as if trying to remember. "Oh, sometimes it feels like forever, but I think it must be about five years now."

"I see. It has come to my attention that they may have some designs upon my business. Would you think that possible?"

Sienna was thinking quickly. She had no doubts from who this information probably originated. "Oh, I seriously doubt that. You see, they could have had done business with several other clients in your field, but Thomas confided to me that they were most interested in using your services. They want only the best quality, and they are something of experts. They want and use only the best."

He nodded, but she thought he was not quite convinced yet. "So you do not think they are out to cheat me or use my business connections for their own ends?"

She laughed softly. "No, I would never think they would cheat at business." This was true, since if Porter wanted something under the table, he stole it, and Michael tended to knock people out and take it. "Thomas and Sean can use many channels, but they deal only honestly. You might test them yourself and come to a more definite conclusion after. I have every confidence that they will account for themselves well."

Patos at last seemed satisfied. Her subtle hint that he come to his own conclusions and her equally subtle hint that he was superior to whomever was passing information obviously appealed to his ego.

She relaxed slightly and gave him a sidelong glance. "By the way, I have been thinking about that beautiful sculpture all morning. I hope I did not give offense last night."

He smiled. "No, no offense. Please do not trouble yourself about that." He hesitated slightly then said, "I have several other pieces you might enjoy. Would you care to see them?"

She smiled and nodded enthusiastically. "Oh, yes! But," she hesitated, "I know you are a busy man. I would not wish to impose on your time."

He smiled at her, his eyes very bright. "No, I have no meetings until this afternoon. Please, would you like me to escort you?" He held out his arm. She smiled graciously and stood, taking his arm.

He led her from the room, nodding to his secretary as they left. "I won't need you today until the meeting later. Please call me at 1:45." She nodded.

"Now, my angel, let us see what speaks to you."

He led her through a hallway and a room. He seemed to be considering where to take her. "Ah, I think I know exactly where you might like to go!" He smiled. He opened a door at the other end of the room.

It was a conservatory of sorts, full of plants and blooming flowers and a waterfall. There were artfully placed benches and chairs with café tables scattered through the private park. Sienna was

151

impressed. This was a truly beautiful space.

"How heavenly!" She exclaimed.

"Yes, heaven for my angel."

She smiled appreciably. "This would be such a lovely place to have a picnic in."

"What a brilliant idea!" He pushed a discreet button and a few minutes later a butler appeared. "We would like a couple of bottles of wine, some cheeses, and some bread brought here. The lady would like to have a picnic."

The butler bowed and left.

Sienna walked slowly through the gorgeous space. She knew Patos was watching her. She stopped by the waterfall, admiring a particularly bright spray of flowers. She held them up to admire them better. She noticed something hard and smoothly cold in the pot when she touched it. It was undoubtedly a bug; she had enough experience with electronics to recognize them when she touched them. Now the question was to whom did it belong? If it were Patos', that was understandable, but it might have been planted by someone else. Beatrice had been here for a while, and she undoubtedly had been loyal to her mission at the beginning. It might be a state bug. One easy way to find out.

Sienna frowned slightly. Patos came over curiously. "Yes, Angel? Is there something wrong?"

She looked back at him and back at the flowers she still held. "Oh, I thought I felt something odd in these flowers. It's probably nothing. I may have imagined something."

"Show me."

"No, it is most likely my mistake."

"Show me." He insisted, coming closer to her. She sighed and turned to face him.

"Very well, but if it is nothing after all, I hope you won't hold it against me." She gently took his hand and directed it towards where she had felt the electronics. "No, you must come closer!" She admonished softly, looking up into his face, not at her hand at all. He took a step closer, sliding his hand around her waist. She continued to look him in the eyes, even as she slowly directed his hand to the bug.

"Oh, here it is." She whispered softly still not looking at the plant.

He carefully pulled the bug out of the pot. While he looked at the electronics curiously, he didn't let go of her waist.

"What the hell is this?" He was angry. It wasn't his. Good, she would be able to use that. He crushed the bug between his fingers. When he got angry, she could see the true persona that he hid under that cover of politeness. It was not pretty.

"Do you have so many enemies, sir?" Sienna whispered. "Why not forget them, just for a little while?"

"I don't like being watched." He glanced at her quickly. He probably meant to look away again, but he seemed unable to. Sienna slowly reached up and took the electronics from his hand.

"No, you wouldn't. But then, perhaps you might like to give them something to listen to, something to be truly jealous of?" She dropped the broken circuitry on the ground, still looking him in the eyes. She smiled a slow, naughty smile. "I bet they would be very interested to spy on that. Want to give them something to listen to, sir? I bet I can think of all sorts of things that would make for interesting listening."

He seemed unable to speak. He carefully put his hand up to her face. She closed her eyes and raised her head a bit. He ran his finger very gently over her lips. She parted them slightly. She could feel his attraction now. This was exactly where she needed him to be.

There was loud knock and the door opened. The butler had reappeared with the basket. "Sir, the food you requested." He said respectfully.

Patos jerked himself up abruptly. He was irritated, and he didn't like being thwarted. "Yes, very good."

Sienna stepped back, letting his hand slide across her back

before it fell away.

She glanced artfully to the side, as if embarrassed. Sometimes she could even work up a good blush. Not always.

Patos cleared his throat. "Where would you like to set up this picnic, Angel?"

She smiled at him. "Where ever you would like, sir. I trust your judgment."

He smiled at her. His eyes still burned with desire, and she rather liked the fact that he had been thwarted twice now. He was enthralled. Maybe she could keep this up.

Patos gestured to a table a little distance from the waterfall and farther from the door. "How about this one?"

She smiled. "Yes, this is lovely."

She sat carefully. The convenience of a café table was that it allowed him to touch her knees underneath. He brought the basket over, and when he sat, she made sure she brushed the inside of his leg with her knee, as if it were accidental.

He poured two glasses of wine. She smiled and accepted hers, again looking him in the eyes. She raised her glass slowly to her lips and closed her eyes as she inhaled the bouquet of the wine.

"Ah, what a heady scent." She said softly.

He didn't say anything, but he did take a quick drink himself. She took a small sip and set her glass down. They chatted a bit about nothing important. Sienna noted that it was one-thirty. She didn't have much time left to get him keyed up again. She glanced at the basket. "I am a little hungry. Might I ask you for some bread?"

He pulled a piece off a loaf and held it out to her. She took his hand and carefully bit off a piece of the bread as he held it.

She smiled at him. She noticed that his hand trembled slightly. He leaned over the table slowly. She closed her eyes and leaned in to him. There was a slight tapping noise. Perfect timing again. It was like she had this to the second.

Patos was quite angry. He jerked his head to the side, exhaling

154

sharply. "Yes!"

The secretary opened the door and, looking down at the ground, said, "Sir, the men you wished to meet with are here. They are in the antechamber."

Patos nodded shortly. "Fine. I'll be there in a minute."

Sienna was still leaning over the table. She caught his sleeve gently. When he looked back, she put her hand behind his head and brushed his lips with hers. "Just so you don't forget about me this afternoon." She smiled as she whispered.

"No, I won't."

She stood and nodded her head to him. Then she went to her own room. Later, at dinner, she would have to make sure she kept Patos talking about Porter and Michael. She would encourage him as much as possible. However, she had no intention of being alone with him after that, not tonight. The hint of being forbidden would be enough.

Chapter 12

Sienna was at breakfast early again. She was anxious to tell Porter and Michael how she was doing on her end. She knew that they were doing well, since Patos had talked about nothing but how they knew a good thing when they saw it and they would be a great outlet for him at dinner. Beatrice was there and had glared the whole time. Sienna had stayed quiet, since she did not want to get more embroiled in the power struggle of this fucked-up house.

There was some business that Patos had after dinner, so Sienna went back to her room. She made sure to lock her door to keep Beatrice out. She doubted she would show up, but one never knew.

At eight o'clock precisely the next morning, Porter came into the breakfast room. Sienna, who knew him so well, saw that he was upset about something. The casual observer would miss it; it was the set of his shoulders and the way he buttoned his jacket as he walked in.

She rose and greeted him. He bowed over her hand. "You look amazing, Marie. May I join you for breakfast?"

"Of course, Thomas. You know that you need not ask." She gestured and an efficient waiter brought them plates of food.

"Where is Sean? Surely he isn't sleeping still?"

"Sean has business elsewhere." Porter said calmly, laying his hand over her own on the table.

She felt his fingers gently touching the back of her hand in a rhythmic way. It was a code that Porter and she had worked out. It was based on the code Porter had read Thomas Edison and his wife used; tapping Morse code on a knee or hand. Whether or not Edison had really used it didn't much matter.

While they said very simple things to each other, his fingers told her another story. "Sienna, one of Patos' secretaries sought out Michael yesterday. He was sheltering her when I came up. It was full of guys. Michael and I took care of them. It was tight. We think they were there to bring Karen back."

"You all right?" She tapped back. "You seem upset."

156

"Somebody got in a lucky cut. Got me in the arm. I am fine."

"You are lying."

"Maybe. Beatrice has been telling Patos that you are plant."

"Fuck. You stay safe."

He nodded. "I'll come again tomorrow morning. I need you to be safe here."

"I will, Porter." She tapped back. "I have no interest in being a pawn."

"Good. I need you."

"I know. I need you to."

"I will. I love you. Try to have a headache today. We will get a new plan ready."

"You better come for me soon."

He smiled at her then. She saw that he was very worried about her still. He kissed her gently and stood to go. "I will return tomorrow, Marie. I apologize and I am very sorry that you are feeling unwell."

She also stood. "I am sorry that I do not feel well, Thomas. I hope to be better tomorrow."

"It isn't your fault. Try to sleep some today. Perhaps that will help."

"I will. I love you."

He saluted her. She sat and watched him walk towards the door. A man servant reached out to detain him, but Porter jerked his shoulder out of the way and grabbed the man's hand so quickly that Sienna didn't see his movements clearly. She was always a bit surprised by his reactions.

"Don't fucking touch me." Porter said dangerously.

"Sir, I was ordered to keep guests here until Mr. Patos is informed."

Porter disdainfully threw the man's hand from him. "Fuck that. I can't wait around until he shows up. You saw me, and I treated you badly. You can let him know that." He walked out of the room without further trouble.

157

The man servant quickly looked to Sienna for help. She shook her head in warning. Porter was on edge and anyone who got in his way was probably going to get hurt. The man servant nodded helplessly.

Sienna was going to pretend to have a headache all day. Porter didn't want her to get into trouble before they had the plan worked out. She couldn't move without them knowing what she was doing. That would be dangerous for them all.

Patos came in around nine. Sienna was staring out a window and pretended to not notice.

"Angel, are you all right?"

She gave a feigned start. "Oh! I am so sorry, Mr. Patos. I didn't notice you there. I have the most tremendous headache today! I think the weather must be affecting me."

"Do not trouble yourself, my angel. I was coming to excuse myself for the day. There has been some unexpected personal business that I must attend to."

"I am so sorry, Mr. Patos."

"It is all right, my angel. If you will excuse me?"

She nodded and he left.

In order to maintain her headache fiction, Sienna wandered slowly back to her room. She was determined to eat nothing that day and drink water or tea only. Because her room had listening devices in it, she would have to be quiet. What to do? She pushed the jackets and suits in her closet aside idly. Something sparkly caught her eye. There were some party gowns in the back. She pulled them out. Some of them might even fit. She took off her dress and tried on several. A strapless off-white column dress fit fairly well, but Sienna personally didn't like strapless gowns. They sometimes shifted at inopportune moments. The other gown that fit well was a black tank dress covered with sequins.

Admiring the dress in the mirror, Sienna thought that the fit could be better. She had enough time, and she had nothing better to do anyway. She went and got the little mending kit she carried with her. Porter might be better at sewing but Sienna was more than competent. She removed the dress and began to modify it. She wanted it to absolutely hug all of her. One never knew when one might need a well-fitting and beautiful dress.

After a while, the dress fit better. She took it off the hanger and put it back in the closet and put the other hangers back.

She sat at the vanity. This whole situation was getting more difficult. If there was a mole, it was almost certainly only Beatrice. She had very specific information that she was passing. However, it would appear to the narcissistic Patos as if it could be anybody. She might be able to play that up. She wouldn't act until she was surer of what he thought about her. She smiled slightly. Well, besides physical attraction. Nobody could miss that.

Later, towards dinner time, she heard quiet footsteps outside her room. She had the lights off anyway, so she slipped quickly into bed and pulled the sheets up as if asleep. She could act like she was asleep with the best of them.

She heard the doorknob turn, catch on the lock, and then it was unlocked and opened softly from the outside.

A very quiet voice murmured, "You see, sir? She is there. I have it from the staff that she has not left this room, nor called for any help or food all day. No one skips meals without a reason. I think she might be ill."

There was a pause and a voice she recognized as Patos' said back just as quietly, "You're right, of course. I only want her to be well for tomorrow night. We have the soiree at the embassy, and I need to show her off."

"Yes, sir. Will she mind dancing, though?"

"She dances exactly like you think she does. She is heaven to lead."

"Ah, yes. Well, you might ask her. If she has rested then she might not mind."

"Just look at her. If her Thomas was not such a perfect business partner, I would take care of him and Sean and dump them in the river to have her all to myself."

"I do not think she would necessarily mind, from what I have heard."

"She might, but I can change minds."

"Yes, you are a master of that."

There was another pause before Patos resumed speaking, still in the quiet voice. "When you find that damned Bubblegum, you bring her back and lock her in a small room with the lights off. She hates the dark and then she will be quite pliant by the time I can deal with her."

"Yes, sir. Since that one glitch yesterday, she seems to be moving slowly around the city. I think she is looking for shelter. Once she settles, I will send out another gang. That first one seems to have taken the money and left with it. Most distressing. But we should have her soon."

"Good. I think I will wake this angel soon. Did you look at that bug yet?"

"Yes, it is not one of ours. The corrosion on it makes me think it was not put there by her to fool you. It seems to be older. She could have faked it, of course."

"No, I would be prepared to swear that she didn't know what it was or how important it was."

"No," The second voice sounded humored. "She seemed quite intent on other things than a bug."

"I am not lying when I say that she is intoxicatingly luscious. I would gladly kill that man myself to possess her. Too bad he is too valuable. Ah well. Let's see if I can catch an angel. She seems to fly just out of reach. I want to change that tonight."

"Good luck, sir. I will go back to the observatory room. I'll let you know if anything happens with that other girl."

"Very good, Xi. I will call on you later."

Sienna maintained her fictitious sleep for all of this

conversation. She felt the bed dip under the weight of someone sitting at the head. She sighed deeply and rolled towards the dip, still feigning sleep. Fingers touched her bare arm gently and slowly traced up to her shoulder, then to her neck and cheek. She sighed again and opened her eyes.

"Oh, hello, Mr. Patos. I did not expect you." She smiled and sat up. Glancing down, she quickly pulled the sheets up as if embarrassed. "I apologize, sir; I did not mean for you to see me like this."

He smiled at her. "It is my fault. I came to ask you if you are well enough for dinner?"

"Yes, I feel much better. The headache has receded almost all the way now. I would be honored to be your escort."

"Then while you change I will wait outside."

Dinner was the same type of grand affair. Sienna ate very little and spoke less. She was still faking her headache. After the dinner was cleared and the dessert was being brought in, Patos looked at her speculatively.

"Tomorrow, I have to attend a party at the Irish embassy. We must have our guest-visa renewed and that means being seen at the right times. My angel, do you think you will be well enough to attend on my arm?"

Beatrice glared, but Sienna ignored it. She pretended to think about it. Inside, she was exultant; the US had an extradition treaty with Ireland. If they took him there, they could be done with this by the next day. If Michael kept Karen safe and she could find the warehouse that would be taken care of. Sienna had no doubts that Michael was completely capable of his job. She was worried about Porter shuttling between the two places. Aloud, she said, "I would love to go with you, Mr. Patos. Thomas will not mind if I do."

"Very good. And you, my queen, you will be escorted by Mr. Xi. You have been his consort before, so you should be comfortable with it."

Beatrice nodded shortly. "Yes, sir."

"Any other questions?"

Sienna raised a finger. "Will there be dancing?"

He smiled indulgently. "There is always dancing at such events."

"Perhaps we should practice a bit first, so that I don't trip."

"No, I would not wish to appear clumsy."

She looked around speculatively. "This room is a good one to practice in; the floor is fairly open, after all."

Patos laughed. "You are right! After dessert, we can try a few dances."

True to his commands, the chairs and table were cleared and the mysterious Mr. Xi appeared. Sienna remembered that it had been his name that Patos had said earlier when they thought she was asleep.

The first notes of some music swelled out of hidden speakers. It was a tango. Sienna had taken lessons since she was a teenager. Porter had been absolutely correct when he said she loved to dance. Anything with a Latin flavor was fun, and she had some unorthodox moves that would probably be just as distracting as the physical proximity itself. When she dropped that lovely, sexy salsa move, Patos actually missed the next eight counts. When the song ended she threw a hot enganche to give him something else to focus on.

The next song, a waltz, began, but Patos didn't move to begin. Sienna was quite content to let him stay entranced.

"Angel, you are bewitching." He breathed.

"Yes, I know." She lowered her eyes coquettishly. She gave him a long look through her eyelashes and leaned up to whisper in his ear, "You haven't ever flown on angels' wings before. You have a queen, but she's tied to the ground. She needs someone strong to lift her up to fly. Who does she turn to when you aren't here? But even fallen angels fly; I can show you heaven, or, should you be brave enough, I can show you hell."

His hand on her back trembled violently.

She laughed softly, still whispering into his ear. "I am not sure that kind of dance is sanctioned on the dance floor, Mr. Patos."

"To hell with that!" He said hoarsely.

She laughed again and slowly ran her lips across his jaw line. Beatrice made a loud sound of disgust.

Sienna had him tight, now she would have to back off subtly. She gave a slight cry and straightened as if she was shocked by something.

"What is it?" Patos asked sharply.

"Oh, it is probably nothing. I thought for a second that I had been stung on my left arm. Perhaps a wasp? It is gone now." Beatrice was to her left.

Patos glanced over at Beatrice, his eyes narrowing in distrust. "Yes, I think I understand. Well, my angel, I think I would not like to fatigue you after your recent indisposition. Might I escort you to your suite so as to make sure you are unmolested?"

Except by you, Sienna thought. Out loud, she said, "Of course, sir. You are the soul of courtesy."

Chapter 13

Once in her room, Sienna put her hand to her forehead. "Ah,
Mr. Patos! I had completely forgotten, but I have no party gowns here.
I did not bring any with me!"

He smiled at her. "There are several in your closet." He pushed
the other clothes aside to show her.

She smiled and clapped her hands. "Oh, you are right! I never
thought to look!" She lied, and then began to look through the dresses
as if seeing them for the first time. Patos sat at the vanity and watched.

Finally, Sienna held up the two she had tried on earlier. "Which
do you think, sir?" She held each one up to her for inspection.

"I prefer black." He said, his eyes very bright.

"Very good; I do too." She said, carefully laying the off-white
one aside and admiring the black one. There was a discreet knock at
the door.

"Come." Patos said shortly.

A man servant opened the door, holding a mug of some hot
drink on a silver platter. "The lady's drink, sir, as ordered."

Patos looked up sharply. Sienna wasn't paying much attention
and she took the cup up while half-distracted. It was full of something
hot and rich, very dark and sweet-smelling. She took a sip. It was
wrong with a bitter aftertaste. She knew immediately that she'd made
a dreadful mistake. She put the cup down quickly.

Patos was still glaring at the server, who had gone very white.
"I ordered nothing for this lady. What is this?"

"Please, sir, I only received an order from the head cook that it
was ordered and that I needed to bring it up right away. I know nothing
else."

"Out! Get out." Patos glanced at Sienna. He stood up quickly.
"You already had some, didn't you?"

Sienna nodded. She felt a numbness starting to flow through
her. It was almost like a lazy grey fog was swimming up. She shook her
head, trying to clear it and focus on what she was supposed to be doing.

164

Patos swore and pulled out his phone. "Chen, get up here. Angel's room. Now."

He came over and sniffed the cup. "Hell!" He said violently. "Someone's playing games here and I don't like it!" He paced around the room in anger while they waited for Xi to get there.

Sienna felt the fog take hold of her arms and legs. They felt like soft lead. She was starting to lose feeling in them. It felt a little like sodium pentothal, but there were differences. Xi and Beatrice came into the room, the latter smiling cruelly when she saw Sienna.

Patos was furious. "What the hell is this, Chen? Why are you giving her Xoria?" He demanded of Xi.

"I don't know, sir. I ordered nothing. I never use that without your express approval. Perhaps the cook can tell you where the order originated."

Patos jerked his head impatiently. He was clearly not in the mood to call all over his house to find the answers he wanted. He happened to look at Beatrice and seemed to understand something. He strode quickly over to her and grasped her arm tightly. "What the hell did you order?"

"I... sir... I did it to protect you! She is scheming against you!" Beatrice squirmed, trying to break his grip.

"You gave her Xoria? You idiot! She's been sick all day! You are going to kill her!" He struck Beatrice in the side of the head in rage.

Sienna felt the grey fog swirl into her brain. She lost all interest in the room. Everything was dull and numb; she had no connection with anything. Some part of her mind screamed at her, trying to focus, to remember. She was supposed to do something. What was it? It was important; what was it?

The floor loomed up in her vision. She was falling for a very long time, landing gently. There was no feeling of impact. She rolled over slowly and stared at the ceiling. It somehow registered that Xi and Patos were bending over her. They were speaking urgently to each other. Sienna forced her mind to sharpen, to listen, to fix what she saw and heard in her mind.

"You need to get that into her now or we will lose her." Patos was saying.

Xi nodded. "Yes. Hold her down. I'll get this arm. She is going to go crazy once it starts. We can't let her hurt herself."

Sienna noted dully that there was some pressure on her now. Her right arm was firmly held and stretched out to the side. She looked on incuriously as Xi put a hypodermic needle against her elbow. He must have gotten it from somewhere but she didn't know where. He set his knee on her wrist and put his right hand on her upper arm. He leaned all his weight on her arm and pushed the needle in. Sienna didn't feel anything at all. Then he began to depress the syringe slowly. At first, Sienna felt like she was still in the grips of the horrible grey fog. There was no change. Then fire started to burn up her arm. The fire raced all through her, burning away the fog and setting all her nerves aflame. Rather than dulled, her senses became hyper sensitive: the light stabbed, the air burned her lungs. Dimly, in her agony, she heard someone screaming. Her body clenched to the utmost. Her heart fluttered violently and began to falter. She was dying; she knew it. No one could endure the agony for long.

Then, after untold minutes of hell, the fires began to recede. As the burning left her body, it was replaced by pain and violent reaction. She began to tremble uncontrollably. She was as weak as she had ever been. Her throat was raw: she'd screamed it that way.

Finally, the fires burned out. She trembled and tears fell from her eyes without her noticing.

"Oh God." She whimpered finally. It was all she could do. She shivered with sudden cold, the opposite of the heat she'd felt only minutes before. Every muscle hurt, her heart ached, her stomach churned. She hoped she wouldn't throw up on the floor.

Xi looked at her clinically and took the weight off her arm where he still knelt on it. He took the empty syringe form her arm and put a small bandage over the spot where blood began to well up. "She'll be

166

fine now. It was touch-and-go there though."

"Yes. What the hell did she give her that for? Xoria isn't a truth drug." Patos said, standing up and looking at the crumpled form of Beatrice by the door.

Xi also stood up. "No, but she has watched us interrogate using it before. It might look like one from the outside. I am just glad the Kickstart worked quickly enough."

Patos nodded. "She had enough Xoria in that cup to kill anyone. It's lucky Angel only had a little, or it wouldn't matter about the Kickstart at all. Why the hell would she do it though?"

Xi smiled slightly. "Well, she is rather jealous. Jealousy can be a good tool, but it can become misplaced sometimes."

Patos glanced at Sienna, who still was too weak to move. "What about her? She'll be all right, won't she? I want her to be with me at the embassy tomorrow. Something as beautiful as she is needs me to show her off."

"She should be fine. She is strong and the effects should wear off after a few hours. She'll have bruises though."

"And she won't remember any of this, right?"

"No one else has. The Kickstart seems to erase any memories when it leaves. She'll sleep it off and not have a clue what happened in the morning."

"Excellent. Let's get her to bed and then we can decide about this other one. She might not be worth it anymore."

"That is your decision, sir. She has been quite useful in the past."

Patos grunted and they lifted Sienna and laid her on the bed. She still trembled and her muscles ached. Then they took Beatrice between them and left. A few minutes later, a man servant entered the room and tidied up. He came over, removed Sienna's clothes without any emotion, and laid them over the back of the chair. He covered her with blankets, took the cup and platter, turned off the lights and softly shut the door.

167

In the darkness, Sienna finally gave into her pain and fear and she cried, shaking and silent, until she fell asleep.

Chapter 14

Despite Xi's assurances to the contrary, Sienna did not forget anything. Terrible nightmares and memories jerked her awake many times, sweating heavily and breathing quickly. Many of her nightmares involved Porter being tortured or changing in front of her eyes. She was so afraid that he would be different, that he would reject her now, that he would no longer want to be with her. She dreamed several times that he changed into Patos or Xi and took cruel pleasure in her pain. Then she dreamed that they were hurting him and he was screaming and she was paralyzed and helpless.

By six, she was done trying to sleep even though she was still exhausted. A long warm shower helped stabilize her mood and set her for the day. She still had a job to do and people were counting on her to do it. It would have probably been easier for her to kick it if she hadn't been low on energy from losing weight earlier.

By seven, she was down in the breakfast room. It was bright and cheery in there with fresh flowers on the tables. She ordered a cup of hot green tea. She was afraid to drink anything dark and she would order only drinks clear enough for her to see through. As a name, "Xoria" meant nothing to her, but there must have been some reason it was in a dark and thick drink. A person must have been able to see whatever it was and become suspicious. Therefore, she wouldn't drink anything dark. She was too afraid to.

Even when the tea came, she sat holding the cup for a while, still wary of drinking anything. Eventually, she got up the courage to take a sip. It tasted fine.

At seven-thirty, Porter came in. Sienna hadn't expected him that early and she almost dropped her cup as she hastily stood. He looked exactly the same: gorgeous and strong. It must have been obvious to him that something was wrong. He came to her quickly and held her.

She clutched at his shirt so hard her fingers ached. "Please, please take me away from here." She pleaded softly into his chest.
169

He held her comfortingly. "I can't, not yet. If I could ensure that you would be safe, I would." He breathed into her hair.

Of course he couldn't. It hadn't been an option. Hearing him, feeling him gave her steadiness for now. She took several ragged breaths and then straightened, pulling back slightly.

"Yes," She said softly. "I understand."

His beautiful eyes were desperately concerned. "Are you all right? You seem a bit sick."

"I should be fine. Perhaps it is a holdover from yesterday."

He nodded, still concerned. "Have you eaten breakfast yet?"

"No, I have no appetite."

"That is a sure sign to me that you need to eat, and lots of protein." He put his fingers gently over her lips to stop any protest. "We aren't going to argue about this, are we, Marie?"

"No." She sighed.

They sat, Porter signaled a waiter and ordered for them both, and then he put his hand on her knee. She laid her hand over his.

"Tell me." He tapped.

"I was careless. Beatrice slipped me something and then Chen Xi and Patos had to give me an upper. It was the worst thing ever."

"What was it they gave you?"

"Xoria and it was in some dark drink. The upper was called Kickstart and they injected it. Neither means anything to me."

He shook his head distractedly. "Are you all right?"

"Yes. I am weak. The upper was very painful. They held me down. Bruised me all up."

Porter gently pushed the sleeve of her sweater up on her right arm. There was a large purple bruise where Xi had leaned on it. He carefully recovered it, but Sienna could feel him trembling with rage.

"Porter. No. I cannot lose you." She tapped sharply.

He took a deep breath, closed his eyes, and let it out slowly. "All right. You are right. There is some party at the embassy. Is he invited?"

170

"Yes. You always were good at finding out secrets."

He winked at her. "You need to go."

"What's the plan?"

He winked again. The waiter appeared with their plates of food. Sienna stared at hers. She said, "Thomas, you have to be fucking kidding me. There is no way I can eat this much."

"You're going to try."

She sighed and picked up her fork. As she did, she glanced towards the French doors and started violently. Mason was there, talking earnestly with some servant and gesturing towards them.

Porter saw her stiffen and turned. "Ah, Jonathon? Here?" He said casually. He raised his voice, "Jonathon!" He waved and Mason came over.

He pulled out one of the chairs and sat, winking at Sienna. This had to be serious if Mason were here. Porter and Michael could usually work through problems.

Porter picked up his fork. "What the hell are you doing here, Jonathon? I seem to recall I gave you very specific instructions back at the shop."

"You did, sir, but the new shipment came in. I thought you would be anxious to see it as soon as possible. Mr. Connor directed me here." Mason reached into his jacket and pulled out a flat green velvet box. Sienna recognized it immediately. That's what Porter needed. There must be a new plan then. Sienna felt somewhat better.

Porter opened the box and glanced over the contents. Each little compartment had jewels or casings separated into it. He nodded. "Very good. You did quite well to bring this to me. And, now that you are here, there are some things I will want you to do for us."

"Yes, sir." Mason stood up and smiled at Sienna. "Lady."

"Jonathon." She smiled back.

"Sir, I will go and see what Mr. Connor has for a list." He looked at Sienna again pointedly. "My lady, I will see you again soon." He touched the table eight times. It was on for eight o'clock tonight. She nodded slightly. He winked again and left.

Porter again laid his hand over her knee.

"This is the plan. You must go to the embassy tonight. Mason and our handler will be your chauffeurs. You need to get Patos to the unoccupied south wing by eight. We willisolate him into a room. You will never have to face him. Make sure you get clean. No one must trace you. It is paramount that you are safe. Do you understand?"

"Yes."

"Use an emerald. You know how. If it needs more use a diamond. I will rescue you when you are in the dark hallways. I promise to be there."

"I will. It should not hard. Just make sure you come."

"I'll always come for you."

"All right. You better kiss me."

He smiled slightly. "Marie, I hate to leave you," He said out loud, "But with Jonathon here, I have some adjustments to make with luggage and securing purchases. You understand?"

"Of course, Thomas. I am perfectly fine here."

"Then I will see you again tomorrow morning?"

"I look forward to it."

He leaned over to kiss her, his hand softening on her knee. Her fingers touched his wrist.

"Mr. O'Flynn!" Patos voice interrupted the kiss. Porter drew back. His hand left her knee as he turned genially towards the host. Patos was staring at the box. "These are quite unique." He ventured at last.

Porter smiled easily. "Yes, they are rather nice, aren't they? This is the latest shipment from one of our suppliers and my assistant thought it prudent to bring to me immediately for my perusal."

Patos nodded, still staring at the box and its contents. "If this is the level of quality from your other suppliers," he said at last, "then we shall have a very profitable business relationship indeed."

Porter shrugged. "Sean and I deal only in the best." He stood up, meticulously checking over the contents of the box. Once he was satisfied, he shut it carefully and took Sienna's hand. He reverently kissed her fingertips, and she felt the two small gems he carefully pressed between her fingers. She smiled at him and he left.

Patos watched him go which gave Sienna a second to transfer the gems to a hidden pocket on the inside of her bodice. It would appear to be adjusting her clothes to anyone watching.

By the time Patos returned his gaze to her, she was again sipping her tea. "And how are you this morning, Angel?"

Sienna smiled at him. "Quite well, thank you. Although I do think the headache has left me a tad tired. And I seem to have caught my arm in between the bed and the wall or something. I have a bruise I don't remember getting." She showed him her arm. He made a disconsolate noise while looking pleased. "Other than that, I am perfectly fine."

"I am glad to hear it. I had hoped that you would have no ill effects from the headache. I must beg your pardon again. Until this evening's engagement I shall be quite busy. Pray excuse me."

"I shall. I will be sure to rest up until then." She rose and smiled at him.

"Please do so. Will you require anything?"

"Shoes, I think. I have no appropriate shoes."

"Very good. What size do you wear?"

"7 US size, or 4 ½ European."

"I shall have some sent up for you to try. Now, please do excuse me." He bowed slightly and left.

Sienna went back to her room and locked the door. She laid out her makeup to do a smoky eye. She also pulled out a small perfume bottle. She hardly ever wore perfume; this bottle contained only a little rubbing alcohol. She carefully took out the emerald Porter had passed to her and dropped it in. It dissolved away. Obviously, it was no emerald. She next took out an ornate and heavy-looking gold bracelet. Touching a hidden lever made a spring open part of the filigree to reveal a small cavity. She dropped the tiny diamond inside and closed it again. She also pulled out a slip and some other under garments. The bruises on her shoulders made her apprehensive about wearing them, but she would need to. She sighed and took them to the bathroom to wash them and wring them out to dry. Washing them would also destroy any tracking devices that might be on them.

Finally all her preparations were made so she took off her clothes and climbed into bed to sleep some more. Hopefully the thought of Porter would keep the terrible dreams at bay. It didn't.

A soft tapping at the door awakened her some hours later. She groggily threw on a robe and opened her door. A man was standing there with several boxes.

"Shoes for the lady?"

"Oh, yes, come in." She stepped back.

The shoes all fit, but the best were the gladiator-style sandals. They were almost certainly tracked. She'd be leaving everything but the bracelet and the perfume bottle behind. She wanted to get the ring out because Porter had made it, but everything else was collateral and would be left.

An hour before they were to depart, Sienna sat down to get ready. She swiftly put on her makeup, opting for dark blue and gray. Her hair was naturally straight and needed little more than a quick brushing and a touch of enhancer to make it shinier.

She put on the dress, letting it settle on her. Glancing in the mirror, she smiled to herself. Putting on makeup always made her look different, even to her; the dark, dramatic eyes definitely helped. She had a small clutch and she put a makeup removal swab in for later.

She took the tiny perfume bottle, shook it carefully and worked the tight stopper out. She carefully touched it to her clothes two or three places. Then she touched it to her neck and the insides of her wrists. That should be enough. She put the stopper back in the bottle and put it in the clutch as well. The gold bracelet was already on. She laced up the sandals and stood. Too bad about those bruises; they

174

showed under her straps and on her wrist vividly. Oh well. It was Patos' fault anyway, and if he didn't like them, that was too fucking bad.

There was a knock at the door. Sienna opened it. It was Mason. He smiled at her, his eyes twinkling mischievously.

"Your car is ready, Lady. Mr. Patos wishes you to come when you are prepared to." He bowed.

"Thank you, I shall not keep him waiting." Sienna came out and closed her door, carefully slipping the perfume bottle from her clutch to Mason's pocket.

Mason nodded and she turned towards the stairs. Mason walked right behind her. "You look amazing, as usual." He murmured in a hardly audible voice. "Although that damn perfume is fucking hard to miss."

"Thank you. The bruises are a nice touch, no?" She said in a voice just as quiet.

"They in no way detract from your beauty, great lady."

"You have been hanging out with *him* too much. I can tell. His outrageousness rubs off on everybody. Plus, you must think this is going well."

"Everyone has their own faults."

She stopped at the top of the staircase to survey the entry hall. She intended to command the attention of everyone as soon as she could. Patos was talking quietly with Xi and he turned when he heard the footsteps. His eyes lit up when he saw her. "Ah, Angel! You look as ravishing! Yes, quite ravishing…"

Sienna smiled and came down the stairs regally. She held out her hand and Patos bowed over it. He straightened, still holding her hand and turned. "The wrap, Chen." He suggested to Xi. He left and returned quietly with a shimmering silk shawl that settled on Sienna's shoulders smoothly.

"This is beautiful! Thank you!" She said, admiring it and looking at herself in the mirror. "It sets off the dress to perfection."

Patos was looking at her greedily. "Oh, I think that is you and not the wrap, my angel."

She blushed prettily.

He held out his hand to her. "Shall we go?"

Chapter 15

The ride to the embassy wasn't long. It took perhaps ten minutes. Patos couldn't keep his hands off her the whole time. He had to be touching, kissing, anything. It seemed very clear that Sienna would not have to use the diamond to keep his attention. When the car had stopped, it took Patos a full minute to realize Mason was holding his door open. He got out quickly, arranging his tie. Sienna also got out, winking subtly to Mason. He kept his face completely impassive. He always did have a good poker face, Sienna acknowledged as she took Patos' arm and they went into the party.

The time was seven-thirty. Good. She only had to maintain her part for half an hour more. She curtsied gracefully to the ambassador and various officials and allowed herself to be complimented outrageously. Patos obviously wanted her to himself; being thwarted in that was frustrating to him. Sienna noted it and made sure that she flirted with a handsome diplomat within his view. The diplomat asked her to dance, and she allowed herself to be lead in a lovely foxtrot.

Patos stepped forward and claimed her for the waltz that started next. Sienna noted that the time was two minutes to eight. She smiled gaily and as the dance ended, she again leaned in to whisper into his ear, "I think I must leave the dance floor. Will you escort me? Preferably somewhere private and where the lights are low? I think I must have some personal attention, and soon."

Patos swallowed hard. Several times. She noted with satisfaction that he was far from his usual polished self. He nodded and she took his arm.

Her sense of direction was good, plus she could see that the southern rooms were not lighted. A long boring administrative hallway stretched off south with every tenth light on to provide minimal illumination.

They walked down the hall slowly. Suddenly, the lights all went out. Sienna dropped Patos' arm in feigned alarm. She stepped back, towards the wall. At the same time, she felt a strong arm encircle her
177

waist and a hand over her mouth, lifting her off the ground and silently carrying her into a dark side hall.

She momentarily grasped at the arms then she let herself be carried. Once she was set down, the hand over her mouth gently changed to a finger to warn her to be silent. She nodded. Porter breathed into her ear, "You need to get clean now. Just leave it all here."

Again, she nodded and pulled off the dress, the shoes, and took out the makeup swab. She left everything else in a pile on the floor. Porter took her hand and led her down another hall. It was very dark. Sienna stumbled once or twice. Porter picked her up and carried her gently to a room. There was a large window on one wall looking into another room. The other room was softly lighted with a lamp and a table and chair stood in the middle.

"One-way mirror?" Sienna whispered. Porter nodded. He set her down and Sienna looked around curiously. The room they were in was obviously an observatory room. There were speakers from the other room to here and the one-way mirror was an old trick.

"Sienna, my love, are you all right?" Porter said softly, still looking very concerned.

She smiled at him as she took the makeup off with the swab. "My dear Porter, I have never been happier to see you, even if you did scare me pretty much shitless." She looked around her for somewhere to throw it away.

"I am sorry. I am sorry for everything." Porter said quietly. Sienna heard something in his voice that was different. She turned quickly back to him. He looked very upset.

"Porter, you have nothing to be sorry for. None of this was your fault. I don't blame you at all."

"Perhaps not, but I blame myself."

"Fuck that!" She said sharply. "It was my own fucking fault that I got careless!" She found she was getting angry. Not at Porter, precisely, but at the situation. Perhaps it was the relief of being out of

178

the dreaded house finally, but she suddenly felt very upset herself. She stepped up to Porter and grabbed his shirt with both hands. She looked up into his face wanting to shout at him so he would hear her. "Do you even fucking hear me? It was my own damned fault! Don't fucking take it from me!"

He looked at her gravely for a second or two then suddenly grinned. "No, I won't take the blame if you want it so badly!"

Despite herself, she laughed. "Fuck off, Porter."

"No, I won't do that." He leaned down and kissed her.

The anger turned to something just as hot. Sienna put her fingers in his hair. It was longer than usual, and she could get quite a bit in her hands now. She smiled, even during the kiss, and muttered, "Don't think you can fucking get away from me now, bitch."

He smiled too. "Don't you think I wanted to."

Before things could get more interesting, there was an amused cough. Sienna let go and pulled back slightly. Mason was there, a smile on his face.

"I take it that you have convinced Porter to quit being a fucking idiot about all this?"

Michael came through the door, quietly leading another woman. Sienna recognized her as Karen.

She smiled back at Mason. "I was working on that when you came in. If you had waited just a bit longer, I might have been more effective."

"No, I think you were plenty effective." Mason said solemnly.

Sienna laughed. She went to Mason and threw her arms around him. "I am so very glad you came, Mason." She said, still laughing. She kissed him exuberantly. Mason blushed.

Then Sienna went over to Michael and did the same thing to him. Michael coughed in embarrassment. "Sienna, you're not really dressed and the perfume is almost impossible to ignore." He said, uncomfortably.

"Oh! I forgot. I am sorry, Michael." She took Karen's hand

gently. "And you, my dear, are very brave. Thank you for your help."

Karen smiled at her. "I am so glad to be out of there. Michael and Porter are really very good to me. They keep telling me good things about myself and I almost believe them."

Sienna nodded seriously. "I should warn you that they will lie about almost anything, but not to people they love."

Karen blushed. She looked down at the floor shyly. "I doubt that." She mumbled.

Sienna took her shoulders firmly. "No, my dear, that is the truth. Just like it is the truth that you are really free of that horror and you can go with us back."

Karen blushed some more but didn't say anything.

"He should be in the room soon. There isn't anywhere else for him to go. I closed all the exits." Mason said softly. "We will have to keep it down in here, but he won't see or hear any of you if you do."

Sienna moved back over by Porter. She felt cold. It could be the fact that she was wearing only a slip and some undergarments. Could be. "What's the plan, Mason?" She asked, shivering slightly.

"I will have the great privilege of interrogating him, which in this case means rubbing his face in the fact that we caught him. Then we are leaving and they can do what they want with him. And... here he is. Let's give him a few minutes to get comfortable."

Patos had wandered into the room. Mason waited until he was in then pushed a lever on the wall. The door behind Patos shut soundlessly and locked. With a small cry Patos turned towards it to force it open but he was too late. Now he turned back to the room, his face wary. They watched as he inspected the table, chair, and walls. Sienna began to shiver more as he came closer to the mirror. Maybe she wasn't cold after all. She could feel anxiety washing over her. What if he found the mirror or could see through it? What if they couldn't get out? She shivered harder. The terrible thoughts kept coming, even though the logical part of her mind tried to stop them. She reached out to make sure Porter was really there, that this wasn't some terrible nightmare again where everyone disappeared or everything went wrong. He was there, beside her. His arm was warm and strong. She hugged it tightly, shivering still. She was terrified. It felt like some of her dreams were coming to life.

Porter was no fool. He must have sensed that she was going through something. He calmly and gently moved her in front of him and put both his arms around her. She couldn't stop shivering, but she felt much better.

Mason looked at her for a moment. He looked at Porter and said softly, "She's reacting. It could be any number of things, but she's reacting badly. Keep her warm and keep her safe. She needs you very much right now."

"I know." Porter said just as softly. "You do your part, Mason, and let me have your jacket when you get back. I don't have one."

Mason looked at him questioningly for a second. He nodded. "Show time." He breathed and opened a side door.

Patos was still examining the room he was in. Mason came in through a hidden panel, closing it quietly behind him. He had a small sheaf of papers in his hand.

"Ah, Mr. Patos. Please, have a seat." Mason said genially, glancing through his papers. Patos sat warily.

"Yes, thank you for joining me. We have some things to discuss, I am afraid." Mason continued in the same even tone.

Patos rallied. "You must be mistaken." He said.

Mason raised his eyebrows. "Oh? No, no that is impossible, I am afraid. We have you from several good sources."

"Well, what are you doing then? Am I under arrest?" Patos demanded.

"Under arrest?" Mason laughed easily. "No, not from me! I am with no official force! I just needed to make sure you were here and secured! After that, my paid job ends." He glanced back at his papers. "I think that the embassy might have plans for you on that front. They concern me not at all. Just to warn you what you might expect. We

181

both know the Irish have an extradition treaty with the US. Yes, I think you are in for rather a bad time. But I don't give a flying fuck about that." He paused again. "You might feel better knowing that your house was raided a little more than fifteen minutes ago. Beatrice and the other ladies you kept there are in custody. Oh, and that warehouse... yes, that was raided too. The pictures are all safe now, and your jewelry plant has been neutralized. You see, we have detailed information. Anything you have touched, we have seen to. Enjoy the rest of your party, sir. It's the last one you'll see for a long time."

Patos fell back in his chair, his face very pale and angry.

Mason turned as if to go. He straightened as if remembering something. "There was one other thing, Mr. Patos," he said, turning back.

Patos looked at him warily again. "Yes, what is it?" He ventured.

Mason walked towards him. "I have a personal message to deliver from a few of your acquaintances."

Patos shrank back. "Don't touch me. That's illegal. I have rights!" He blustered.

Mason leaned in closer. "I don't fucking care about your rights. As far as anyone else knows, I don't even fucking exist. You think you can use people and throw them aside when you're bored? Let me teach you the finer lessons in human relations." Mason hit him with a left-cross. Patos hadn't seen it coming. He slumped, unconscious in the chair.

"That's for Sienna and Karen, bastard." Mason sniffed, shaking his hand absently. He came back through the door.

Sienna gave a tiny cry. She was free of him. It was like a shadow was lifting from her mind, slowly, very slowly. She clutched at Porter, still expecting him to disappear. Her shivering increased.

Porter held her gently. "Shh, love. It is all right now. I'll take you away."

"You're real? You're not one of my nightmares?" She

whispered desperately, not daring to turn around.

Michael laughed. "Well, I wouldn't say that necessarily."

Porter sighed. "Michael, shut the fuck up."

Michael laughed again. "Hey, she asked if you were a nightmare. I can't help it if it's a totally relevant question."

"Listen closely, Michael. Shut. The. Fuck. Up."

"Listen closely, Porter. Like. Hell."

Mason came back in, handing his jacket to Porter. Porter gently put it over Sienna. She shied away from it suddenly. It was too heavy. "Ow, no, it hurts. My shoulders. It hurts. Please don't!"

Porter took it off immediately. He looked helplessly at Mason. "What else can we do? She needs to warm up, and soon."

"Then we get the fuck out. Now. We're done here."

Porter nodded and picked up Sienna again. She buried her face in his shoulder. Then she suddenly remembered his arm. "Oh, Porter, your arm! I'm too heavy." She struggled, trying to get down.

"Fuck that, Sienna. It was only a scratch."

"You're lying." She protested, still trying to get down.

"Not this time." Michael said from just behind them. "It really wasn't much more than a scratch. He should be up to his usual shenanigans and other shit in no time."

Karen laughed softly. "You guys are really something else. I have never heard anyone insult each other like you do."

Mason shrugged. "It's because we love each other. That's how men show they love someone, they insult each other. Very lame, I admit, but there it is."

Karen giggled. Sienna was only half-listening. They were going through darkened hallways still. Mason finally opened a door to the outside. He glanced out. "All right, it is clear. Let's get out of here."

Chapter 16

In the car, Sienna started shaking again. She was reacting from everything. The dreams were such confused impressions, and they had merged with the fantasy landscape that was Hong Kong at night. To her tired eyes, the blinking and bright lights were stabbing, glaring nightmare creations. She burrowed into Porter's side, shaking badly. The lights were too much. She squeezed her eyes shut and covered her face.

Still she shivered.

She heard Porter talking with Mason. "I'm worried, Mason. She hasn't stopped yet. What else can we do?"

Mason answered quietly, "We can't do anything until we get back. Whatever they gave her probably gave her nightmares all night, and she is tired now. She is hurting, and she never got her weight and energy up from before. Those things are blurring the lines for her between nightmares and reality."

"You talk like a psychologist or something." Karen ventured.

"I am." Mason said absently. "We have to keep her safe all night. She is probably going to be this bad, possibly for days. Karen worries me, too."

"You're right." Porter said. He hadn't let go of her since they'd gotten in the car. "I'll keep her safe."

Sienna gave a small sob into him. She was still afraid that it would all evaporate into nothing.

Karen said something. Sienna only heard the last part. "...Sounds exactly like something Michael said to me."

"Of course," Mason sounded amused. "We're all the same type. We want to keep our friends safe. You should have seen the last time Porter lost it. And Michael. At the same time. Keeping these two fucking morons safe is much harder than watching out for boogey men is for you and Sienna."

"What happened?" Karen sounded very interested.

"Do we have to drag up ancient history?" Michael asked in a

pained voice.

Mason laughed. "Oh, because a couple of weeks is so fucking long, Michael! But no, I won't tell her how you two had a fight in my entry hall, had a cry-fest in my study, and dropped the worst fucking news I have ever heard like it was nothing. Nope. I won't say a fucking thing."

"That was fucking cheap, Mason."

"Too fucking bad. You are both way fucked up still, and these two ladies need to understand all your fucking quirks so they can help, if they want. You do realize, Karen, that you will have to make that choice on your own. Possibly not right now, but soon. You have to choose for yourself. We can't keep you, and we can't protect you forever without your choice to be protected by us."

Porter stirred slightly. "She isn't ready yet, Mason."

"No one ever is, Porter. I am just setting it up. We all deserve knowing what is expected of us."

"You never set anything up for me."

Mason snorted. "Since when? I give you all sorts of fucking set-ups. If you think back, you might even remember some of them."

"Like asking about sensitive personal information?" Michael asked.

"Of course. It isn't just to hear all your fucking sob stories. I ask to get you two idiots to face your own demons. No one is so strong that they don't need help, right, Michael? Not even the strongest man in the world."

"Mason, please." Michael sounded pained. "We all know that is fucking shit."

"Do you? Do you really, because you still act like you are going to muscle your way through everything. Still! Between the two of you, I am going to go crazy myself."

"I'll get help, once we're back."

"No, I want you to go to someone else. Whomever it is that you are seeing is not helping you right now. I can recommend a few people for you, but I am going to make it a stipulation that you go. Both of you. Twice as often. Especially you, Porter."

"Twice!"

"At least." Mason said firmly. "You are still way fucked. You can't be the support Sienna needs when you can't even let her make mistakes on her own. And Michael, same with you. You both are blaming yourselves for something that you could in no way have influenced. Assuming guilt for no reason and catastrophic thinking are not good for anyone, especially not for any of us. These ladies need the space and freedom to make mistakes without the added guilt that they might cause you two to fucking lose it. I need you two to be able to take things in stride. Right now, you are both so touchy that I am not sure when that will be. Therefore, you are both ordered to go to therapy at least once a week until I think you are better. Do we understand each other, gentlemen?"

Sienna felt Porter heave a big sigh. "Fine, Mason, whatever." He surrendered.

"Who do you want me to see, Mason?" Michael sounded a bit upset.

"We'll discuss it later."

"What about Sienna?" Porter asked.

"I'll make arrangements with the ladies separately. They are a lot more damaged than you two idiots. They need special handling."

"Fucking not fair."

"I never promised to be fucking fair, now shut the fuck up about it. I'm your friend, I'm your employer, and you had better fucking do what I tell you to."

"Fine, whatever. Still not fair."

"Life's not fair."

All this went by Sienna like it was s dream. She felt like her limbs were leaden again, like the grey fog was coming back. She started to shake harder. The car slowed.

"Goddamn traffic jam at ten o'clock at night. I hate the fucking city." Michael muttered.

Sienna suddenly knew they weren't getting away. There were people who had stopped the traffic to grab them and drag them all from the car. They were going to drag her back and put more Kickstart into her, they were going to do it to Porter, right in front of her. It was going to be her fault that he was hurting. She couldn't let him hurt. She started fighting wildly, crying frantically. She had to get away. They were all going to die because of her.

"Mason! She's losing it! I can't hold her enough! She's too fucking strong and she's going to hurt herself!" Porter said sharply.

Mason had a hypodermic out. "Dammit, I didn't want to do this. Michael, get her arm. She is going to fucking hate it."

Porter held her as still as he could and Michael held her arm still. She arched against them both, screaming and thrashing.

Mason, his face pale, pushed the needle into her arm quickly and injected the medicine. He pulled the needle out just as quickly.

Sienna was screaming, trying to get away. She didn't know where she was, who people were, why she was there. Everything had faded into some terrible merciless vagueness; she couldn't tell who was around her or where she was going. She knew only that there was some nameless terror trying to get her and that she had to get away. She had to get to safety. She had to... Suddenly, it was all gone. She sagged limply against Porter again, sobbing uncontrollably.

Porter held her close. "What the fuck was that?" He demanded of Mason.

"I can only guess, Porter. I think it was a reaction from the drugs they gave her. She may have episodes like this for a long time. Maybe it has done something to the chemicals in her brain, who the fuck knows? And it is just as likely that the fuckoff gave something like it to Karen. Now you two understand why I said they are more damaged."

Michael had his arm around Karen, who looked terrified. "That man is lucky we left. I would tear various important parts off him for this shit."

Mason nodded. "I know. While I can't condone it, I totally agree with you. If what he did is permanent, then I might have to find out where he is being held and take further steps."

"What steps?" Karen whispered.

Mason smiled at her. "Don't worry your pretty head about it. I do not think I will need to do anything at all. Officially, he hasn't been arrested. He exists now in a state of limbo, for as long as the government wants to keep him there."

"And... you really think he gave me something that made me afraid of the dark?"

"No, I think it very likely he gave you something that has enhanced your natural fears. Your fear is excessive, and there isn't really a reason for it. Until we can get some sort of analysis of your mental state, I doubt that there is some trauma that you are hiding from. I think you are, therefore, being fucked with by drugs. But what they are and how they work, that is anyone's guess. There are hundreds if not thousands of chemicals that might affect us, and we have charted only a few."

Karen suddenly started crying. "Oh, thank God! I was so worried that I was really that messed up!"

Michael held her close to him and she buried her face into his arm.

Mason shook his head, his face a picture of disgust. He glanced at Porter. "This is what a truly self-centered fuck does to the people around him. It can go overboard the other way, too, though. A truly co-dependent person will try to fix the self-centered fuck by themselves. Do you see why I need you and Michael in therapy, and why I have to get the ladies in for further analysis?"

Porter sighed. "Yes, Mason, I do. I'm sorry I can't do it on my own, is all."

"We all are, but we are only made stronger by letting others help. Right, Michael? We can only learn our weaknesses by sparring others, since we only see our strengths."

"Yeah, you're right. I wish he hadn't hurt these two so badly. This is killing me."

Mason nodded. "Me, too. They are more precious than any diamonds, or paintings, or anything."

Sienna gave a tired little sigh. "You're lying, Mason. You do that a lot."

"No, actually I don't." He looked at her very seriously. "Look, Sienna, we all came for you both. What does that tell you?"

She tried to think of something, but her brain moved only sluggishly. "I... I... fuck, I can't think at all!" She started crying in frustration. She began hit herself in the side of the head, frustrated and angry that she couldn't think.

Mason held her arm after that. "Fuck, Sienna, don't do that!"

"Am I really going to be like this forever?" she practically begged.

Mason looked at her with great tenderness. "Sienna, I don't know. Even if you are though, I still love you."

She just stared at him. Nothing was registering. The car inched along.

Mason took her pulse. "Porter, she's starting to drop again. We might have to give her a gentle upper. But if I do, she might go too high. I want your honest opinion. If she drops too low, we might end up with her falling asleep and slipping into a coma. If we up her too much, she might have another psychotic episode."

Porter's face twisted with sudden conflict. "Why the fuck are you asking me?"

"Because, idiot, you want her to marry you. It's for sickness and health, not just health. You want to be her husband then you are going to have to man up. Marriage doesn't mean everything gets rosy-pink shit. It means you share your shit even more. Now, which is it?"

Porter hesitated. Sienna drooped. She felt like the world was swimming by. She was in the middle of a void and the world was going away. Maybe it had never been real to begin with. She looked incuriously as the lights all flowed into one continuous blur, then began to fade entirely.

Gradually, she began to be aware of things again. She was not in the car. They were in the apartment. She was lying somewhere. The lights were on. She hurt. She looked around, trying to focus.

"She's back." Mason said from beside her, standing up. He had a syringe. Sienna recoiled from it. "It's okay now, Sienna." He said gently. "I know you are afraid of this. The thing is, you were slipping away and I had to bring you back. I had to use a drug to do it. Your brain is still trying to rid itself of the toxin that you ingested yesterday. One of the ways it is doing it is by shutting off certain parts, but in doing so, it might also shut down too much. Do you understand me?"

Sienna nodded.

"No, you need to use words." Mason said, looking at her very intently.

"Y..yes." Sienna managed to get out.

"Good." Mason looked at her with great compassion. "I had to know if your brain had shut down your speech centers. I am sorry."

She nodded. Porter was standing behind Mason, looking terribly worried. She looked at him and found she couldn't look away. Mason said something, but it didn't register on her at all.

Porter stared at her and she at him. It was probably ridiculous. She finally reached out a very unsteady hand to him.

He came to her and picked her up so gently. "Sienna..."

"No. Don't. Just... don't put me down. Ever."

He nodded. "No."

He carried her to the room he had in back. "Will you be okay with the lights off or will you need them on to sleep?" He asked.

"I don't know. Don't leave me alone."

"I won't, Sienna. I just want to make you comfortable right now."

"Would you bring me a damp wash cloth then? I want to wash

190

off everything I can of that dreadful place. And some water?"

"Of course. Whatever you need."

"I need you, now, and probably forever."

"Good, because you are stuck with me."

"About fucking time."

Chapter 17

The night seemed to stretch forever. It seemed like Sienna slept only for a few seconds each time. She kept waking up, screaming, thrashing, shouting, weeping. Each time, Porter held her and talked to her until she calmed down. Once, Mason had to give her another upper. Sienna was so tired by the time that the sun came up, she was drifting in a state verging on unconscious. Porter must have been exhausted, but he didn't seem to mind much.

Mason came in as they dozed.

"Yes?" Sienna heard Porter whisper.

"Is she asleep yet?"

"No, she hasn't really slept all night. This is gonna be a fun trip."

"Yeah, fun; exactly what I was thinking. Once we get back, we'll need to get her into the clinic. She needs to be seen, immediately. You are going to have to take her. I'll come too, but she needs you."

"I know. I appreciate your help, Mason. I know I am not the best for this job."

"Fuck that. You are the best because of who you are. She doesn't need fucking Superman, she needs a man."

Porter was silent.

"What?" Mason said. "You think I am lying?"

Porter sighed. "No, but I almost wish you were."

Mason snorted. "Superman lived in a fucking Fortress of Solitude made of ice. He couldn't handle the world. He was just a fucked as you are."

"Hadn't thought of that. Yeah, I guess you are right."

Sienna started shaking again. She was so very tired, and she started to cry in frustration. Why was she not able to control herself?

Mason stood up quickly. "She's losing it, Porter! Watch her!"

Porter held her a little more closely. "I am, Mason, but she has done this all night. I don't think I can do anything to make a difference."

"That doesn't matter much; I need you to tell me if she needs something."

192

Porter hesitated. "What if I'm wrong?"

"Porter," Mason said firmly, "I trust you with my own life, and with the lives of my teams. Fucking get it together. I trust you. Learn to fucking trust your own damn self."

"You have such a way with words."

"Fuck off. We need to get out of here, and now. This is too dangerous, and the sooner she can be somewhere she trusts, the better. You're going to stay with her, right?"

"Yes."

"Good. Then you better have a big enough bed for the both of you."

Porter shifted a bit uncomfortably.

Mason said nothing more and left. Sienna had heard everything and most of it had rushed right past her. Her brain was struggling to even focus, let along comprehend.

Porter held her and kissed her head. "Shh, Sienna, it's okay."

"I can't fucking stop! Why can't I? Why am I so damn pathetic?"

"You're not pathetic. You're just indisposed right now."

She didn't even bother answering. She knew the truth; she was useless. More than useless, she was a danger to the team. If she could have figured out a way to get out on her own, she would have left and let them be free of her.

Finally, she calmed down enough to think more clearly. Porter still held her.

"You must be tired, Porter."

"It's nothing. I do this to myself sometimes. Staying up all night doesn't hurt me."

"Are we leaving soon?"

"Probably after breakfast. You need something to eat. Would you like me to make it for you?"

"Yes, please."

Porter got up and raked his hair back. "God but I hate this hair."

He muttered to no one. He pulled on his shirt and left quietly.

Sienna tried standing. She was a bit unsteady, but she could do it. She looked at the small window in the far wall. The alley behind was empty but for the usual detritus of cities. If she could get it open, she could get out it and leave. No one else would have to deal with her uselessness anymore. It was hard to think that she wouldn't see Porter again, but she didn't want him to resent her. She pulled on a robe and softly went to the window. She carefully pushed a chair under the opening and tried to move the sill. It seemed to be very heavy. She pushed as hard as she could and it budged an inch or two, grudgingly.

"What the fuck do you think you are doing?" She hadn't heard Mason come in. He was looking at her knowingly from the doorway.

She couldn't find an answer. She looked at the window longingly. Mason sighed and walked over. "Sienna, you can hardly fucking walk. What makes you think we couldn't find you again, possibly within a few minutes?"

Slowly, she flushed. She was terribly embarrassed. Mason firmly shut and locked the window again, then he put his arm around her waist and picked her up off the chair. He set her on the bed and sat in the chair, facing her. He was quiet for a while. Sienna turned her face away, mortified. Finally, Mason said, "You know, I had a feeling you would try something like that."

Sienna didn't say anything. She was ashamed. A tear slid down her cheek.

Mason continued, "There is no way you could have pulled it off. And why would you want to? Do you think I will let you hurt yourself just to prove you can?"

Sienna shook her head. He didn't understand. This wasn't about her.

Mason continued in that calm voice. "Do you really think Porter can't handle this little episode? He is a lot stronger than he seems. You know, there is really only one reason he didn't do the exact same thing that time. Do you know why he didn't do it?"

Sienna shook her head again.

Mason smiled slightly. "No, you don't, and he doesn't really, either. But there is one reason he couldn't do it. It isn't because he isn't strong enough, or weak enough. It isn't even because he wasn't in despair. In the end, it is because he could not, absolutely *could not*, hurt you. He could not be that selfish. He loves you that much. Are you going to throw that away and take even that from him?"

Sienna stared at Mason, feeling guilt starting to creep up in her.

Mason shook his head gently at her. "Look, I am not that stupid. You have been through something extremely difficult. The easiest thing in the world is to run away from something like that. The problem is that you can't run away, Sienna. It is part of you now, and you cannot run away from you, no matter how hard you try. Porter wants to share everything you go through, everything. Are you going to cheat him? You said not too long ago that you wanted to share all his pain. It doesn't work just one way. That's not love, that's selfish. You're not a selfish person. You would never forgive yourself for doing that."

Sienna closed her eyes. Her stomach lurched and twisted. It hurt to hear it because she knew it was true.

Mason sighed again. He sat beside her on the bed and put an arm around her shoulders. "Look, Sienna, I can get you help, but I can't do it if you run off, literally or figuratively. You have to decide to get help. It has to be your choice or it won't work."

"I know." She gasped out. "It's so impossible!"

"Right now, it is." He agreed calmly. "If we get the right help, it won't always be. Are you willing to try?"

"Yes. Just, please, don't tell Porter about this. Please. I don't want him to think it was because of him."

Mason smiled. "You mean that you don't want him to know you were weak?"

"Well..." She trailed off.

"No, I won't tell Porter. You will. He told you his worst secrets.

You can't keep yours locked up just because you are afraid to be weak in front of him."

They sat there for a little while. Sienna, lulled towards sleep again, leaned against Mason wearily. "Please don't tell him?" She whispered drowsily.

"No, I won't, Sienna. Sleep, beautiful; we will get you better soon."

As if she were waiting to hear that, she slept.

When she woke, it was slowly. She had no idea how long she had been asleep. She seemed more alert though. That was promising. She sat up and stretched a little. Mason was still sitting there where he had been. Porter was sitting in the chair across from them, under the window. To Sienna's eyes, he looked a bit upset. She flushed guiltily. No one said anything, but Sienna suddenly knew what she was expected to do. Very carefully and slowly she stood up and took a few unsteady steps to where Porter was. Just as unsteadily, she knelt down in front of him and, looking up at him in desperation, she said, "Porter, I am very sorry. I thought, if I ran away, you would be rid of me and my shit."

Porter looked tremendously surprised. "What the hell is this?"

Sienna couldn't hold her emotions in anymore; she laid her head on his lap and started sobbing violently.

Dimly, she heard Porter say, "What the fucking hell just happened?"

"She is letting you share her weakness, Porter. What the fuck do you think?"

"I don't care about her being upset by this. That's normal. Who the fuck wouldn't be?"

"I know that, Porter. That doesn't mean she doesn't feel like a burden to us right now."

"Fuck that. I will carry her if I need to."

"You will need to. She can't walk, not even to the end of the alley."

Porter gently smoothed her hair. "Sienna, what the fuck?"

196

"I am so pathetic right now!" She wailed. "I know I'm different. I can't do anything right! I am so afraid you won't want me anymore, that you will just want who I was! What if I can't be that person anymore? I'm so afraid of it! I don't want you to not want me!"

"Fuck, Sienna, of course I want you; I love you. I don't love who you were any more than I love you right now. I would never want some ghost of who you were just because it's what I know. I want you, as you are, right now, forever."

She started sobbing again. Somehow, it was exactly what she had needed to say, to tell him. And he didn't care! It was the best and worst thing she'd done all week.

She heard Mason laugh softly. "I fucking told you she didn't need Superman. You are the man she needs, not some fake bullshit. Are you starting to get it? Now do you see why she needs you?"

"Sort of. But what the fucking hell did she even try to do?"

"She tried to open the window and get out, what did you think?"

"Oh, Sienna." Porter sighed despairingly. "You beautiful little fool. You perfect, perfect wonderful girl."

"Anyway, I figured she'd try something like that. PTSD is pretty insidious. She feels like a burden to us, and the logical way to solve that is to remove the burden. So she was going to run away and take her presence away so she wasn't hurting us anymore."

"That's not logical, Mason."

"No, but it is exactly the same thing you tried to do, isn't it?"

"Yes, I suppose so. Kinda how the priests say suicide is the final, most selfish act?"

"Why the fuck would she think we would fucking care?" Michael's voice floated in from the door area.

"Because she isn't thinking clearly right now; she only sees the hurt around her, nothing else. She thinks she has caused it, and she wants to take that away from you. She really is a very loving woman and she never wants to cause pain to her friends."

"I completely understand." Karen whispered.

"I know you do." Mason agreed. "This is why, as soon as we get out of here and back to the states, I want both you ladies into a clinic to have some tests run. PTSD can be treated, but it takes a long time and lots of work. And tons of support, of course." The bed creaked slightly as he stood up. "Now, here is what is going to happen. We are going to go and eat. All of us. Then we are going to leave. All of us. No arguments."

"Don't take this as an argument," Michael said, "But won't that jet only hold four of us?"

"Yes, which is why you are going to act as co-pilot."

"I've never flown one of these before, Mason!"

"I know, but it should be close enough to one you have flown."

Porter leaned over and whispered to Sienna, "Are you better now?"

Sienna shook her head, still keeping her face hidden.

"Well, I am sorry, my love, but you can't stay hidden forever."

"Why the fuck not? Who made up that damn rule? I want to strangle whoever it was."

"I don't know, but it is the rule so you have to come eat with us."

Sienna stood up very shakily. Porter looked at her, amused. "What the fuck are you smiling about?" She snapped at him.

"What the fuck do you think? Since when do you have to act so fucking macho all the time? Let me help you."

Sienna was about to say something back but she stopped. He was right. Why was she afraid to show weakness in front of him? "All right. Please, Porter, would you help me?"

He stood up. "Of course I will." He bowed grandiosely. "Would you like to walk and have me support you, or would you like me to carry you?"

"Oh." Sienna wasn't sure. It seemed an awful lot like the same thing. "I don't know. You're going to be carrying me a lot today. Will

198

you be able to handle it?"

Porter smiled at her. "I think so, yes. You don't weigh all that much, and even if I am a little sore later, I shouldn't strain myself that much with it. Especially since my idiocy made you lose weight. I am still pissed with myself about that."

"Well, can I walk a little, just to see if I can? I really do hate having no control over anything."

"I understand, Sienna. I've been there myself. Lean on my arm if you need to."

Chapter 18

They went into the little kitchen area. Karen sat very close to Michael. She looked strained. Sienna sighed. Whatever the fucking bastard had done to her, it was awful.

She made it to the table and Porter held her chair for her. He did that often anyway, but she knew one of the reasons he did it now was so that she wouldn't strain herself. She sat down wearily.

Michael looked at her for a second. "Porter, do we have something other than that robe for her to wear?"

Porter thought about it as he gathered the plates and the food he'd made. "I honestly don't know. I will look after we eat."

"If you want, you can have some of my things." Karen offered.

"Thank you, I would like that very much." Sienna smiled at her slightly.

Karen smiled back. "I can only imagine what these two would come up with without our assistance."

"True." Sienna looked on as Porter began to dish up eggs and fruit. "Porter, for once, listen to me. I can't eat much today; I feel like I will throw it all back up. That would be a very bad idea for all of us."

Porter looked at her steadily. Mason, who had been out of the room, came in and shook his head at Porter. "She knows what she is talking about. Do what she says."

"Fine." Porter surrendered ungraciously.

Mason ignored that. "Sienna and Karen, I have been on the phone with one of my colleagues at the clinic I sometimes am affiliated with. They often treat people who cannot reveal certain parts of their backgrounds, and there is a higher instance of patients with PTSD who are assigned there. My colleagues are willing to see you once we get back. However, I need some information from you both, personal information. I can get it in one of the rooms here, and no one needs to overhear."

Sienna nodded shortly. She was annoyed by this although she wasn't sure why. "Whatever, Mason. I can do it wherever."

"Don't make that sort of statement without knowing what you are agreeing to, Sienna." Mason admonished sharply.

"Fuck off, Mason. I can't fucking walk anyway. Just ask the damn questions."

Mason looked at her quite steadily. "No."

Sienna hadn't expected that at all. She stared at him incredulously. "What the fuck did you say?"

"I said, 'No', Sienna. Fucking what do you think I am, anyway?"

"What the fuck! Why not?"

"Because, my dear, you are out of control. I will not do something that I think might embarrass or demean you in front of other people. Fucking drop it. I'll ask later."

Sienna was very angry all of a sudden. She was about to respond but Porter took her hand firmly. "Fucking drop it, Sienna. He knows what he is doing and you are out of line right now."

"Fuck off, Porter!"

"No."

Sienna tried to shake him off. "Let me go!"

"No. I am still stronger than you are and I will hold you all day until you calm down."

She started to cry. "That's not fucking fair!" She accused.

"Whatever. Are you finished with this yet? Would you like to eat now?"

"Fine, whatever. Let go."

He did. Sienna glared at him then started to eat her food furiously.

Mason was still looking at her with that calculating look. Sienna finished quickly. Mason had eaten hardly anything, but he stood up as soon as she was finished. "Let's do these questions in Michael's room. Now. Without anyone else."

Sienna shrugged. "Whatever."

Mason shook his head. "No, not 'whatever'; this is important."

"Fine, Mason. Do the fucking questions!"

He came over and picked her up. "We'll be in the room, if anyone needs us." He called over his shoulder.

Porter gave a stifled snort of laughter. "Enjoy!"

Mason set Sienna on the bed casually and shut the door. He sat on a chair facing her. "What the fuck is driving you?"

"Is that one of you damn questions?"

"No, it's a question of a friend. What the fuck, Sienna?"

"I don't fucking know. Ask your damn questions."

Mason looked at her for a long minute. "Hm. You're doing worse than I thought. Maybe breakfast was a bad idea."

"Why?"

"Because it delays our departure by that much. You need help, and as soon as I can get it for you."

"Am I really so fucking broken?"

"Just damaged right now, yes. You really think I would ask you penetrating and personal questions in front of everyone? Give me some fucking credit."

"What does it fucking matter? No one fucking cares."

"Like hell. I am not going to let you hurt your friends just because you are feeling belligerent any more than I will let Michael go tear Patos' arms off or Porter go find the leader of the gang out there. Just because you are hurt doesn't mean you get to hurt everyone around you; you are as fucking bad as any of them right now. Worse, actually, because you can't stop."

"Maybe it's just fucking hormones."

"No, this is more than that. You are over-reacting violently." He shook his head distractedly. "Aw, fuck, this is getting nowhere. Okay, I am issuing an ultimatum to you, here and now: either calm the fuck down, or I will sedate you for the entire flight."

"What? You wouldn't!"

Mason just looked at her steadily. "Oh?"

Sienna knew, without a doubt, that he would. She still wanted to bluff him out. It made no sense, she knew it, and she couldn't stop at all. The rational side of her observed in detachment as she said as insultingly as possible, "You don't have the fucking balls, Mason."

Mason didn't get angry. He just sighed, stood up, and opened the door to the room. "Porter. Michael. I need you two in here."

They came in with questioning looks.

Mason sighed again. "I really, really didn't want to do this, but you are becoming too erratic. Your impulses are becoming too strong. I can't take the chance that you will act unexpectedly on the plane in a way that might endanger yourself or anyone else. Right now, I can't trust you, Sienna. Therefore, I am truly sorry and I hope that someday, someday in the future perhaps, you will forgive me." He turned to Porter and Michael. "I have to give her a depressant. You two are going to have to hold her down. She is going to go fucking crazy."

Sienna stared at them all with rising alarm. Mason reluctantly pulled out a small case from his inner pocket. He took out a vial and a syringe. Sienna saw him carefully load the syringe with the drug from the vial. Porter and Michael were holding her firmly. She started to struggle against them, even though she knew it was utterly hopeless.

"No, Mason! No, I'll be good! Please don't do it! I promise, Mason! Please!" She screamed, writhing and twisting.

Mason looked terribly sad. He quickly swabbed her arm and pushed the needle in.

"No!" She screamed, still trying to get away. "No, Mason, no!" The world was spinning out of her control. She stared wildly at Mason.

"I am very sorry, Sienna." He said gently. "Someday, perhaps, you will understand. God alone knows if you will ever forgive me."

"Please don't!" She begged.

"It's already done. I took the needle out over a minute ago." His face was full of compassion.

Sienna shook her head. That was impossible, she was not drugged. He couldn't have done it that fast. He just couldn't have…

The room started to fade out. She clutched at Porter. "Porter, please, don't…" Whatever she was going to say faded out. She didn't lose consciousness completely. It was more like a suspended dream or something where she was completely unattached to her body or emotions. She could still see, hear, smell, all of it, but she didn't care. She couldn't direct her eyes or thoughts at all. She was a passive observer in the ultimate sense of the phrase.

"Why did she have to do that?" Michael's voice drifted in.

"I don't know. Whatever she is reacting to is heightening her natural aggression beyond what is normal. You think she was bad at the table, she was ten times worse in here. You two remember that one night where you beat the hell out of each other?"

"Yes."

"You remember how uncooperative you were at the beginning, before you started to let yourself heal?"

"Yeah, I suppose I do."

"Well, that, only much, much more frightening. You had a good, solid reason, in that you had trauma in your past that you had never faced and had suppressed. Sienna may have a trauma in her past, but I kind of doubt it. My instincts are telling me that this is completely unnatural and that scares me. She could do almost anything if she gets that far gone again."

"God but this is hard." Porter said softly.

"We'll get her help, as soon as we possibly can. She can't hurt herself now. She can still hear and see us, but it's like her brain doesn't care. She might even sleep in this state. But the main thing is she can't hurt herself. She also can't move herself. All right, gentlemen." Mason's voice became businesslike. "She needs to be dressed and she needs to be carried. We're not going to be wusses about this, are we? Good. Let's get his done as quickly as possible and get the hell out of this damn city."

Very gently, she herself lowered to something and equally gently she felt something being put on her. Dimly, she thought that maybe there was something she was supposed to be paying attention to, but it was too hard to remember, so she stopped concentrating.

Mason's voice came from somewhere. "Karen, here's the thing: we can't afford to have you or Sienna reacting in a violent and dangerous fashion, especially not when we are in the air and can't do much. Therefore, I am going to warn you now, as urgently as I can, if you start to display behavior that I find dangerous in my professional opinion, I will not hesitate to use this drug on you, as well. I simply cannot risk you doing permanent damage to yourself while in a state that is not your own. Do you understand what I am saying to you?"

"Y-yes, but, well, what do you mean, you can't risk it?"

"I, for one, Porter, for another, and Michael, for the third and most important, care about you too much to allow you to do things that you will regret later. Is that clear enough?"

"Um, yes, I think so."

"We're leaving, now. Porter, I know that I have acted in a manner that you may not agree with. I apologize, and I hope you can forgive me."

"Mason, you are my friend and I completely trust you. But, next time, could you give a little goddamn warning first?"

"Or a lot of goddamn warning?" Michael chimed in.

Sienna felt someone picking her up. She thought maybe she should care about who it was, but she couldn't make herself.

"No, I can't give you any warning, idiots. What do you think, I have some goddamn play book that I just leaf through and find the right fucking play?"

"You mean you don't? Aw, fuck!"

The ceiling was moving. No, that was wrong, she was moving. She was just looking at the ceiling. Or, maybe it was moving. She no longer cared.

Then they were outside. The sky was overcast but still bright. "Here, Porter, hand her in." Michael said from somewhere below.

She felt herself floating. There was another ceiling. It must be a car.

After a while, there seemed to be a confused welling in her

impressions; was she floating? Was she even alive? Was she dreaming?

She fell into a spiral of loose unconnected impressions. Nothing made any sense, nothing connected to anything else. Her mind took snapshots that made no story. Then they were all gone and she just floated into nothing.

Gradually, she floated back. It was very slow, but she regained her senses. She didn't have full control, but she felt like she could do things again.

"Water?" She whispered. She was so thirsty.

"Of course." Mason leaned over and very carefully helped her drink a little. "Are you feeling better?"

"Yes." She whispered again. It was a lot of effort to talk. She paused for a moment and then whispered, "Porter?"

Mason smiled slightly. "He's here, Sienna. We're over the ocean. You've been out for quite a while." He sighed softly. "I am truly sorry."

Sienna took a few moments to think her slow way through that. "I know."

Mason laughed. "You are delightful, do you know that? Anyway, once we get there, in about five more hours, you are going in to the clinic. I am going to watch you and Karen until then, because you are not going to scare me that much again."

Sienna closed her eyes. Too much was happening for her to process any more.

"Rest, Sienna. You need to be as calm as you can be for as long as you can."

"Yes." She whispered. She slept then, for a long time, and even though she was tormented by terrible dreams, when she woke back up, they faded away into sunlight and she didn't remember any of them at all.

They were still flying. Mason was chatting softly with someone off to the side. Sienna still couldn't move very much, and she still seemed slow in thinking. She did feel a bit calmer. That was a definite improvement.

She was thirsty again. "Water?" She whispered.

Mason turned immediately. "You are awake again. Very good." He said pleasantly as he held the water bottle for her to drink. "We're still over the ocean, but we are only about an hour out now. Are you feeling better?"

"A little." She closed her eyes for a moment. "Still slow."

"You will be for a while; that is one of the downsides to this depressant. No drug is perfect."

"Is Karen okay?"

Mason sighed. "No, she isn't. You had a bad dream at one point and she started to react to your being upset. I don't know what that guy gave you two, and it might not even be the same thing, but it is pretty damn potent. I had to restrain her too. She didn't need as much, but then, she isn't as strong as you are."

"I'm not strong."

Mason smiled. "Maybe not terribly physically strong, Sienna, but you are mentally much stronger than most people are. Karen has been brutalized for God knows how long. She has been under a great deal of psychological and physical abuse for quite a while. She has been helpless and told she is useless. One of her hardest jobs is going to be working through all that. Yours will be different. You already know you are a very talented and beautiful person. Your biggest obstacle is probably going to be learning to repress these wild impulses, at least until we can find out what he gave you."

"You think you will?"

"Well, they did raid the house, and I did specifically request that they forward any and all chemicals to a lab I know right away for analysis."

Sienna thought about that. It took a while. "You did that?"

Mason rolled his eyes. "Why am I surrounded by people who always seem amazed when I do things for my friends?"

Porter said softly, from right behind them, "Because you

deserve the annoyance."

Mason shook his head despairingly. "No, I deserve a goddamn medal. Yes, I requested it. It was more than a request, and it is already being done."

Porter whistled softly. "You must have a hell of an influence."

"Of course I do, Porter. How the hell did you think we even get hired for these things, anyway?"

"I hadn't really thought about it."

"Clearly."

Sienna closed her eyes again to think. It helped to block one sense out. "You think we can get better?"

"It will depend on what he gave you, or rather what Beatrice gave you, since I am more inclined to think it was the initial Xoria shit rather than the Kickstart. It may have changed your brain fundamentally. I can't say right now."

Sienna sighed involuntarily.

Mason put his hand on her arm gently. "I know, Sienna. It is hard to face the prospect of being so very different from whom you were, and that it might be forever. We are completely willing to help you, and we are completely willing to give you what you need. However, you have to tell us what those things are, once you understand them better yourself."

"What if I can't do this anymore? What if I'm useless to you?" She whispered, near tears.

"Then we won't ask you to. But we will still be your friends."

From behind her, Porter said gently, "If you can't, Sienna, then I won't. I won't rub your face in something I know will cause you pain."

Mason nodded. "Sienna, none of us are to be hired for several months. That was part of my stipulations from this job. We have time to get better, now. All of us. Right, Porter?"

Porter exhaled noisily. "Yeah, fine, whatever."

Mason shook his head again. "Not whatever!"

"Okay! You win! Yes, I will get better!"

208

"Good! Now, Sienna, when we get there, Porter will get you to the clinic, but he really needs to get to his own therapist while you are being analyzed. I promise to stay with you and Karen the whole time, but Michael and Porter are going to have to start their own treatment. This is very hard on them, you know. They will probably be back before you are done, but I can't promise that. Do you understand?"

"Yes. I just wish..."

"I know, but seeing you two go through more will be too hard on them. They need a safe place to recover. Especially since they won't admit to it."

"I understand."

"Good. We will be landing in about fifteen minutes. Porter, Michael, you two heard me. You are going, as we discussed. You may bring the ladies to their clinic and then you will take the car and go to your own appointments. Right, gentlemen?"

They both assented. Neither sounded happy about it.

"I am sorry; I can't chance it."

"We get it, Mason." Michael said from off to the right.

"Good. You better get up to assist the pilot if he needs you."

"All right."

Chapter 19

The landing and the car trip were mundane and uneventful. Sienna still had no control over her larger muscles, and she still felt slow. Mason was on his phone for a significant part of the trip. Michael held Karen; she was almost completely out of it still.

At one point, Sienna thought she heard Mason say, "I don't know. I think we should scan. MRI never hurts in these cases."

Sienna whispered, "In a tube?"

Mason glanced at her. "Just a moment, John." He looked at Sienna for a long minute. "I'm afraid so. We need to know what your brain is doing and not doing. MRI is really the best way to find that out. Will you be able to do that for us?"

Sienna closed her eyes again. "I suppose. It is scary."

"Yes, it is. I do not want to take away from that."

Sienna didn't open her eyes, but she felt a tear run out and down her cheek.

Gently, Mason wiped it away.

"Okay, Mason. I will try."

"That's my girl." He said softly.

At the clinic, Sienna looked around with her limited range of eye movement. It was sober and quiet and clean. Mason went over to talk to somebody.

Sienna realized suddenly that it was almost time for Porter to leave. "Porter, don't go." She said suddenly afraid that he would disappear and never come back for her.

"Sienna, you know I have to. I can't handle much more. Mason was absolutely right about that."

"Please don't leave me."

"Sienna, I will come back. I will always come back. I will never leave you for long. And when you are done for the day, I will take you to my house. No, not yours. You are going to stay with me. I won't let you be by yourself. Mason will be here with you while I'm gone."

"It's not the same."

210

"I hope not! But besides that, he is the best person for this. I trust him with much more than myself."

"I do too, I guess. I am afraid though."

"I'll come back."

"Okay." She took a deep breath. "I am sorry I keep being selfish. Go to your appointment."

Porter kissed her very gently on the forehead.

"You better not think that is all you are going to do."

He smiled and kissed her on the mouth. "I will be back soon, my dear."

Mason was back. "They're ready. This way, and then you two better get going."

After Porter and Michael had left, Sienna felt Mason gently putting something on her arm.

"Sienna," He said calmly, "this is an I.V. drip. It won't hurt you, but there might be reason to use it. Will you be all right with this?"

Sienna thought about it. "I think so, Mason."

"Let me know immediately if not."

She felt a small sting and that was all. "I'm okay."

"You always were a strong woman. Okay, they are going to scan you and Karen at the same time, separate rooms. I will be observing you both. Let us know if there is something that is a problem."

"Yes, Mason."

He carefully patted her head. "Then you are ready."

The scan was not too bad, considering. Sienna forced herself to breathe deeply and calmingly through it. The tight quarters were definitely not a good thing. She started having a little trouble maintaining towards the end.

Finally, she was slid out. She had regained some of her muscle control. She turned her head and saw a man in a white coat smiling at her.

"You must be Sienna, Mason's friend and colleague. I'm Dr.

Matthews."

"Doctor." Sienna nodded very slightly.

"It will take a few minutes to get all the scans uploaded. In the meantime, I thought we should have a little talk about some of your background. At this clinic, we see many patients who cannot tell us everything. I want you to speak of what you can, but do not distress yourself if you can't reveal certain things. We can usually work around some specifics if we need to. Also, Dr. Briggs has given us some of your information."

"Dr. Briggs? Oh, Mason."

"Yes, that was who I meant."

"Sorry, I forget that he is a doctor."

"He is your friend, first and foremost. Here, he is a colleague. He is most interested in your health." Dr. Matthews looked at his charts quickly. "How old are you, Sienna?"

"Uh..." Sienna had a little trouble remembering. "36."

"What is today?"

"I have no idea, Doctor."

Dr. Matthews made a notation on one sheet. "That is fine, by the way. I am not worried about it. I am just noting it in case it can help pinpoint later on."

"I understand."

"Good. I am glad that you are such a good patient. Now then, you were in Hong Kong, according to Dr. Briggs. He has indicated that you ingested some drug and another was administered to rectify the first. Do you happen to know what those drugs were?"

Sienna closed her eyes. She was getting tired again. "No, I only know the names they called them by."

"What were those names?"

"Xoria was the first. It was in a drink, so I must assume it was soluble in some liquid. The second was a hypodermic they called Kickstart."

"I see. We'll see if we can't find those out soon. We have all

212

the chemicals they seized."

"Do you think I will get better?" Sienna asked quietly.

Dr. Matthews considered. "Well, it is hard to say for sure, as I am fairly sure you know. However, the scans that I saw did not indicate extensive damage or anything like that. There were some worrying things in the scans, but what those are, I can't say yet. That's also just based on me seeing only a few, not the whole of them."

"I understand. I am worried about that."

"I would be in your place, too. My initial assumption is that you will heal completely, but it will take some time and you will have to work to contain the symptoms. Dr. Briggs has alerted me to some of those, as well. In truth, I am more worried about the heightened aggressive tendencies."

"It might not be just aggression. I am having trouble controlling all emotions. It feels a little like I am trying to balance with an inner-ear infection and keep overcorrecting from one side to the other. Sort of. It is like I know it is happening but I can't stop it, either."

Dr. Matthews wrote something down. "That is a good observation. Anything like that will be helpful to know."

"I think it gives me terrible nightmares. I haven't slept well in days. That might be part of why I am forgetting things now."

"That could be a part of it, certainly. In fact, I would like to start there. Until we have a more complete picture of what it is and what it's doing, I want you to be able to sleep. I warn you that this will make you sedentary and slow. It is sometimes difficult for people who come here to handle that sort of lethargy."

Sienna thought about it. "I think that it will be okay. I would rather not be flying off at every little thing."

Dr. Matthews nodded. "Very good, then. Dr. Briggs and I will discuss this. If you would prefer, we can do it right now, in here. Some prefer to have any and all information."

Sienna thought again. "No," She said at last, "I trust Mason completely. He won't do anything to hurt me."

"Very well. You just relax, then. It may take a little while for us to come to a consensus. If you feel anything like discomfort or anxiety, I want you to push this button, all right?" He put a little remote with one button on it in her hand.

"Yes, Doctor."

He left quietly. Shortly there was a soft knock on the door. "Miss Byron?" A female voice said.

"Yes?" Sienna responded.

"There is a Porter here. Drs. Briggs and Matthews said that, if it is all right with you, he can come in."

"It is all right with me."

Porter came in. He was tall enough that Sienna didn't have to strain to see him. A tear slid back and into her hair.

"Shh, Sienna, don't cry. I am here now." Porter came over and sat beside her, taking her hand gently.

"I can't help it, still. I was so afraid that you would leave and never come back."

"I know. I shouldn't have told you to not cry. What I should have said was, 'Damn, you look amazing and I am in awe of you all over again.' That's what I thought first."

"Don't make fun of me."

"Never."

"Bullshit."

"Okay, you are right. But only a little and only over things that don't matter."

She sighed. It was good to hear him and know he was there. She closed her eyes again.

"Are you tired?"

"Yes, Porter. I haven't slept in days. The dreams."

"Oh. Is the doctor going to give you something?"

"Mason and he are talking about it now. How was your meeting?"

"It fucking sucked. What did you think? But I feel better now."

214

"Good." She sighed again and started to drift off. "I'm going to try to sleep. Don't leave me."

"I won't."

She didn't really sleep. It was more like drifting in and out of fantasies. Eventually there was another knock on the door. "All right, Sienna," Mason said, "Dr. Matthews and I have a plan."

"Oh, good." She mumbled.

Dr. Matthews came over and checked her vitals quickly. "You were sleeping?"

"More like dozing, I think."

"Did you have any of the bad nightmares?"

"No, just the usual nonsensical dreams."

"Very good." He made some notes. "Dr. Briggs and I have decided that you should have a gentle drug to help you sleep. That is of paramount importance right now, since it is through sleep that our bodies do the most repair work, especially of our brains. The problem is that you will need to be monitored for the first night at least to make sure that there are no reactions, and if there are, you need to be corrected quickly. Dr. Briggs has assured me that he has this under control. I am just warning you about it."

"I understand, Doctor."

"Further, we need you to come back in tomorrow. Will that be a problem?"

"I can't remember. Will it be a problem, Porter?"

Porter shook his head. "There is no reason she cannot be back, Doctor." He said firmly.

Dr. Matthews nodded again. "You are Porter, then?"

"Yes, sir."

"I would like to speak with you for a moment. Dr. Briggs will stay with you, Sienna." Porter rose and followed Dr. Matthews out of the room.

Mason sat in his chair. He absently took her pulse. "You are starting to get stressed again." He noted.

215

"Maybe it is because Porter left."

Mason smiled. "Probably some of it. Here's the thing, Sienna. You have to stay at my house for at least tonight. Both of you. I have to make sure you are safe. Dr. Matthews is giving Porter some instructions, but I have to be there in case this goes to hell, for either you or Karen."

Sienna smiled slightly. "I get it, Mason. Will I be able to eat?"

"It will really depend on you."

"Okay."

"New topic. Can you move your arm for me, beautiful?"

Sienna concentrated. She managed to raise it a little before she had to let it drop. "It is pretty hard."

Mason nodded, carefully writing something on the papers beside the bed. "That's good. How about a foot; can you wiggle a foot for me?"

Sienna tried moving various large groups of muscles at Mason's promptings for a few minutes. She managed to move them all, although none of them for long or very far.

"That's pretty consistent with our findings in general with this depressant. You are doing well."

"Except for the part where I even need the fucking thing."

"That's not your fault. We can allow for that." Mason hesitated. "While Porter is out, Sienna, I have to ask some questions. How much do you weigh?"

"I don't really know. I was at 120, but then the stress and all made me lose some and the last few days probably did too. Maybe 110?"

Mason nodded. "Also, while Porter is still out: are you pregnant right now?"

Sienna smiled slightly. "Impossible, Mason."

"I figured, but I have to ask. The medicine could be very dangerous for a developing baby."

She smiled again. "Still a virgin, Mason."

216

"We do seem to tend towards that in this select group. I think that is a total of... everybody so far."

"Really? We must be the most pathetic and boring group I know then."

"No, I think we are the smartest and most selective."

"Like that makes any different."

"I think it does."

"No wonder we are so much fucking fun at parties."

"That probably contributes, it's true. Anyway, when we get to my house, I have to get things ready. Like, beds, things like that. Porter and Michael will have to help. The depressant will continue to wear off and you might even be able to walk around or move on your own."

"Okay, Mason. Thanks for all you are doing."

"It is nothing. It should be a standing offer from me."

"I understand, but that doesn't mean that everyone will do it."

"The ones who matter will, and that is really all that matters, when you think about it. During the night, if one of you ladies loses it, I might need help from Porter and Michael. Just to warn you in case you wake up alone."

"I understand."

Mason smiled at her sadly. "I am so sorry this has happened, Sienna. I know it is scary to think that you might never be the way you were."

A tear slid down into her hair again. "Yes, it is. And I am still very afraid that it will be too much for Porter and that he won't want me anymore. That he'll leave. Terrified, in fact. Just don't make fun of me for it."

Mason nodded. "I know. It has to be something he chooses. But if he is even half the man I think he is, he won't hesitate at all."

Sienna smiled weakly even as another tear slid into her hair. "God, I hope you are right."

Mason looked at the chart again. "One more personal question that we never got around to asking earlier; have you ever had anything traumatic in your past that you may not have mentioned or might be suppressing? We might need to know if there is something else contributing to this."

Sienna thought about it. "No, nothing that I know of specifically, other than this fucking irrational fear about you all hating me for this."

"We don't hate you."

"Not yet, but if I never get better, you might."

"Nope. We'll never hate you."

Sienna smiled but more tears ran down.

Mason seemed to know she was having trouble believing him. "I haven't been wrong yet, Sienna. Well, not on that front, anyway."

"I was going to say…"

"Shut up."

Chapter 20

The men set up a bed in the middle of the living room. Sienna sat by feeling generally useless. She hated this.

"Okay, looks good." Mason said, standing up. "Let's go make sure that the bed in my room is good enough, then I will set up a sleeping bag in the study or the other room or something. I am going to have to check like every two hours. However, I trust you gentlemen to tell me immediately if you suspect there is a problem. I have to know in order to act."

Porter nodded. "Got it."

"Michael?"

"Yeah, man, but are you sure I will be able to tell?"

"I trust you, Michael, so you better believe that you can."

Michael still looked dubious, but he nodded.

They went back to do their chores and Sienna was left with the semi-conscious Karen. Sienna glanced at her curiously, then carefully stood up and made a very unsteady way over to the couch. She sat on the floor and carefully checked Karen's pulse.

"Ah, my dear, we are in some serious shit." She said softly to herself. "I guess I am gonna have to start praying to whatever God Porter has found that we can get better."

"Yes." Karen breathed so softly that Sienna wasn't sure she hadn't made it up.

She kept checking on Karen while the men were occupied. After maybe ten minutes they came back out.

Mason nodded gravely to Sienna. "Thank you, Sienna."

"You're welcome, Mason. I needed to do something useful."

Porter smiled slightly.

"What are you laughing at, Porter?"

"I know exactly the sort of thing you are talking about."

"Oh? Do tell."

"Nope. That is something I can't revisit right now. Who's hungry?"

219

Michael laughed at him. "You always change the subject right when it gets interesting."

"Yeah, gee, I wonder why? Wait, no, I fucking don't!"

"Whatever, I think you are afraid of it."

"Well, no shit, Mikey. I told you before, I am terrified of it."

Michael shook his head.

Porter sighed. "Look, I can't do too much heavy shit at once, it sends me on a downward spiral, okay? This is hard enough without me losing my shit all over again."

"I get it, man, I am just observing that when the conversation starts to get personal or interesting, you change the subject."

"I'm not the center of attention here."

"Maybe you should be, though. You hang out on the peripheral all the time, but you are almost never at the center."

"You know, you can't really fucking talk, buddy. You only sit in the center when we make you."

Mason sighed. "You are both idiots. You both do the same shit. Do you have to fight over it?"

Michael shook his head. "No, but we will anyway."

Porter smiled. "True, that."

"You two are going to drive me out of my mind." Mason complained.

Porter shrugged. "Sorry in advance."

Mason snorted. "Enough. What are we doing for food?"

Michael opened the refrigerator. "Ooh, look, you have steak! That! We're doing that for dinner."

Porter kept a straight face. "Okay, I am glad that has been decided. What else?"

Michael stepped aside. "Why don't you look, master chef?"

Porter elbowed him out of the way. "Shut up. Ooh, corn. And lots of lettuce."

Michael laughed. "And you were just making fun of me." He forced his voice up a few octaves. "Ooh, and this tomato is just luscious. I must have it!"

"Shut the fuck up." Porter said absently. He didn't even look over as he surveyed what Mason had to eat.

Mason started laughing. "God, but I missed you guys! I am actually glad that you are here tonight."

Porter laughed as well. "I am pretty glad, myself. I got tired of having to watch every fucking thing all the time."

Michael snorted. "Whatever, man. You are so keyed up all the time I am shocked that you can sit still."

"And why on earth did you think I took up boxing anyway?"

Sienna sighed. She stood up slowly. Mason was there in a second. He didn't help her; he was just there if she needed him to be. "Thank you, Mason." She said very softly.

"It's no problem." He said just as softly.

She made it to the high bar and managed to sit on one of the stools. Porter glanced at her once but didn't say anything.

"Glad you could join us." Michael said.

"You two need to be kept in line." Sienna said.

"Indeed we do." Porter agreed, slicing vegetables. "Especially 'muscles' there."

"Me?" Michael protested. "At least I don't steal everything outright."

"Yeah, whatever, you just beat someone on the head and take it. Same thing."

"More sporting."

"That's only like a sport if the punching bag is an active participant."

Michael smiled. "This particular one was that one time."

Porter laughed involuntarily. "True! Okay, you win that one."

Michael saluted him.

Sienna shook her head gently. "You are incorrigible, both of you."

"They know. They do it on purpose." Mason said. "They are

very worried about you two and they are trying to bluff out of it."

"Ah, man, you ruined the fun!" Michael protested.

"Yeah, well, I will reinstate the fun. Juan is coming over to help with this whole mess."

"Awesome. We just needed tons more energy and irrepressible annoyance running around this house. I knew it was missing something. Like noise."

Mason smiled. "He is very worried, to be honest."

Sienna sighed. "Of course."

Mason gently took her hand. "It will get better, Sienna. Someday, I firmly believe you will be done with it all."

"How can you be so sure?" Sienna was desperate to know how she could ever expect to be over being useless to everyone and needing so much watching.

"I just feel it. Also, the lab hasn't found any chemicals that are permanently alternating yet. They haven't gotten results on them all, but the ones they have are temporary so far."

Sienna felt her trembling starting again. She so wanted to be herself again. "Really?" She whispered.

Mason gave her hand a small squeeze. "Really, Sienna. I think you will kick the ass off this drug, and it will be no more than terrible memories for you soon."

"I'm afraid to even hope that right now."

"I know you are. I don't blame you."

"None of us blame you." Porter said softly. "You must realize that, my dear. We all want to help you and support you and none of us see it as a burden or something distasteful that we are just going through the motions for."

Sienna nodded awkwardly. She couldn't quite believe any of this. She still had no control over herself; how could that not be a burden?

Michael shook his head at her. "I think I know what you are thinking. Stop. What Porter and Mason are telling you is the truth.

None of us is really any good at lying to you, anyway. Not for very long. Please, let us help you. I need to make up all that I have done wrong anyway. You are one of my best friends, I think. Please let me help you?"

"Michael, you know I can't just say 'yes' and then be all okay with this."

"I'm not asking you to. I am asking you to let us help you, not let us do it all for you. I would pull you through fire and water if I could, but I can't. Not this time. I lost someone once, to a sickness, and I have had to accept that I cannot fight everything. Mason keeps trying to teach me that. Hopefully, someday, I will even learn it."

Sienna was overwhelmed. She couldn't hold anything in, so she put her head down on the smooth marble of the counter and cried into her arms.

Mason said, "Porter, I will finish that. She needs you, and you need to do this."

"Should I take her somewhere?"

"No, I need to know if she worsens. I am afraid that you have to keep her here, even though it is awkward for all of us."

"Understood."

Sienna felt him put his arm around her waist gently. He just sat beside her while she hid from him and everyone else for a while. If she kept her head down and her arms over her face, it was almost like she could pretend that she was alone and that she wasn't bothering anyone. Eventually, she drifted off to sleep.

It was a dream that woke her up. One of those hideously frightening dreams where she couldn't tell if she was awake or asleep and then everyone around her changed into the most monstrous forms she could imagine. It was worse because the monsters weren't terrifying; they were completely believable, but just a little wrong. When she shuddered back to reality, she was confused for several minutes.

Mason was there, checking her pulse. Sienna was more than a

little afraid that he would suddenly become a caricature of himself and that she would be driven mad by it. He didn't change. Porter sat beside her, still with his arm around her. She couldn't even bring herself to look at him until she was sure it had been a dream. Seeing him change into something else would have been too much. She realized that she was sweating heavily and breathing quickly. Once she was sure the world was right, she asked for some water.

Juan brought it to her immediately. He must have come in sometime during her sleep. He looked more upset and grim than Sienna had ever seen before.

"Thank you, Juan." She whispered.

"It is nothing, Sienna. You know I always jump to serve pretty girls." He tried to keep his tone light; he failed, but Sienna appreciated it anyway.

"Liar." She looked at the glass and then at her trembling hands.

"Would you let me help you?" Porter asked.

"I am afraid I have to. I can't do it alone."

"You shouldn't have to do it alone, Sienna."

"And you shouldn't have to help me with everything."

"Perhaps not. I want to, and it won't be forever."

"You don't know that."

"No, but I believe it."

"Whatever, just give me the water."

Porter helped steady the glass but he didn't do it for her. She had to bring it up and do the work.

"Thank you, Porter." She whispered, deeply ashamed.

"You're welcome, Sienna. Did you really think I would take it all away from you? I know how independent you are, and how you cannot be tied down. Freedom is important, and I would never want to take it from you, you know. Part of being free means the ability to say 'no', even to drinking water."

"I guess you are right. I hadn't really thought of it before, but maybe that's what freedom really does mean: the ability to say no."

Mason nodded. "It does."

Juan looked skeptical. "You are all confusing me now."

Mason laughed at him. "What does it mean to choose something, Juan? It means that you say 'yes' to one thing and must necessarily say 'no' to all other options, right?"

"I guess so. I guess I have only heard freedom applied to saying 'yes'."

"I know. We are kind of obsessed with that here in the US. It's all about what we say 'yes' to, but we end up not paying attention that saying 'yes' also means eliminating the other options. Nobody can say 'yes' to everything. Who would even want to? A person would never get anything done that way."

Juan nodded. "Yeah, it makes sense. It is like choosing one path for the current. It can't go somewhere else if the conductors are set a certain way and the path laid a certain way, otherwise it won't work. It'll all burn up."

"Exactly." Mason stood up. "I am checking on Karen for a second. Carry on."

Juan looked over at Porter wryly. "You ever get the idea that we are totally weird for having these types of conversations all the fucking time?"

Porter smiled slightly and shrugged. "Probably, but I am pretty weird anyway, so it doesn't bother me. Besides, I like philosophy."

Juan shook his head. "Yeah, you are weird."

"Hey, you're the one who pulled an electrical solution out of your own head, not me."

Juan thought about it for a moment. "Okay, you're right. I am just as weird."

Sienna smiled. "Good thing we are all like that."

"So, Mikey," Juan said casually, "How come you got the hot girl this time? She must be somethin' special for you to bring her back with you."

"She is, Juan, but you knew that."

Porter nodded. "Juan is jealous, Michael; you can hear it absolutely dripping in his voice. And, if you had brought back some new prototype along with a pretty woman, he would probably collapse in despair right here and now."

Michael laughed. "He could have any number of his own girls."

"I know that but he doesn't."

Juan snorted. "Whatever, you two idiots. We've had this discussion before."

Porter returned his snort. "You're absolutely fucking right! I just had it with Michael, multiple times! And he has to tell me, multiple times!"

Juan shook his head again. Sienna laughed very softly. "You don't believe them, do you, Juan?"

"Porter has you and Michael found this Karen girl. Well, look at me, Sienna. Who the hell wants someone like me?"

Sienna looked at him very seriously. "Juan, I am telling you the exact same thing I have told these two fucked-up idiots; you are very attractive, you are smart, and of course women want you. Just because you don't see what we do doesn't mean it isn't there. And fuck off Porter," She said as he opened his mouth. "I know exactly what you are going to say, so fuck it. Juan, you need to start realizing, just like we do, that what other people see isn't our flaws but our strengths."

"Sienna, you don't have any fucking flaws!"

"My dear, I am just as flawed as anyone."

Mason spoke up from over by the couch. "I read a famous quote by a great philosopher once about that sort of thing. He said, 'I am a man and therefore have all devils in my heart.' None of us is better than another, or worse. Merely different. What we choose to ignore or act with our own devils determines how we are much more than our weaknesses do."

Juan still looked extremely skeptical. "Yeah? Who said that?"

Mason stood up with an ironic smile on his face. "G.K. Chesterton. Michael, would you come over? She is doing much better, and I think she would like you to be here."

Michael put down the knife he had been using on some green beans and went immediately. Porter looked at Sienna. "Would you mind if I finish making some food?"

Sienna shook her head. "No, you go do what you must."

Juan was watching Michael and Mason conversing softly. Porter took the steaks and went outside to use Mason's grill. Juan looked over at Sienna quickly. "Are you being serious about all this, or are you making fun of me? I don't mind if you are, you understand, but I want to know for sure."

"Juan, I wouldn't make fun of you for something this important."

Juan sighed. "I was afraid of that."

"We're all afraid of it. That's why we are all in various therapies now. I am terrified that I will be useless forever and that Porter will get too overwhelmed with it and leave."

"He wouldn't do that, Sienna. Not after he came back for you from Tergistan and Hong Kong."

"Maybe, Juan, but I am still scared. Do you see what Mason meant about us all having demons in our hearts? Who do you think whispers to us and makes us unsure?"

Juan shrugged. "I never wondered before. But it kind of makes sense. I like the idea of a logical argument, and this seems to be pretty logical to me."

"Well, then, try this one on; we keep going places and girls seem to always find a reason for hanging around you. The other men, too. Women are just as logical as men; why would they hang out if there was no interest?"

Juan looked taken aback. "Oh, well, now that you mention it, uh, I have to think about this. I am not trying to say that you are wrong; it's just a little hard to think about that way. That's all."

"I know it is. Just don't take too long."

Juan sat, looking off into the distance for a while, toying with his glass. Sienna knew that Juan always considered the logical ramifications of anything he worked on, so she let him think his way through his own way.

Michael brought Karen over to the bar area. He gently set her beside Sienna. "Are you going to be all right here, Karen? I should go help Porter."

"Yes, I think so." She said softly.

Mason sat beside her. "I'll be here if you need anything, all right?"

Karen nodded.

"Hello, Karen. Ready to take on the world?" Sienna asked with an ironic smile.

"I don't think I am even ready to take on food."

"Same thing."

Karen smiled slightly. "I am not looking forward to tonight."

"Oh, me, neither, my dear! Me, neither! But at least we have the most attractive bunch of nurses I have ever seen! The fucking hotness alone should cure us."

Juan smiled. "You are making fun of me now."

Sienna sighed. "No, Juan, I said I don't make fun of you for the important stuff. Fucking accept that you are hot already."

"Now you sound exactly like Porter."

"What the hell did you expect? Karen, this is Juan. He is another one of our rather select and special group. As I am sure you heard he also has his own shit to work through."

Juan laughed. "Gee, thanks, Sienna!"

"Oh, fuck off."

Juan laughed again and reached out to gently grasp Karen's hand for a moment. "Charmed, lovely lady. Michael is a lucky fuck."

Karen blushed slightly.

"Juan," Mason said calmly, "She has the exact problem with believing that sort of thing that you do right now."

"Oh. Well, you are lovely, and Michael is fucking lucky to have found you."

Karen looked away. Juan was quite shrewd and he often hid it behind his bouyant personality. "Also," he continued, "I think that Michael knows he is lucky and he is very grateful that you came to him for help. I think you are quite courageous and intelligent. You chose the exact right person, you know. Not many have that ability."

Mason smiled. "Now you just need to listen to your own damn self, Juan, and you will be doing it right."

Juan grinned. "Hey, baby-steps!"

Karen looked confused still. "I don't disbelieve you; it's just so hard to trust."

"Yeah, well," Juan said easily, "That's because you've hung out with too many fuck-ups. Now you can hang out with awesome fuck-ups. We'll get you better."

Mason laughed. "Juan, you are impossible."

"I know. It makes me so damn irresistible."

Sienna smiled. "That's exactly right, Juan. I have been telling you that."

"I know you have. I am working on it."

Porter came in with the steaks. He raised an eyebrow. "Oh, really, Juan?"

"Yes, really, for once. I am being serious. Sort of."

"Good. I am getting tired of saying the same damn thing over and over."

"Whatever. You like hearing yourself."

"Maybe, but I like it better when the person I am talking to fucking listens. Now, who's hungry?"

Chapter 21

Once they were done with eating and were all ready to sleep, Mason pulled out a small case. "Ladies, this is the drug I'll be giving you. Dr. Matthews and I agreed to use the same one for the two of you in different doses for tonight. We'll see if we need to make adjustments tomorrow. However, it is a hypodermic needle, and it will need to be injected. Also, I will need to check on you multiple times during the night. Michael, Porter, and Juan have all agreed to help with that, but you will have to trust us implicitly. We can't take the time to explain everything if we need to act. Is all this clear?"

Sienna nodded. Karen looked very scared as she slowly nodded.

Mason carefully measured two syringes full of whatever it was. He laid them on a clean towel on the counter and set everything else out. "It will take up to half an hour to really work. You will start to feel a little tired, perhaps dizzy. The side effects are minimal. The only problem is that it might not be a strong enough depressant to suppress the nightmares I know you both suffer from. If you are having night terrors, you won't be able to wake up easily from them. You both need to sleep so your bodies can recover. That might mean sacrificing your dreams for sleep right now. It is a hard trade-off to make, I know. We had to weigh the options."

Again, Sienna nodded. She didn't want to dream those frightening dreams all night but she knew she wouldn't get better without sleep.

Mason looked very serious. "I need to inject you both now. Will you be all right with that?"

Sienna sighed. "I know you won't hurt me, Mason, even if I wish you didn't have to do it. I will try to hold still for you."

"Thank you, Sienna." Mason said simply. He gently rolled up her sleeve on her right arm, exposing the nasty bruise on her wrist.

"Whenever I see that," Porter said conversationally to Juan, "I want to go back to Hong Kong and kill that man."

Juan's eyes glittered dangerously. "I'll fucking help you."

Mason carefully swabbed her arm and quickly injected the drug. He was very good and she felt hardly anything. It was the idea that was making her apprehensive.

"Are you all right?" Mason asked.

"Yes, you are good at this. I didn't even notice it."

"Experience, my lovely." Mason turned to Karen. "Karen, I know you don't want this and that you might not trust me yet."

Karen straightened a little on her chair. "If everyone else trusts you, I can't really give a good reason not to." She put her arm out, even though it shook with her fear.

Mason was as efficient at it with her.

"All right. Gentlemen, you know what we have discussed. I trust you all. You better fucking trust yourselves. These ladies depend on you. Got it?"

They all nodded.

Juan held up one hand. "Question, Mason."

"Shoot."

"Where did Sienna really get that bruise from? That was no ordinary fighting bruise or falling bruise. That was serious and deliberate."

Sienna closed her eyes and leaned against Porter. She didn't want to talk about it. She didn't want to remember it. He gently put his arm around her waist.

Mason said, "She was given a depressant by the agent we were supposed to be using. In order to counter it, and keep her alive, Patos and his chief lieutenant gave her an upper of some sort. In order to do it, they had to hold her very still, and I assume one of them knelt on her wrist and pushed on her upper arm to keep it still. I can imagine that, as strong as Sienna is, she tried to throw them off very hard. They must have had a difficult time holding her still enough to get it all in. That sort of thing has to be injected very slowly or else it overwhelms the body too much. She has bruises where they pushed on her to hold her down, on her wrist, her arm, and her shoulders."

"Fucking hell!"

"Enough, Juan!" Mason said sharply.

"Oh, fuck off! I am going to fucking kill him myself."

"I said enough! You can't get to him!"

"And he did that to Karen, too?"

"We don't know yet, Juan. It doesn't really matter much; you can't get to him. I won't tell you where he is and you can't do anything without knowing that, so calm the fuck down."

"Juan, drop it." Michael said softly. "These women need us here now, not us gone."

"This is fucking messed up, Mikey."

"I know it, Johnny, but what the fuck would it help if you did off him, anyway? He still did it."

Juan slammed his fist on the bar. "Fucking hell!"

"Enough!" Porter said shortly. "We can't do anything. Fucking pull it together."

Juan took a deep breath or two. "Okay, okay, you are all right. Just... just let me go for a walk for an hour or so. I didn't expect this and it has caught me by surprise."

"All right, Juan, but I expect you to be back, soon. I rely on you." Mason said pointedly.

"I know, Mason. I will be here. I am going to need to calm down though. I am too wound now to sleep. Just let me go for a bit. I promise to be back and calmer."

"Okay. Go."

Juan went, muttering darkly to himself.

"Why is he so angry?" Karen asked, sounding a bit tired.

"Because he cares about you." Mason said distractedly.

"But... but he doesn't even know me!"

"No, he doesn't, but he knows Michael, and he knows that Michael is not frivolous or flighty."

"But that's Michael, not me."

"Right now, my dear, you are part of Michael's life. That means that we care about you. Later, you might choose to be otherwise. We will still care about you. Juan is upset because this has caused Michael and Porter to be in pain, as well as you and Sienna. He loves Michael and Porter like brothers, maybe even more. Because of that, he is angry that they are being hurt by this. He loves Sienna like a sister, and also because she is part of Porter's life. He loves you because you are part of Michael's life. Juan is very transparent in some ways. He is fiercely loyal to his friends, and when they are hurt, he gets angry. Fortunately, he also can get over it, unlike certain pig-headed people I might name."

"Hey, now, Mason," Sienna said gently. "I am trying to get better about that."

Mason laughed. "Nicely done, Sienna."

"I rather liked it. Could we please change the subject? I would much rather not remember anything about that night."

"No, I imagine not. The good news is that the bruises will fade after a while and that will help."

Sienna yawned. Her eyes had been closed for all this, and she felt like she was drifting off, as if gravity were pulling her to the side. Her perceptions began to be confused.

Porter tightened his arm around her. "Are you all right, Sienna?"

"I don't know. I feel very strange. Like I am…falling…"

"Okay. Let's get you to bed then. You need to lie down."

"Whatever. I can't concentrate that much."

"I'll do it."

She was flying, maybe. Or maybe not. She felt like she was moving. The world seemed to be spinning lazily. Then she wasn't moving, but the world kept spinning anyway. She was cold, then she was too warm. Then she was falling into empty space and it no longer mattered.

It seemed like she was asleep for a long time. She woke partly up and realized that she was alone but it didn't seem to matter too much and she fell back asleep quickly. The dreams were horrible and it

233

seemed that the night stretched forever. Towards morning, she thought she heard someone come into the room through the door. She stood up to see who it was, and the world spun away into a grey nothingness and she was suspended in a paralyzed fear. Then, she heard the door open again, she stood again, and it all happened again. When she heard the door open a third time, the grey nothing caught hold of her immediately and she hung in that nameless, space less fear.

Then the lightening sky woke up her up; she was in Mason's living room. Porter was still asleep beside her, which was itself a minor miracle. She couldn't remember the last time he'd been asleep when she woke up. She heard the door open and was afraid waiting for the enveloping grey. She stood up anyway.

It was Juan. He looked tired, but not exhausted. When he saw her, he smiled broadly.

"Good morning." He whispered.

"Depends on which side of it you are on." Sienna whispered back, yawning.

Juan nodded. "I bet it does. You seemed to be okay most of the night. Well, except for like all of it. What I mean is that you didn't seem to be terrible."

"I guess not. I feel terrible though."

"Well, you look fantastic, as always."

She smiled involuntarily. "You are the worst liar I know."

Juan smiled back. "Nope. He's still on the floor."

Sienna nodded. "You're probably right. And I think I will lie back down for a while."

"Good idea."

Sienna was so thankful that she hadn't been thrown into that fear again. It had been a bad prospect to face. Porter appeared to be still asleep, but he could have been acting. Sienna didn't much care. She carefully lay down without disturbing him too much, then decided that was trash and snuggled into him.

Porter woke up instantly. So he had been asleep. "Mmm? Oh,

good morning. Now, I am going back to sleep." He said drowsily, glancing at his watch.

"Yeah, you'd better." Sienna closed her eyes.

When she woke up again, the sun was up. Porter was gone from beside her. She could hear him moving around in the kitchen. She felt much better this time.

"Good morning. Again." She said to Porter as she stood and stretched.

"Same to you. How did you sleep?"

"Awful, but the last part was better."

"Good."

"And you?"

Porter sighed. "Karen had a terrible time." He said softly. "She is very afraid of the dark, so when she woke up partially from nightmares, she was damn-near hysterical. Very hard."

"Is that why you were still asleep this morning?"

"Probably. And the fact that it was fucking four-thirty."

"Oh. Well, whatever. You should be glad that all I wanted to do was sleep, then."

Porter blushed slightly.

Sienna laughed gently at him. "Only joking, love."

"I know. I am glad that you are able to do that, again. It tells me that you are not feeling as hopeless today as you were yesterday."

Sienna stretched again. "Maybe it's the sun. I always feel better with the sun out."

"You're a damn cat."

"Possibly. Want me to be your sex-kitten?"

Porter dropped the bowl. "God! Dammit, Sienna, don't do that to me this early in the morning!"

"Ooh, I like this power..."

"You always had the damn power."

"You never reacted like that before."

"It's because I am fucking tired. Trust me, you always had the

235

power. I about fucking lost it the first time I ever saw you and it hasn't changed much since then."

Sienna came over to the bar and sat down. Porter passed her a cup of steaming green tea. "I thought you might not like a black tea yet."

"No. Thank you, Porter. You are good to me, even when I tease you."

Porter shrugged. "You keep me in line."

Sienna watched as he mixed things. She sipped the tea slowly. Even after sleeping, she felt a bit sluggish. "What are you making, anyway?"

"A couple things. I am really tired today, I need to be doing things or else I might fall asleep again."

"You can, you know. The bed is still there."

"No, Sienna. I have to be up. Karen really had a hard night, and I have to be up now. It's my time for it."

"Your time?"

Porter smiled at her. "Did you really think we only slept last night? Mason has a schedule for us, too. You didn't need much, but we guys all were on a time schedule. And Mason has been up all night. Thank God he didn't ask me to that. All the strain of the last days has about fucking done me in. I couldn't have done it."

Sienna stared at him. "You guys all stayed up for shifts to make sure we were safe?"

"Well, hell, Sienna, why does that surprise you?"

"I don't know, it just does. I feel all confused about it, or something."

Porter came around the bar and put his hands gently over hers. He looked at her in the eyes. "Look, my love, you are still tired. That makes it hard to think. Trust me, I know. But we all would and will do this again, for as long as we have to. You would do the same for any of us."

"Yes, but..."

236

He reached up and put his finger on her lips. "No, no 'but'. We all love you, just as much as you love us."

"I know, but..."

Porter smiled. "No, there isn't a 'but' to go with it, Sienna. We all agreed to it, without reservation. Well, maybe with a little reservation. But we all agreed to it." He sighed then. "Poor Michael; he is the most hurt by all this. He had a little sister once, and she died from pneumonia. He is reliving that particular helplessness all over again."

Sienna looked down quickly to hide her shock.

Porter took her chin and raised her face again. He looked at her for a moment, searchingly. He didn't say anything more but he went back around the bar to start making food again.

There came a soft cry from the back of the house. Porter jerked towards the sound. He looked back at Sienna quickly. "Will you be all right for a few minutes?"

"Of course, Porter."

He whisked down the hall in a second. Within a few minutes he was back. "False alarm." He said and started measuring again. Sienna enjoyed watching him for a while.

Porter put something in the oven.

"What's that?"

"A Dutch pancake. It puffs up then the center collapses and I will put fruit in there."

"I wish I'd known you were so good at this the first time I met you; I'd have not tried to show off quite so much."

"Whatever, Sienna, you are a better cook than I am."

"No, I can't improvise the way you can."

"Like that makes me better; that means when I make something bad, it is terrible."

"Oh well, you look damn good doing it."

He smiled. "I think I am way down the list on that, too."

"Whatever, Porter. Didn't you ever wonder what I saw the first time I saw you?"

Porter paused. "Uh, no... not really."

She smiled at him. "Oh, too bad, because I am going to tell you anyway. I thought there was no way I could be so lucky to be on a job with someone as tall and hot as you."

Porter snorted. "You're making that up."

Sienna shook her head seriously. "Not this time; sometimes I might, but this time, I am telling the truth. I couldn't believe that you were really the one I was supposed to be meeting from the train. When we pulled into the station and you were standing there, I thought how fucking lucky would it be if I were paired with you."

Porter shook his head.

"Do you really think I would lie to you, Porter?"

"No, but you couldn't even see me."

She laughed at him then. "My dear, you were at least six inches taller than everyone else on that platform! Plus, I was in the coach, I was higher up than you! Besides, you are very handsome; how could I fucking miss seeing you? Think back to that stupid Gala; how many random strangers asked you to dance? I am certainly not in the minority in my opinion."

Porter didn't say anything. He continued measuring and mixing.

Sienna sighed. "My dear, you can tell me you aren't ready as often as you want, but life will not wait for you. You are beautiful, and you need to start to realize it. I'm not just talking about what you look like, either."

Porter poured whatever it was into another dish and put it into the oven. "I know, Sienna. It is still hard to hear."

"I am sorry for that, but I won't stop saying it. Never."

"Never is a long time."

Sienna nodded. "I know. Would you please pour me more tea, beautiful?"

He laughed softly. "You are impossible, my dear." He poured her some more hot water.

"I know. I do it on purpose. I learned it from you." She grabbed his hand before he could pull it back. "I mean it though."

For a long time, he didn't say anything. He merely looked at her. His dark eyes twinkled and a small smile hovered on his mouth. The oven timer went off. "Ooh, I need to get that." He gently pulled away from her and pulled out the Dutch pancake.

Sienna sipped at her tea again. She was content; he was at least listening to her about it all now. He was getting better. Now she just had to get better herself and it would all be good again.

"What did you mean that one time in the shop when I said something to Michael and he went all rigid? You said something about 'it happens sometimes'." Sienna asked, remembering.

Porter sighed. "When we were trying to bring Cinna out, she would say things about us all, things we absolutely couldn't believe and also absolutely couldn't dispute. You say some things that are just like it occasionally, and we all fucking lose it for a minute or two."

"Well, she must have been pretty damn perceptive then."

"I think so. Anyway, that is what I meant." Porter looked at her shrewdly. "Are you jealous?"

Sienna thought about that as she drank some more tea. "No, I suppose not. Not jealous, really, more like a little sad that I didn't share it with you. Just like I am a little sad that I didn't share other things with you. She must have been quite a woman."

"She was. But I had to come for you."

"Was it.. Was it hard?"

Porter sighed. "It was one of the hardest things I have ever done, my love. She knew I would be forever divided though, I think. I still can't believe that it took two of you to get me to get my shit together. I must have serious problems."

"We all do, Porter." Sienna drank some more tea. Idly, she looked at the time. It was only six-thirty. "What time are we going back to the clinic?"

"Oh. Uh, around nine. You should be pretty good, to be

honest."

"Good. Maybe I will have time to lose this fucking blonde hair today then."

"I think we can probably arrange for that. Mason sent Juan for some clothes for you from your condo, by the way. If you want to shower, we can make that happen, too."

"Ah, that sounds heavenly."

"Heaven for an angel?"

Sienna almost spilled her tea, she started shaking so hard. "Fuck! Don't say that, please!"

Porter was immediately there. "What is it?"

"He called me that. It was my nickname. Please don't."

"I won't. I was only teasing. I would never call you an angel. You are a saint, maybe. Angels don't have bodies."

Sienna started at him. "Really?"

"Well, that's what the priests say. I figure they probably know better than anyone else."

"Oh. Yeah, probably. You just startled me."

"I apologize. I won't do it again."

"It'll probably be okay, just not this soon."

Porter nodded. "Anyway. Yes, we should be able to get you in to the stylist. Think she'd do my hair?"

"Are you kidding? Who wouldn't?! You are completely hot! She'll freak over your hair."

Porter blushed. "You are teasing now."

"No, still not. She will. She about jumped Michael."

"Maybe I will wait then."

Sienna smiled at him. "Oh, I like it longer. I can pull it so much better that way. So interesting."

Porter laughed. "You almost make me want to keep it!"

"You should; hot black curls like that are hard to resist."

Mason came out from the back. He looked very tired. Sienna felt a pang of guilt. She stood up immediately.

Mason smiled faintly at her. "Hmm, I look that shitty, do I?"

"No." She lied.

Mason laughed. "You are so lying right now, young lady. I will fucking spank you."

"Ooh, interesting notion."

Mason laughed again. "Got any coffee, Porter? I am not ready to face the day non-caffeinated."

Porter poured him a cup. "How's she doing?"

Mason sighed and sat down. "Not well, but the morning is making it a bit better. I think the light helps."

"It helped me." Sienna said.

"I am not surprised. Anyway, we'll get you back in today, but I think you will probably be okay."

"Thank you, Mason. I can't tell you that enough."

Mason shrugged. "Just try not to do it again."

Porter nodded vigorously. "Fuck yes."

Sienna laughed softly. "You have my word on that!"

Chapter 22

The meeting with Dr. Matthews was not too bad, considering. Mason was with her for about half of it, and that helped tremendously. He was able to give very detailed information about the important things. When he left to check on Karen, Sienna was able to give her more personal observations.

Towards the end of the interview, Dr. Matthews put up some colorful scans. "These are from your scan, Miss Byron. They look fairly normal, except they show a heightened sensitivity in the emotional centers of your brain. Nothing we have analyzed yet gives us any reason to suspect that this will be permanent. You yourself are already noticing that you are steadier once you have slept. That is going to be one of your biggest assets, and also one of your biggest challenges. I realize from what you have said and Dr. Briggs has confirmed that it is harder for you ladies to sleep at night. I do not think this is due solely to a drug or chemical, but it might be. I think it is due to heightened sensitivity to a normal fear. Dark is frightening, if only because we humans cannot see the dangers that might lurk in it. Therefore, it makes sense to be afraid. You are irrationally afraid, however. I think this has heightened that particular emotion as well and will wear off. Once we have a definite answer on the chemicals, we will be able to instruct you better."

Sienna nodded. "I understand, Doctor. Thank you."

He smiled slightly. "I should be thanking you; you have given me a challenging problem with enough information that I might actually be able to solve it. Most people who come through here can't or won't give me enough to make a good diagnosis."

"Well, you're welcome. I am glad I could add some spice to your life."

He laughed then. "You are a unique sort of person, you know."

"So I've been told."

"It's true. Well, Miss Byron, we are done here. I want to see you again in a week if we don't have anything before then."

242

"Yes, sir." Sienna slid off the table and walked carefully out to the waiting area. Mason, Porter, and Juan were there, talking softly. They stood quickly when she came in.

"Oh, please, continue on. You don't have to stand for me." She waved her hand grandly.

Mason grinned. He bowed. "As my lady commands!"

Dr. Matthews, who had followed Sienna out, laughed again. "You certainly are a fortunate man with friends like this, Dr. Briggs."

Mason shrugged. "Just lucky. I am going to confer with Dr. Matthews here for a bit. Sienna, if you want, Porter can take you to do your errand and I will see you back later."

"Of course. Thank you, Mason."

He inclined his head.

Porter took her arm gently. "Are you ready?"

"Yes, let's go lose this fucking awful hair."

"As my lady commands!"

She laughed at him.

Once they were in the Stylist Corner Salon, Porter glanced at her. "Do you want me to come with you, or will you prefer to be alone?"

"Why don't you come? Unless you'd rather wait out here, of course."

"I don't much mind either way. I will come."

Stacey smiled at them both as they came in. "Hello, Sienna. It is nice to see you again! You are right on time." She turned. "Emma, she's here!"

Emma came out quickly. "Ah, hello, Sienna, gorgeous! You ready to lose the Playboy Bunny look?"

"I think so. It isn't working for me, even though you did a fabulous job. You did the best anyone could do. It's just not me."

Emma nodded seriously. "Oh, I totally agree. You're not plastic enough for that look to work well. So let's get it off you!" She paused and looked curiously up at Porter. "Would you like to come back with us, sir?"

"If I may." Porter said gallantly.

Emma smiled. "I am totally okay with someone as hot as you coming back!"

Sienna laughed. "Oh, Emma! You are so irrepressible."

"I know. I should try harder, but, damn, girl! You have the hottest bunch I have ever seen. Think he'll let me do his hair?"

"You could ask him." Sienna said pointedly. "He is right there."

"True. I'd like to just run my fingers through it. Hotness."

Sienna winked at Porter. "Told you." She said softly.

Porter smiled slightly. "So you did. I should have believed you."

Sienna shrugged. "I know it is hard for you still."

Emma led them back to the cutting room. "Now, beautiful, what can I do for you?"

Sienna sat carefully and considered. "I think I want to go back to my natural color for a while. You remember what it is?"

Emma thought about it while she put the cutting apron over Sienna's shoulders. "I think I have it somewhere. Or else Manuel does. Actually, let me get Manuel. I know he has a promo with you in it somewhere with your natural color. Then I can be sure." She called down the hallway. "Manuel! You got a promo of Sienna with her natural color?"

Manuel came in soon after with a picture. "Here, Emma. Did she bring that luscious Michael with her this time?"

Emma laughed. "No, but she brought something just as good!" She gestured towards Porter.

Manuel nodded towards him. "Dang, girl, you have some serious luck. You have all the hotties in the city. Are you cutting him today, Emma?"

Emma shrugged. "I don't have him scheduled, but I probably could do a quick one. He has the most gorgeous hair I think I have ever seen on a man."

Porter was flushing. Sienna laughed at him. Manuel smiled

slightly. "Oh, yes, it is beautiful. Love the energy in it." He looked at Porter, considering. "You are pretty hot, you know. You don't have the body that Michael does, but something about your face and eyes is completely arresting."

Porter sighed. "I will have to take your word for it. I am in no position to judge, but I know you are an extraordinary artist."

Manuel was still considering him. "Well, if you want Emma to cut your hair, I would be willing to take some shots of the two of you, gratis, of course."

Porter promised to think about it.

Emma carefully dyed Sienna's hair and set the bag over it to let the dye take. She turned to Porter with a business-like air. "So, gorgeous, you want a cut while I'm waiting on Sienna's hair to set?"

Porter smiled. "Why not? You've disarmed me!"

Emma laughed. "Come over here, sugar!"

Sienna smiled and watched as Emma cut Porter's hair. She cut it longer than Porter usually had it. Sienna privately liked it a bit longer. It was so damn sexy that way, especially because it kept falling into his face.

"Okay, Sienna, let's see how this looks." Emma looked and declared that it was ready. She quickly washed the dye out. "Let's do a quick cut, too. I don't like this bob with that color as much. Too modern and structured for this color."

"You're the expert, Emma! You do what you want to!"

Emma didn't take off too much; she merely gave it some layers in front to soften the look a bit. "How do you like it?" She asked, turning the chair so that Sienna faced the mirror. Sienna sometimes forgot what her hair looked like, especially when she had to change it for more than a few days. Rediscovering the light brown was always a little surprising.

"Oh, you are a master, for sure!" She marveled. Porter didn't say anything but Sienna knew he liked it better.

Emma smiled with pleasure. "You always say that."

245

"I'm always right, too!"

She laughed. "Want to do another shoot? I like the way these two turned out. Not as dramatic as last time, but I like these two a lot all the same."

Sienna shrugged. She didn't much care. "Up to you, Porter."

Porter sighed. He looked towards the ceiling. "Why do I get the idea that I am going to do this regardless? Fine. But I'll only do it with Sienna."

"Yay!" Emma clapped her hands. "I bet Manuel already has a place all chosen and lit. He is just as bad as I am."

Sienna laughed. "So true."

Manuel did, in fact, have it all ready. "Sienna, love, you must bring all your friends. We have the best shots from you and them. I may never have to hire a contract model again, and I love it. So here is what I want. You two are much more natural-looking than the last one. I want you to lie down, Porter, on your back on this nice drapery, and Sienna, I want you to lie on top of him and you look at each other. Make it natural. Also, Porter, do you have on an undershirt? Would you take off your outside one?"

Porter shook his head gently. "I do have on an undershirt, but I have a bandage on my right bicep."

Manuel looked interested. "Really? I like that!"

Porter smiled slightly. "Okay, so long as you know." He unbuttoned his shirt and set it aside.

Emma whistled. She turned to Sienna. "You are the luckiest girl in the world."

"You are just too outrageous." Sienna let Porter get positioned where Manuel wanted him.

"Okay, Sienna, you can come in now."

She carefully lay down on top of Porter's stomach and chest. "Ready, baby?" She whispered, raising her eyebrow very suggestively.

"I'm pretty sure this isn't that kind of shoot, Sienna." Porter replied calmly, brushing her hair back from her face.

246

"We could make it that way."

"Ha. I bet Manuel would have some issues with that. The focus would be all off. Need one hell of a wide lens. And then, if we knocked over the flash, it would cause problems."

She laughed. "I think we could contain it."

"No fucking way. Besides, there'd be some serious noise. That doesn't translate well to still pictures."

While they were talking, the flash had gone off several times. "And that's it. Perfect! You two are so sexy together, you are going to melt my camera with much more." Manuel announced.

Sienna laughed at that. "All right, all right. I will take the hint!" Porter helped her up, then stood.

Manuel looked very pleased as he clicked through his pictures. Porter looked as he buttoned his shirt back up. Manuel nodded. "I told you the bandage is hot. Makes the eye draw to your arms, then to the face. And Sienna wearing ivory right above makes it look planned. You are beautiful together."

Porter smiled. "You truly have an eye for this. I am in awe of your talents."

Manuel flushed with pride.

They went out to pay. Stacey handed the usual receipt to Sienna. It was blank, and Sienna left a large tip.

Porter handed some money to Stacey. He turned and handed something to Manuel, too. "Just in case." He smiled. Manuel also smiled and nodded.

Sienna linked her arm in his. "What was that?"

"A large tip. And a business proposition for him on the side." Porter responded calmly. "He is one of the best photographers I have seen in a while, and I might want to pay for some shots for my lines. If I am going to be semi-respectable, I may have to actually promote the store."

"You'll never be more than a rascal."

"Probably true, but I can fake it. Just don't tell anyone."

247

"Are we going back to Mason's now?"

Porter squinted up at the sun. "Damn, I wish she'd cut this shorter." He muttered.

"It looks smoking hot on you. I like how it falls."

"It's going to drive me bat-shit crazy. Anyway. Uh, Mason's, yeah. I think we can find something to do for a while before we have to go out. Want to go see how the store is doing for a little bit?"

Sienna shrugged. "Sure."

James was glad to see them. Sienna thought he always was a bit relieved when Porter came back. Porter trusted him implicitly, but James might not be ready to go out on his own yet.

"I am glad you are back, sir."

Porter smiled. "Thank you for cooperating with my friend. We couldn't have done it without you."

"You're welcome. Nothing new to report, although I have noticed an increase in interest in your diamond lines. Not a lot, but there have been inquiries."

Porter nodded. "I did go to the damn Gala this year. Undoubtedly, someone is fishing."

"I thought so, and I haven't said anything firm about any of it."

"Good. Let's keep them guessing a bit longer. I think I will have to dedicate some energy and time to making a good promo and that will take planning. We will have to coordinate and shit like that. Also, I want to showcase some of your stuff."

"My stuff? It's not good enough."

"My decision. I think it is."

James shook his head dubiously. "Whatever you say, sir."

Porter looked over the books and looked at the stock they had acquired, then he shook James' hand. "I'll probably be in and out all week. Sienna here will be back soon, although perhaps not for a full day right away. Also, I might have another lovely young lady to take some shifts."

James smiled. "So long as she is pretty. If I have to look at her all day, I want a pretty one."

"Oh, she is that!"

Back in the car, Sienna, who was dying of curiosity, grabbed Porter's arm. "You aren't going anywhere until you tell me who it is."

Porter looked a bit surprised. "Karen, of course. She is going to need a job and the store isn't so busy that she will get overwhelmed."

Sienna nodded slowly. "Yes, that's a good idea."

"I knew that. And I have another good idea right now."

"Oh? What?"

He grinned at her. "I am not telling you yet." He teased.

"No fair!"

He laughed but he didn't say anything else.

Sienna pouted. It didn't matter. Porter ignored it. He drove around the streets for about fifteen minutes. Sienna privately thought it was a shame that he knew she was so curious and liked to use it against her. It did make for fun surprises though.

Finally, Porter pulled into the driveway to his small house. "I thought you might like to relax for a little while before we go back out to Mason's house." He said simply.

Sienna was speechless. She hadn't even considered it.

Porter smiled at her. "You can sleep, if you want. Or watch television, or whatever you want to do. I will even leave you alone."

"Like hell. You are coming with me."

"Well, I admit that I had hoped so."

Sienna hadn't been in Porter's house very much. It was small and sparse, but it was quiet and peaceful, too. She wandered through the two bedrooms and the living room area., deciding what to do. Porter got some water.

"All right, I have decided on what I want to do." She announced.

"And that is?"

"I want to sleep. With you. Among other things."

"All right. I can manage that."
"Good. Now get in there."

Chapter 23

Sienna continued to become more normalized. The wild mood swings started to calm down, although she could fly into a rage at the slightest moment occasionally. Mason seemed inclined to think that she would just have to learn to live with that.

Karen was still afraid at nights. Sienna didn't know if she would ever get over that, but she might. It had been a week since they had returned. Dr. Matthews had looked at them both and said that Sienna was probably fine. So far, all the chemical analysis had come back as temporary. The damage was in the memory of the event, not from the drugs themselves. Sienna privately agreed.

After the appointment at the clinic, Porter and Sienna sat down with Michael and Karen.

"Karen, we wanted to offer you a position." Porter said quite seriously. "I own a small jeweler's store and I am always looking for someone to help work the counter. My apprentice and I are often trying to produce or fix jewelry, and it is imperative that we can do that without having to provide excessive customer service. It would be part-time to begin with. Sienna has offered to help you as much as you need to become comfortable with the system and the store. Would you like to try it?"

Karen looked at Michael for a minute. He smiled at her. "It has to be your decision. I won't say anything either way."

"That's not fair."

"I know, but it still has to be that way. If you think about it, I am sure you will see why."

Karen looked down at her hands for a while. She had been told that she couldn't make decisions for a long time and she had been told what she had to do instead of making any. Michael was right: she did have to decide for herself and on her own. Sienna thought this was a very hard idea for her. No one said anything.

Finally, Karen looked up. "Okay, I want to try."

Sienna smiled at her. "Oh, good! I need someone to help keep this thieving pirate under control!"

Karen giggled, then looked a bit uneasy.

Porter smiled as well. "Karen, you can have your own opinions now, even about us. Don't be afraid to joke with us, to laugh at us as well as with us, and to correct us when we are wrong."

Karen looked back at her hands.

Porter continued as if nothing had happened. "I am afraid we can't give you very much to start with. I am currently trying to mount a new line, and the promotions and such for it will be high for us. However, we should be able to go at least twelve an hour. Will that be acceptable for the start? It is always open to raises and incentives." He pulled out some paper work.

While Karen read through and signed the contracts, Michael looked at Porter with a knowing expression. "A new line?"

"Yes, I guess I could actually expend some effort for once."

"Are you getting professional ads done?"

"Why, yes, I hired Manuel to shoot some. Want to model for him?"

Michael looked horrified for a second, then he seemed to think of something. "Well, if you are serious about it, then I might try it for you."

Porter seemed a bit surprised. "Damn, okay. Yes, I was serious, but I didn't fucking think you would take it up."

Michael shrugged. "I fucking need to work on stuff too, Porter. It isn't just you."

Porter smiled. "I can get a time scheduled with Manuel for you. It should be within the next two weeks."

"You're moving fast."

"I have to. There has been interest generated by the Gala appearance. I want to capitalize on it. Besides, I want to get James' work out, too. He deserves to get a start, and I can give him one."

Michael suddenly smiled. He turned to Karen. "Would you like to shoot some promos with me, my dear?"

It hung between them for a moment. Karen was obviously still a little afraid of seeing herself. She smiled a bit hesitantly after a minute. "Um, okay, I will try it."

Porter shook hands with Michael. "You, sir, are a fucking genius."

"Why thank you, Porter."

Then Porter shook hands with Karen. "Thank you, Karen. Would you be available tomorrow to start? The mornings are usually slower and will afford more time to learn. The store opens at 8:30 am. I know it is early, but the early people appreciate it."

Karen nodded. "I should be fine with that."

"Good. Please be there by 8:00. We have some things to take care of first." He stood up and extended his hand to Sienna.

Sienna also stood and looked quite earnestly at Karen. "No one will abuse you there, Karen. James and Porter are the absolute soul of courtesy, both of them, even though we all joke with each other outrageously, and they will not tolerate anyone who is not a gentleman. They have turned men out of the store before. Do not hesitate to ask for help if you find yourself in a situation you cannot handle."

Karen nodded, her eyes wide. "I will try to remember that."

Sienna smiled up at Porter. "We all make fun of him and he is outrageously self-deprecating, but Porter would gladly lose business to keep us safe."

Porter smiled back at her. "Business is fleeting. It comes and goes on a whim. Tomorrow then, lovely."

Sienna was sharing Porter's house for the time being. She didn't have as many nightmares as before, which was nice. She did still have them and Porter worried about her being alone. Sienna wasn't about to argue; she liked sharing his life. She did not want to intrude, however.

"Porter, are you sure I am okay in your house? It is yours."

"Sienna, everything I have is yours, too. I want to share all of my life with you. I can't very well hold my house back, especially not if you need it still."

Sienna blushed. Sometimes when he made statements that were so obviously the truth it caught her by surprise.

Porter glanced at her as he drove. "I mean it, Sienna. I want you to feel as comfortable as you can in my house, and I in your space. I think that is pretty important for me. I have always tried to keep my life separate, and I don't want to do that anymore. Part of that is letting you in, everywhere. If you are uncomfortable, though..."

"No, I am perfectly happy there. I would ditch my place in a second to live in your house."

Porter was looking out the windshield, but Sienna noticed that he looked happy about that.

She smiled. "Do you think I am exaggerating?"

"No, Sienna. I was desperately hoping you would say exactly that."

"Well, it is the truth. I haven't brought it up before because I was afraid of encroaching on what might be your space. You still need places to have to yourself, privacy, things like that. It would be very selfish of me to take everything from you."

Porter nodded. "And it would be the same of me to ask you to give up your own freedom. We should probably discuss this some more, preferably when I am not driving."

"Very well, Porter. I think you are right."

"Of course I am right. I am always right."

"Well, I wouldn't go that far, but you are right this time. All right, new topic, then. Karen will be starting tomorrow, hopefully. What should I do to help her?"

Porter tapped the steering wheel gently, thinking. "I think it will be best if we don't start her on the counter right away, but maybe helping with the displays. She'll still be asked to do some customer interaction, but much less than otherwise."

Sienna nodded. "That is a good place, I think. Plus, she can be on display, herself. She needs the esteem boost, and compliments do

254

that."

"You're the expert there, not me."

"Shush. You are doing better now that you know you have to accept compliments at face value. Besides, you don't get all blown up on flattery. There is a difference, and realizing the difference is important."

"You're right, of course."

"You might have to be careful if you get lots of critical acclaim for this new line though. If you become as famous as I think you will be, it might be difficult to tell the difference."

"Not really. Compliments come from friends, flattery comes from people who don't know me at all."

"Sometimes, it is true. Sometimes, compliments can come from strangers though."

"Sienna, my love, you get compliments all the time because you deserve them."

"Porter, my love, you do, too. We're not going to argue about this, are we?"

"No, I suppose not."

"Who besides Michael and Karen are you going to have modeling these new pieces, anyway?"

"Well, my dear, I would ask you, but I don't want you to do it just for me. I want you to do it only if it is something you want to do. Nothing else."

"I promise to think about it. But I think you should do some, too."

Porter laughed. "I promise to think about it."

Sienna knew that was the best she could get from him for the time being. He had trouble adjusting his thoughts when it concerned what used to be his private life.

"By the way, what did you mean about Michael being a genius?" She asked. It was nagging at her.

Porter smiled. "No, my dear, I can't tell you that. I promised."

"Dammit, Porter!"

"I am sorry, Sienna, but I did promise, and you don't really need to know. It is nothing to do with you."

"Oh, like that makes any fucking difference."

The next week went without much a hitch. Karen started her new job and seemed to fit in quite well. Sienna had not exaggerated when she said James was the soul of courtesy. He had all the old-fashioned charm that Porter himself exuded, and they both were talented artists. They remained in the back for the most part, both attempting to get the new lines ready for the debut. Manuel was going to shoot the photos for it the next week and they had to make it look good. It was going to be limited-run and exclusive but they still had to be ready.

Manuel stopped in to go over details with them all two days before the shoot. The line was going to be run under the name of "Stone Bare", and Manuel wanted some skin with the jewels. Sex might not always be the most flattering way but it certainly could sell certain things. Karen was pretty nervous over that idea until Manuel explained he wanted the men's line only with shirtless bodies. He thought the juxtaposition would pique interest. For the ladies, he wanted long, formal dresses and staged photos, much like a fashion shoot. Again, the unexpectedness of it would call attention.

"Also, ladies, no makeup. 'Stone Bare' in all ways, please. We'll shoot in a forested area, formal gowns, these beautiful jewels, but you two are going to be the real sellers. Nothing fake. Sexy is going to be in the realness of it all."

Sienna smiled slowly. "This is going to be fabulous, Manuel. Anything you want in particular?"

Manuel looked over the pieces that James and Porter had out for him. Most were diamonds and gold, some platinum, a few pink sapphires, and some of the more unique experimental pieces James had decided on. "Hm. I think I want color. How about purple?"

"I can do purple. Karen?"

"I think I only have ivory. Will that be all right?"

Manuel nodded. "With your beautiful dark hair? I want to shoot with birch trees. Ivory should work very well. If either of you has something else that might work, feel free to bring it. We can always improvise. I want to shoot for a solid two hours, and I want lots of options." He turned back to Porter and James. "Your male models are going to shoot first, here, in that back room. Very sexy feel to that. Very hot, I think. We'll shoot at least an hour."

Porter nodded. "The ladies would also like to shoot at least a few with us, probably out in the woods. Formal, I think?"

Manuel thought about it as he looked over the pieces again. "Yes, I think that would be very sexy and evocative. I have some ideas."

Porter smiled. "I rather thought you might. You always do. All right. Black tie?"

Manuel smiled up at Porter. "Not unless you only have black. I want color."

Porter grinned. "I seem to have a very nice dark blue."

"Good god, you are going to be smoking."

Porter laughed. James was grinning as well.

Manuel left and Porter and James returned to the back. Sienna and Karen took up their positions behind the counters again. Karen still seemed a bit uneasy. Sienna looked at her for a long moment.

"It won't hurt, Karen."

"I know that, Sienna." Karen said, toying with her keys. "It's just I am afraid that I won't be pretty enough for this."

"Stop." Sienna said firmly. "This isn't a contest. The only way you will fail is by thinking that you are not good enough. Manuel is an artist and he would not say anything that was untrue in regards to his art. He wants you to be you, not some fake copy of you. He thinks you are perfect for what he wants. Why do you want to tell him he is wrong?"

Karen smiled slightly. "Well, when you say it like that, I guess it changes it."

257

Sienna also smiled. "Think of it this way; you will absolutely have Michael's undivided attention. Think of how much fun you can have with that. It will help you if you think of it as trying to keep him rather than playing to the camera. He will be like putty for you. I guarantee it."

Karen giggled. "Now that is challenge I want."

"I rather thought it might be. I was going to bring that lovely silk gown I had at the Gala. I think I have a very nice dark pink strapless that might fit you. Would you like me to loan it to you?"

Karen nodded. "I would like that. I don't have too many clothes."

"Let's fix that! I will do your hair for you, if you want."

"I would love that."

"Okay, it's a date!" They laughed together.

Porter looked in from the backroom, a small smile on his lips and his eyes twinkling outrageously. "You two are too much alike. Why do I get the feeling that Michael and I are about to be out-maneuvered by two very devious women?"

Sienna shrugged. "Because you are. Back to your table, boy. Shoo, shoo!"

Porter smiled and went. Karen started to laugh again. "You are beyond belief."

Sienna smiled. "He lets me get away with it all. He brings out the best in me. And the silliest, and the most ridiculous. I rather like who I am when I am with Porter."

The shoot went beautifully. There were no huge problems to overcome and the lighting was perfect. Sienna and Karen weren't in the shop for the men's shoot. Manuel was an expert and Sienna had seen what he could do before. She was looking forward to what this line was going to look like. He had such an unexpected flair and his technical command was good.

The birch grove was gently shaded by the leaves. Sienna wondered about the light and shadow interplay, but then she wasn't

the artist here. Karen looked stupendous. She shone that day.
Obviously, she was trying to keep Michael's eye, and she succeeded
beyond what she might have thought. He hardly looked away. Porter
and he were of course handsome. They always were, and Sienna always
liked men in suits. Manuel shot the full time, Sienna and Karen breaking
to change once.

"Okay, this is going to be the hottest thing to hit the streets in a
long time. I should have these edited and to you for final appraisal
within two days."

Porter nodded. "All right, but I want to buy only limited rights.
You should have the option to build your portfolio with them too."

Manuel looked at him for a while. "Are you sure? That means
that you can't use them beyond this series of advertisements for this
one line."

"I know that. This should not just be about my store. You are
every bit as deserving of being known, and if these are as good as the
other shots I have seen of yours, they are technically good and
evocative. You should be able to use them as well."

Manuel shook his head. "We'll talk about it later. I want to get
these done. I am drooling to see what I have. The sheer sexiness of you
four is enough to make me happy for days."

Porter laughed.

Chapter 24

The photos were amazing. There was no other way to classify them. Manuel had full command of his vision and he executed it perfectly. Porter was more than pleased; he and James pored over them, deciding which to use. Manuel refused to limit the copyright to them. He said he wanted to give them to the store to use. Porter and James agreed only if he would keep the proofs in case he wanted them. It was somewhat amusing to watch them trying to make the other accept the gift.

Eventually, some deal was struck. Sienna stared at the final ads that were going to run. Manuel had manipulated the shots enough that no one person was fully on display. It looked a bit Japanese, with strong, unexpected angles and dramatic staging.

"My God," she breathed, staring at them all laid out on the counter. "This is going to light a fire under every socialite in the fucking city."

"Let's hope so." Porter said calmly. "I want it to be so sexy and exclusive that people will be dying to get it. I like the idea of turning people away."

"Heartbreaker." Sienna accused. "You are a total tease!"

"Damn straight. But then, I did learn for the best. That is you, my little sweetheart. You are the best, or worst, I have ever seen. They call me a charlatan, but it is nothing compared to what you do. You drip sexuality then pull it all back. I love watching you break men and women with just a toss of your hair. Sheer artistry." He glanced at his watch. "I have a lunch date with Michael today. We are going to go over something together. Might meet Mason later, too. Call if you need anything. You have my number."

Sienna looked at him sharply. There was something in that casual tone that was just a touch too casual for authenticity. "Oh?"

She was immediately interested.

Porter smiled. "I'm not giving anything away, Sienna, not even to you. I made a promise."

260

"You do that on purpose. You know I can't help being curious and then you tease me with it!" She accused.

"Of course. But I am still not sharing it yet. I'll see you later." He kissed her forehead and left.

Karen laughed. "Men. Why do they do that?"

"They think it's funny." Sienna muttered darkly. She shuffled through the ad copies again. "Have you looked through these, Karen? You look fabulous!"

Karen shook her head. "No, I am still a bit scared to."

"Well, get over here, girl! Look! See yourself!"

The time passed fairly predictably. Sienna was entering purchases in the books when she happened to glance up and froze. Chen Xi was walking casually up the other side of the street, looking in the windows of the shops with a leisurely air. She stared for a second or two to make sure. Mason had trained her well in observing quickly and she was positive who it was. He went into a store that had jewelry on display in the front window. Sienna was sure he was looking for this store. He would be on this side very soon, especially if the clerk in that other department store directed him here. This demanded action. If they could get Xi, they would have the top two, and he was at least as dangerous as Patos had been. How could she capitalize this?

As she ran through quick options, she suddenly remembered Karen. There was no way she could let Xi see Karen. He would know her in a second. Karen had to be safe. That was paramount.

"Fucking hell!" Sienna swore out loud. "Karen, get in back. Now!"

Karen looked up quickly and went quickly back. Sienna followed her within a few seconds. James was looking up curiously.

"James, I can't stop to explain. Karen needs to be here and you have to keep her safe. There is a man out on the street that will do almost any fucking thing to her to keep her quiet. Porter and Michael will be here as soon as they can. I will try to keep him here until they can deal with it."

"Who is it?" Karen asked, clearly shaken.

"Chen Xi."

"Oh no."

"Precisely." Sienna called Porter. He answered. "Porter, get back here. Chen Xi, Patos' second-in-command, is out on the fucking street right now. I think he knows we have the store, but he doesn't know where."

"Damn! We'll be there in about ten minutes. That's the fastest we can do it. Keep him there, keep him talking. Keep Karen out of sight. It's possible he won't recognize you."

"I will. Get here as soon as you can, but try to not kill him please."

"I will. Sienna, you have to keep him there. You'll be safe only if he doesn't get you away from the front of the store. The windows are big enough to dissuade him from doing anything."

"Okay." The little bell that indicated the front door opening jangled. "I have to go. I think it is him."

"Stay safe, Sienna."

She hung up the phone and tossed it to James. "He's coming." She whispered. "As far as anyone knows, you aren't here. I am the only one here. Stay with Karen. She needs to be kept safe above everything else." Sienna closed her eyes and mentally steadied herself. Then she stepped out from the back room with a bright professional smile.

It was indeed Chen Xi who had come in. He glanced up when she came to the front.

"How do you do, sir? I apologize for being in the back. I rarely have any customers at this time of day." She prattled gaily. Every second she talked and kept him in place was to her benefit. Her heart was racing. Did he recognize her? It couldn't be ruled out.

Xi nodded. He returned to looking at the glass counters. He seemed to be browsing. Finally he pointed at some rings. "Might I look more closely at this shelf?"

"Certainly, sir!" Sienna said in the same bright voice. She

unlocked the display and took the tray out. She tried to move as slowly and deliberately as she could. She had to keep him here and occupied. Setting it on the counter, she asked, "Might I ask what you are looking at specifically? I might be able to better aid you if I knew."

Xi picked up a ring and examined it carefully. "I am looking for something like a piece I once saw. I want to know who made it. It was very unique, and I have an excellent memory for unique things."

Sienna felt her heart give a lurch but she kept her face impassively bright. "Oh? How interesting! We do contract with independent jewelers here, and we have some custom pieces that are available nowhere else. Does anything in this tray catch your attention? We have several pieces by this particular jeweler if it is his work that you are looking for."

"Yes. It was a unique piece. This is similar in some ways." He put the ring back. He looked towards the lone central display case in the middle of the floor. "I think I might be interested in a closer look in this case. I noticed one bracelet in particular that I desire to look at."

Sienna smiled again. "Of course, sir. Allow me to lock these away and I will be right with you." She put the first tray back and came out from behind the counter. "What would you like to see? We have great pride in exclusivity here. Does your preferred jeweler work in gold, silver, or platinum?" She asked as she led him towards the central case, pulling out her keys to open the display.

Xi grasped her wrist in an iron grip. It was the one that he had bruised. Sienna felt intense pain. She tried to hide how much it hurt. "Sir! Please!" She tried to get away but it was impossible. His grip was crushing. Sienna felt him forcing her down to her knees. She was terrified. If he could control her just by this, she would not be able to keep him in the front of the shop. The balance had shifted to Xi in a second and she was unable to do anything about it.

"I think," He said, impassively, "I want to see this." He reached out and took her left hand. He looked at her ring for a moment, still holding her wrist. "This is very similar to what I am looking for. I would bet that it was from the same hand. Where did you get it?"

"It was a gift." He suddenly wretched her arm around. Sienna was forced back and off-balance. She was crying. The pain was incredible. She understood dimly how pain could be used to torture a person without threat of death. It would have been easy to give him the information but she knew she would be condemning Porter and Michael, as well as Karen and herself. She had to stay silent, even if it meant that he killed her or maimed her.

"Where did you get this?"

Sienna didn't say anything. He increased the pressure on her wrist. Sienna felt tears running down her cheeks. It wouldn't be much before she blacked out from pain. She arched back in excruciating agony.

"I'll only ask you once more; where did you get this? Tell me or I break your arm."

"She got it from me, you fucking wanker." Michael said quietly from the doorway. He had come in silently.

"Sean, no!" Sienna screamed. She knew that Xi would know his alias. She couldn't let Michael get hurt because of her.

Xi jerked his head around and stared at Michael. He reached inside his coat and pulled out a small pistol. "Then you must be Sean Connor."

"No shit. And you must be the biggest fucking idiot this side of the ocean if you thought you could break one of my girls that easily."

Xi glanced at Sienna and then tossed her aside negligently with a flip of his hand. He maintained his grip on her wrist but relaxed the pressure finally. Sienna fell, her hand numb and useless for the moment. Her wrist throbbed with pain. Blearily she looked up. She saw Porter come in silently from the backroom. She looked at him and then glanced at Xi and the pistol. The thought that he would shoot either Michael or Porter chilled her far more than any personal danger. Porter nodded once. He understood.

Xi was speaking in the same unemotional soft voice. "You have

Mr. Patos. I want him back."

Michael shrugged. "I don't have him. Even if I did, I wouldn't give him up that easily."

"How about if I kill her?" Xi pulled Sienna up and pointed the gun at her head.

"You don't have the fucking balls. Besides, I have others." Michael made it sound completely believable. Sienna felt afraid that Xi would kill her, just out of spite. She couldn't do much, since he tightened his grip on her again when she tried to get away.

She looked towards the back again. Porter had moved and he was out of her eye line. Xi jerked her up on her knees and pointed his pistol at her, watching Michael's reaction. Michael didn't even blink.

Xi turned slightly. He must have seen movement out of the corner of his eye, because he suddenly jerked and fired at Porter. Sienna had anticipated it and she kicked him in the knee as he turned. The bullet went wide, catching Porter in the arm and burying itself in the wall.

"Thomas!" She screamed. He had been hit and it was her fault.

Xi kicked her away from him, but she had done enough. Porter knocked him to the ground with a hard left cross. Michael was there immediately. He grabbed Porter's arm as he pulled it back. "No, man, don't fucking kill him. He's out already."

Porter was furious but he listened to Michael. "Okay, okay." He shook himself to rid the anger. Blood flowed down his arm and soaked his sleeve. Some of it fell on the floor and on Sienna's skirt. She didn't care. She was far too anxious about him.

Karen and James came cautiously from the back. Michael didn't notice them for the moment. "Fuck, Porter, quit waving your arm around and let me fucking see it."

"It's just a damn scratch."

"Then fucking let me see it, dammit!" Michael examined the cut. "You're right. You know, you keep messing with this fucking arm, it is never gonna heal."

"Gee, thanks, doctor obvious. Just get something on it to fucking stop the bleeding. At least he missed the cases. I'd hate to have to replace anything right now."

Michael quickly ripped the sleeve off Porter's jacket and wrapped his arm.

Porter knelt on the floor. "Sienna, are you all right?"

"Yes. He hurt my wrist."

"God damn fucker."

"Calm down, Porter."

Porter took a deep breath. "All right." He gently held her with his good arm while he pulled out his cell phone and dialed. "Mason? Hey, we got a problem. Well, it might not be a problem... No nothing like that. We have Patos' second here, in the store... No he's on the floor. I knocked him out. He's fucking lucky, because if I'd known he hurt Sienna again, he would be in a lot worse shit... Okay, we'll wait. Bye." He put his phone away. "Mason's coming. James, would you please turn that 'Open' sign around for the time being? Then I think I owe you one hell of an explanation."

Karen stared at Xi for a long time. Her face was very white. Then she looked up at Michael. She took a few trembling steps towards him, her hands held out imploringly. Michael went to her quickly and held her tightly. Then he kissed her full on the mouth. At first, she looked a bit surprised, but then she almost melted into him.

"Aw, so sweet. Adrenaline always brings it out in people." Porter said softly. He turned back. "Now, then, James, I am really sorry you have to deal with this. The truth is that this guy was looking for these two ladies. He wants his boss back, a man who Michael, Mason, Sienna, Karen, and I all helped get arrested. I don't have a fucking clue where the boss is, but he probably wouldn't believe me."

James nodded. Then he smiled. "I figured it must be something like that. I have looked in the mysterious case, Porter. I know it isn't gems."

Porter smiled back. "You are a sharp one, James. But it's

266

probably safer for you to know nothing beyond that for now."

"I understand. You can trust me."

"I already do."

Mason came in quietly. He was paler than usual but otherwise completely in control. "All right, here's the thing that is going to happen. There are two men who are coming. They will take him away, and he will be gone. None of us will know where he is. He'll just be gone."

Karen looked at Mason. "Really?"

Mason nodded. "Really. Then this whole damn nightmare can be over." He came over and gently took Sienna's arm. He pulled back the sleeve of her cardigan. There were five neat marks, four fingers and a thumb visible over the fading bruise.

Porter looked aside quickly. Sienna felt his arm trembling. "Porter, I am all right."

"Fuck that, you shouldn't have to deal with this again."

"Porter," she said softly, reaching up and turning his face back to her. "Really, I am all right. You came when I needed you. That's all that matters."

Tears ran down his cheeks suddenly and he held her very close. Sienna felt him shaking. She held him for a long time with her eyes closed. Neither of them noticed when Xi was taken out of the shop. Sienna never saw him again.

Mason tested her wrist very carefully. "You're going to have another bruise for a while, Sienna. This is pretty serious. Is anything hurting still?"

Sienna kept her eyes closed, wincing slightly. "When you move it to the side like that it hurts."

"I see. And this?" He gently rotated it back.

"Not as much. The sides and the front. Ow, and that."

Mason nodded and set her hand down. "I don't think anything is broken, but you are going to be in pain for some time. I suggest you wear a light wrap or brace to keep your wrist from moving when you sleep. I don't think this is permanent, but it is going to take some time to heal."

"All right, Mason." She whispered. "Suddenly, I feel very weak and tired."

"It's probably the adrenaline wearing off. Will you be able to stay for the rest of the day?"

"I have to. They are getting the line ready to launch."

James sighed. "It is ready. You need to go home, ma'am. I will watch the rest of the day. I know that Porter will probably not be able to concentrate unless he knows you are safe and well. Neither will I. Go home, Miss Sienna. You, too, Miss Karen. We'll launch tomorrow as planned. We're ready."

"Oh, James, you are a very good man." Sienna said. She reached out a trembling hand to him. He gently took it.

Porter stood up, carefully helping Sienna up. "Thank you, James." He said simply.

"It's not a problem, sir. We are as ready as we can be. One more day of worrying won't help, and I can't concentrate if we are both worried about these lovely ladies."

"Agreed. You know what to do. I'll be in tomorrow morning."

"All right, sir." He and Porter shook hands and they left.

Mason assisted Sienna to her car. "You won't be able to drive right now. Will you let me take you home?"

"Yes, Mason. Don't be getting fresh though."

"Never."

"I must be losing my edge if that is your response. Maybe I need to retire."

"No, not really. I think you could make the fish jump out of the lakes for you, if you tried."

"You're lying."

Mason shrugged. "Whatever. I want to wrap that wrist before it gets more damage from moving around."

"Okay, Mason. It hurts a lot."

"I'm not surprised. I am more than a little upset about this. Porter is right; you shouldn't have to deal with it again."

"It was always an option. I knew that when we started."

"Doesn't fucking matter."

"I'll be good, Mason. I'm really sorry. I didn't mean to be a problem."

"You weren't. That he escaped is the problem. I'll be speaking with some people about this. Firmly. That should not have happened. I don't like shoddy work."

Once they were in her condo, Mason made her sit at the table while he wrapped her wrist carefully. He was good, Sienna thought.

"You're very gentle."

"I have practice, Sienna. I also have incentive. If I am not, I will hurt you, and then Porter will probably tear my fucking head off. He is under a lot of stress right now with this new line and he is not thinking terribly clearly. He gets tunnel vision."

Sienna didn't say anything. She felt guilty that she hadn't noticed Porter being more stressed than usual. He'd been so good at paying attention to her. She suddenly realized that she might have been focusing too much on herself and not enough on her relationships. Perhaps it wasn't just Porter who got tunnel vision.

"Oh, Mason, you are so good to us all." She sighed. "I am sorry I don't recognize it more often."

"You don't have to, but thank you all the same."

"I mean it. You are always keeping us in line and watching out for us. I guess I have been pretty selfish to not notice."

"Sienna, you have been under your own stress. I don't blame you at all."

"No, but I do. I shouldn't be this annoying. Don't let me get this self-centered again, Mason. You are worth more than the selfish notions of a silly girl."

Mason nodded and finished the bandage. "Okay, Sienna. I promise. As to your wrist, try to not move it if you can help it. I know that is going to be difficult as you are right-handed, but I think I hear the sound of your knight-errant outside, so I feel better about leaving you. Get better soon, Sienna. You mean a lot to all of us, you know." He kissed her forehead and left. As he opened the door, Porter came in.

"Why thank you, Mason. I appreciate it when someone holds the door for me."

"Don't get used to it. I already wrapped it. Just keep it still."

"As the doctor commands."

"Shut up."

Porter shut the door and came over to the table. He set down the bags he was carrying. "How are you, Sienna? Really?"

"I am really fine, Porter. It hurts, but it isn't so bad that I can't function. I am mostly a bit upset that he found us, nothing else."

Porter nodded.

"Also," Sienna continued softly. "I should be apologizing to you. I have been very self-centered lately and did not notice how stressed you have been. I should not have been so stupid. You have been caring for me and trying to launch a major event. You don't have to do it all alone, Porter. I can care for myself. Just because I like being the center of your attention doesn't mean that I should demand it. Please forgive me for ignoring your needs. I didn't mean to take and not give anything in return."

Porter looked at her oddly. "You haven't ignored my needs, Sienna."

"No? I have, and most grievously. I forget that you are not some super hero, that you get tired, that you have stress from work. I have been taking a lot from you, and I have not been reciprocating. That has to stop. I don't need to stay with you at night anymore, particularly if it keeps you from sleeping as much as you should. I shouldn't be letting you do everything for me, because I can do things for myself. I am tired, but I don't need to make you make food. I can do it. If it is not helping you, then I should start paying attention to that more. You deserve to have space to grow without me all up in it all the time. I am sorry I wasn't helping before. I'll try to do better."

Porter sat beside her. He put his face in his hands. "Oh, Sienna, you are such a good woman." He said softly.

That startled her. What the hell was this? Had he not been listening?

"I will let you do things," he continued, "but I guarantee that I won't sleep better without you. I'll be too worried at night. Please let me stay with you."

"Of course, Porter."

He crossed his arms on the table then and put his head on them. "God, but I am tired all of a sudden." He said.

Sienna put her arm around his shoulders and laid her head on his arm. "Then sleep, love. I will be here."

Whether or not he slept she wouldn't be able to tell, but they sat like that for a long time. It was very comfortable and peaceful. The later afternoon sun came in the window. Sienna liked sitting in the sun. She closed her eyes for a few minutes.

After a while, she felt Porter stir. She sat up again.

"Well, you certainly are helping my needs right now." He said pleasantly. "I feel loved, and that is what I need more than anything else."

Sienna glanced away. She still felt like she was not doing enough to help him and support him. Sitting here wasn't one of those things. He gently took her face between his hands.

"I mean it, Sienna. I feel really loved or accepted. I cannot tell you how much that alone means. You have filled me with something besides darkness and despair. I can't be black and jaded anymore, and it is due to you." His dark eyes were very soft and she felt like she could drown in them and die happy. "I know you think you have been taking from me. But the truth is I want to give to you. I want to give everything to you, then find more and lay it at your feet. You have given me such reason to live. Not just live a life, but live a full life. I am sure Mason has told you why I tried to kill myself, and that I couldn't

271

because of you. It is completely, totally true. I heard you, and felt your pain at what I was trying to do, and I couldn't do it. I couldn't hurt you. I need to protect you and keep you safe. It makes no sense, since you have been taking care of yourself for many years before I was dropped into your world, but I need to. Father Greg says it is because that is how men are wired by God. I would have laughed that off, a few years ago, but not anymore. I suddenly understand how men are protectors in the cosmic scheme. And now I am not making any sense. I hope I helped you understand what I am feeling though."

Sienna laughed at that. "Oh, Porter! I want to be the one you protect, always. I want you to comfort and hold me. You help me be courageous. You help me in so many little ways and big ones. I feel so complete with you. Not that I was less of a person before, but now I am more of one. See? I make no sense, too! We must belong together!"

He laughed with her. "You are probably right. I bet we drive everyone else bat-shit crazy."

"We can only hope. Now, what's in the bags?"

"Food. And the invites for the opening party."

"They're done? And you didn't tell me? Let me see, let me see! Who's invited?"

Porter pulled out several heavy invitations on simple cream cards. They were embossed with the trademark of his store and James' own specific signature. "I thought we'd invite the team, of course. And Manuel. He has to come. James has several people he wants to invite, and I want some specific players in the jeweler world to be invited. If they show, we can introduce James into their peripheral. I don't think he should be playing in the big leagues yet, but they can be aware that he is at least on the sideline, if he wants to get in."

Sienna smiled. "That seems like a good plan. This is next Saturday." She looked at her wrist. "And I bet this pathetic thing isn't ready then. Fuck." She looked out the window distractedly. Porter waited patiently for her. Finally she looked back. "I know this is pretty fancy, but, Porter, I can't even move this right now. I won't be able to put on lots of frou-frou."

Porter put his hand over her wounded wrist gently. "I don't give a fucking damn what you wear. I want you there, because I want you to share it with me. If you don't want to or won't be comfortable, then I don't want you to do it just because it seems like something I want. Do you understand me?"

Sienna nodded. "Well, of course I want to share it with you. I just don't want to embarrass you."

Porter smiled. "I can manage that all on my own, you know."

She laughed. "Okay, fine, we'll see how it is going. But the previous statement still stands. I can't take these clothes off today."

"Oh, I think I can figure out something to do about that." His eyes twinkled mischievously.

"I'll help you."

Chapter 25

The opening party was a smashing success, of course. Porter and James had done a phenomenal job on the push for publicity and there was a line of hopefuls stretched half down the block. Porter and Sienna whisked past them and into the small club they had rented for the event. Porter had a smile on his face as he held the chair for Sienna.

"I love being the one passing everyone by."

"You are a total tease."

He shrugged. "Oh well. It has taken me years of complete anonymity to be able to do it."

The new line was tastefully laid out on various tables along the walls. People could browse but it wasn't the main focus of the room.

James came in with his girlfriend and his parents. He had a huge grin on his face. This was obviously fun for him, too. Porter smiled and shook his hand warmly. "James. You absolutely have them drooling to get in, you know. Some of them are just out to gate-crash, but there are very interested parties out there, too."

James nodded. "I know. But I think they are here for you."

"I'm an old player and predictable. The young ones are here for the fresh blood." Porter bowed to James' girlfriend. "I beg your pardon, lady. I do not think we have been formally introduced."

"Ah, you are right. Porter, this is my girlfriend, Callie Macpherson. Callie, this is my mentor, Porter."

Porter took her hand and kissed her fingertips. "Charmed, my dear. James has excellent taste in everything."

She laughed and blushed. "You are just like he is."

"I know. It is probably just as well, since otherwise I would probably drive him crazy in short order."

"And these are my parents," James gestured to the older couple, "Sam and Patricia."

Porter bowed again and kissed the fingers of James' mother. "I must commend you on your son. He has extraordinary vision and talent."

Sam smiled. "You have certainly helped bring it out, sir."

Sienna sat during these pleasantries. Porter turned to her. "May I introduce Miss Sienna Byron, my fiancé?" He asked, holding out his hand to her.

Sienna stood gracefully. "I apologize for not shaking your hand, sir and madams, but I injured my wrist and I am afraid it is quite painful."

Sam smiled at her. "So this is the famous Miss Byron. James talks highly of you."

"He likely exaggerates." Sienna said calmly with a half smile. She extended her left hand to Callie. "Thank you for coming, my dear. I have heard of you, naturally, and I was terribly curious to meet you."

She laughed.

Mason and Juan came in, both looking very handsome in their formal suits. Porter excused himself to go and greet them. James led his guests off to another table. Mason and Juan came over.

Juan shook his head. "You have them all down the fucking block, Porter. You must have something worth crashing."

Porter smiled. "We'll have to see, but a lot of them just heard there was an exclusive and came out."

"True."

Mason sat beside Sienna. "How's the wrist doing?"

"It hurts a lot still."

"That's too bad."

"It is impossible for me to keep it still."

Mason nodded. "I know. It still should be okay."

Sienna wrinkled her nose. "I hope so."

Michael and Karen came in. Sienna though Karen looked very good in the maroon dress she had on. They came over and sat at the table.

Mason smiled at Michael. "Doing better, are we?"

Michael nodded. "Finally."

Karen looked confused but didn't say anything. Sienna noticed that her dark hair was caught in a beautiful jeweled hair clip. She hadn't seen it before.

Porter came back over, glancing at Karen. A knowing smile touched his face and he winked at Michael. "Karen, my dear, you look absolutely lovely this evening." He said to her.

She smiled. "Thank you, Porter. I am very happy tonight."

Porter's eyes twinkled outrageously but he didn't say anything more about it.

Manuel came in with Emma. She looked to be having a highly entertaining time. They stopped by the table.

Manuel nodded to them all. Emma grinned widely. "This is the most fun I have had in a long time. I never get to cruise past all the clubbies and breeze in while they wait."

Mason smiled. "We are glad that you are enjoying it."

Emma looked at Mason and Juan closely. "These must be some of your friends, Sienna."

"What makes you say so?"

"The absolute hotness, duh. I said you had the hottest group around. I see I am just as right as ever."

Manuel smiled. "You always are right about that sort of thing, Emma."

The various meet and greet activities continued for about half an hour more. Porter did know all the big names, and he was very careful to introduce James to them all. He also was very careful to introduce him as a partner. Sienna liked chatting with her friends. Waiters circulated with trays of drinks and nibbles.

Juan looked thoughtful. "I bet this shindig is costing at least five hundred a person."

Sienna shrugged. "About that, I think. Launches are always expensive and ridiculous. By the way, Juan, there is dancing shortly, and I know you waltz the best of anyone here, so I want in on that now. You save one for me."

Juan laughed. "I do not, Sienna! But I will save you one

anyway."

Mason smiled. "Just be careful of the wrist."

"I will, Mason. I have the brace. No flips or anything."

"No, but I would love to ask you to dance with me if there are any swings."

"I will save you one." She promised.

The music did start up soon enough. It was not a normal way for a launch party to proceed, but Porter and James didn't care. They both liked dancing and they wanted to have fun. As Porter had said, "Besides, we are blowing enough fucking money on this we should be able to do whatever the hell we want. And I want to dance."

Sienna knew that it was traditional for the gentlemen to switch up partners. Porter escorted Callie for a waltz while Juan danced with her. Sienna hadn't been lying; Juan was the best waltz partner of them all. He had the smoothness and feel for the beat. Plus, he had a certain disregard for the rigid rules of the dance that made him a fun partner.

The evening progressed and Sienna danced with many different partners. The few dances she was able to take with Porter were the best, of course. He had always been her favorite partner, even before they were involved more deeply. He was so tall, for one thing, and she liked the way he moved. As usual, the floor was cleared almost completely for the tango. It seemed like most people were afraid of that one dance. Sienna didn't mind; it meant that she got more room with Porter. They had danced it so many times together that it was very familiar. Maybe she should change up a little, just for variety sometime. Not this time, though. She was not going to embarrass Porter in front of clients.

Porter looked at her with a smile. "Want to spice it up a bit?"

"Porter, I promised to be good and not embarrass you."

"Hm, so you did. Fortunately, I didn't make any such promises. You have my permission to let it go for a dance or two."

"Careful, you might not be able to contain it if I do."

His eyes smiled. "Let's find out, beautiful. Burn up the floor, babe."

Sienna had always had a hard time resisting a challenge like that. She smiled up at him with a naughty little look. "Bring it, baby. See what we can do."

It was, in all probability, not the type of tango that most people wanted to watch; it was a lot of fun to dance though. When the music stopped, there was applause. Sienna smiled up at Porter.

"Was that what you had in mind, my dear?"

"Pretty much." He leaned over and kissed her. She was a little short on breath and hot. It didn't matter in the slightest.

The night continued on. Around midnight, it was over. Porter and James saw everyone out. It had been a success. The line would probably sell out in a few days, and there would be an interest in more from all the right people.

At last, James and his girlfriend were ready to go. He shook Porter's hand again. "Thank you for the exposure. I am not ready yet, but maybe I will be someday."

"Even if you never are," Porter said, "You'll have a name out and it is recognized. You could work for anyone now."

"I don't want to work for anyone. Money is secondary, in my opinion. I like your ideas, you let me grow, and you throw awesome parties. I might make more somewhere else, but who else will let me do all that? No one. I'm staying."

Porter grinned. "I hope so. I was just giving you the options."

James grinned back. "Besides, you are going to have to let Sienna teach me how to dance like that. That was the hottest thing I have seen in a long time."

Sienna laughed. She winked at Callie. "Lessons, and just a hint of naughtiness. That's the secret."

Callie blushed and smiled back.

Porter nodded. "That, and we dance together quite a bit. It always helps to know your partner's quirks, in business and in dancing."

"Business is dancing, Porter." James agreed.

Porter laughed. "I can't disagree! All right, James, we'll see you on Monday. I bet that line is completely gone by Wednesday."

James looked skeptical. "I bet Friday at the earliest. My stuff won't move as fast."

"Loser has to work the counter for three days?" Porter challenged.

"Deal!"

When Porter had driven her to her condo, Sienna looked back at him as she unlocked and opened her door. "Are you coming in?"

"Unless you are going to leave me out, yes. And if you do leave me out, I will whine and cry and make a fucking nuisance of myself until you let me in."

"Well. When you put it that way, I suppose I have no choice."

"That was the idea."

She pulled off the shawl she had been wearing and threw it negligently over a chair back. The bruises on her shoulders and right arm had faded. She could still see them, and she disliked that.

"Just ignore the shoulders." She said absently.

"You know, no one can see it but you. I even know what you are talking about and I can't see it."

Sienna snorted; she seriously doubted that. Not that it mattered. She had sort of accepted them for the time being. She still didn't like them. "I am dying for some water. Fucking too much dancing and sweating."

As she drank two full glasses of water, Porter took off his suit jacket and tie. "You're right. It was pretty hot in there."

She smiled over her glass at him. "That had nothing to do with dancing; that just had to do with you."

He laughed. He also drank a glass of water. She sighed and leaned against his chest. "I do love you, Porter."

He carefully set his glass down and put his arms around her. "I love you, too, Sienna."

"Mm. I could just stay like this for a long, long time. I always

279

did go for tall, slender guys."

"Lucky for me, then. What else did you go for?"

"Gentlemen, of course."

"And blondes?"

"Hair color has never had anything to do with it. Beautiful eyes and a sexy body are much more important."

Porter didn't say anything more.

The clock softly chimed the hour. Sienna glanced at it. "Oh, fuck, it is one o'clock. You have things to do tomorrow. You should probably go and get some sleep."

Porter didn't move. "You're right. I should."

"Porter, I am serious; you need sleep!"

"I am serious, too. I am not leaving until you throw me out."

Sienna looked at him helplessly. "You know I can't do that."

"I might have had that idea, yes."

"But you need to sleep! You were going to meet Michael tomorrow!" She was starting to get irritated.

Porter smiled at her. "Yes, I am."

"But..."

He laughed softly. "Silly, silly girl." He said fondly and kissed her very seriously for a long time.

Sienna sighed when he pulled back. "You're not fucking leaving."

"Good. I hadn't planned on it. I just had to convince you."

"Dance with me, then. Just the two of us. No audience."

"All right, but that might get a bit hot again."

"If you're staying, it had better."

"It can't get too hot. I'm not ready."

"Neither am I. I haven't kept it this long to toss it that quick, not even for you."

"Ooh, that's hot enough to think about."

"Just be careful with the wrist. It hurts like a fucker still."

"I know it must. And I am still deeply sorry."

"Porter…" She sighed.

"Yes, I know what you are going to say. It doesn't matter in the slightest. I still feel like it is my fault in some way. I can't help it."

She sighed again. "All right. I give up on that."

They didn't say anything for a while.

The clock softly chimed again.

"It's one-thirty now. You must go to bed."

Porter smiled. "All right, but only if you are coming with me."

"Oh, all right." She smiled at him. Then she yawned.

"See?' He teased.

"Shut the fuck up."

Epilogue

Mason watched as Michael and Karen crossed the street to the jewelry store. He smiled to himself. Porter had done an excellent job on the bracelet and he knew Karen would like it. It matched the other piece Michael had given her almost perfectly. It did have that flair Porter exhibited.

"See, Juan?" Mason said, nudging Juan in the ribs none-too-gently. "Told ya."

"Ow," Juan protested. He rubbed his ribs. "Man, that hurt."

"Boo-hoo. You're coming tonight, aren't you?"

"To Michael's? Fuck yeah."

"Good. How's the new assignment coming?"

"It's all right, but I am not a great coder, Mason. They might not believe I am a hacker."

Mason nodded. "I know, but you are the best I have for it."

Juan shrugged. "I am doing my best, man; it is fucking hard. I might be able to break something soon though."

"Good. Just keep at it. We don't have a strict time-limit yet; I just need someone on the inside within the next few months. Try to keep low."

Juan nodded. "I will. Now, let's eat. I am fucking hungry."

Later, after changing and washing up a little, Mason headed to Michael's condo. He hadn't been there in a long time, and he was curious about why he had finally been invited. Michael must be getting a lot better if he was this much more comfortable with himself. Mason knew that personal spaces tend to mirror personalities and that being comfortable in one meant inviting people in.

He knocked on the door. There was some music playing and voices inside. It sounded like a lively party. Porter opened the door.

"Oh, speak of the devil..." He said.

"Why, were they talking about you again, Porter?" Mason asked, coming in and shaking Porter's hand.

"Probably." Porter smiled. "You're looking remarkably good,

Mason. You must be hiding something."

"Yes. And what is that delicious smell?"

Porter looked at him seriously for a minute.

Mason shook his head very slightly. "Not here, and not now." He breathed.

Porter nodded just as slightly. He said in normal tones, "Michael has brought in half the fucking cow herd to feed us with."

Mason laughed.

Karen came out of the kitchen area. She caught sight of him. "Oh! Mason! I didn't hear you come in! Please, do make yourself comfortable! May I get you a drink?"

"Yes, please. Anything you like."

"You might not want to give me that much leeway." She said with a hint of threat.

Mason smiled. "I dare you."

She laughed at him and went back to the kitchen.

Mason looked around curiously. The last time he had been in here, it had been bare and sparse. Now there were some plants around and pictures on the walls. It was quite comfortable.

Porter smiled. "Yes. He has changed."

"You always were good at reading my tells."

Porter shrugged. "This one is not too hard to read, particularly because I noticed the same things." He looked at a nice portrait of Michael and Karen together. It was very informal. "Besides," he said absently, "I am the same way. You wouldn't believe the things that have started appearing in my house. I actually kind of like it."

"Will wonders never cease?"

Porter smiled again. "No. By the way, I know that you know James is at least partially in the know. He has looked in the case. I wanted to offer it to you as an option; he asked me to trust him with more knowledge next time. I can't make that decision, Mason; it is up to you."

"I will think about it. He is a remarkable young man. I will need

283

to consider his girlfriend though."

"I know. I am just passing it on."

Mason nodded. Karen returned with a lowball filled with ice and scotch. "For my rescuer." She said with a gentle smile.

"I am not your rescuer, just an aid in your rescue." Mason said as he took the glass.

"You made me get better. Without you, I might not have seen how broken I was."

Mason saluted her and took a drink. She was wrong, of course, but he would not be able to correct her on it.

"Your bracelet is lovely, my dear." He said, taking her hand and examining it closely.

"Yes, this old pirate certainly is skilled and almost killed Sienna and me off with curiosity." Karen lamented, grinning up at Porter.

"Me? An old pirate?" He asked innocently.

"You, Porter. You are damn-near evil."

"Yes, I know."

She laughed as the there was a knock at the door. Porter went to it and looked through the peephole. "Mason, it's James. Michael invited Callie and him."

"I know, Porter. Let them in."

"All right, then! No need to get pushy." He opened the door to admit his apprentice and his girlfriend.

The evening continued on cheerfully. Juan was less exuberant than usual, saying he was a bit distracted by work. He went into the living room and was engrossed in something on his phone when Mason sat near him.

"Going that badly?" Mason asked softly.

"What? Oh, no, not really." Juan sighed. "I got in later today, finally, but I have to keep up on it for a few days or they will lose interest."

"Okay, Juan. Don't sweat it too much. Once you are in, they won't forget. Besides, they might want someone who is patient and quiet. The kind who lays low."

"Yeah, I know. I haven't been stirring the pot, but I do want to make a few more contact points before I lay off."

"You're the expert."

James had wandered over. "The expert in what?"

Mason smiled at him. "Ah, that is classified."

"Oh, that sort of thing."

"I am afraid so. Porter has suggested you might be interested. I am not saying either 'yes' or 'no' yet, James, but I am very interested in looking you over. You have some skills that I think would be beneficial and I know Porter, Sienna, and Karen trust you. That means a great deal to me. I need to find out some other things first though."

"Such as?" James asked delicately.

"Well, Callie, for one. I need to look into her. If you are serious about her, then you probably shouldn't keep too many secrets from her. I need to know she is good."

"Yes, that makes sense. All right. I trust you, Dr. Briggs."

"First things first, if we work together, you call me 'Mason'. We're friends."

"Uh, okay. That will take some getting used to."

Juan smiled. "I like him; he has that je ne sais quoi that appeals to me."

"Me, too." Mason agreed.

Sienna came out to join them. "Porter and Michael are putting together some sort of surprise. I know because they told me so, then shoved me out. I am going to fucking kill them both. I hate being curious!" She glowered charmingly towards the back of the condo.

Juan laughed. "They do it on purpose."

"I know, Juan, and I am still going to kill them."

"How's the wrist doing?"

Sienna sighed and sat down next to James. "It still hurts a bit, but it is much stronger."

James shook his head. "That makes me very angry every time I think about it. What was he after, really?"

Sienna glanced at Mason. He nodded. She shrugged. "He was after his boss. He wanted him back and he was willing to sacrifice us all for that."

James shook his head. "Messed up. Are you sure he wasn't after the case?"

"No, he wouldn't know what it was."

"What is it, anyway? I know it isn't gems."

"James..." Mason said warningly.

"No, Mason, I am not that stupid. Either trust me or don't, but not this halfway stuff."

"All right." Mason felt he could trust James enough for this. "Then you are in. The emeralds are a special formulation to heighten natural male attraction to Sienna's specific pheromones. The diamonds make a person more receptive to those pheromones. She used them in Hong Kong to great effect."

"Actually, I only used an emerald." Sienna corrected.

James stared at her, then at Mason. "You basically made her into the sexiest human being on the planet?"

"Yeah, pretty much. Although, to be fair, she is close to that anyway."

"Good golly, that must be interesting to watch."

Sienna laughed. "I am not sure how interesting it is to watch but it gets results."

"Oh yes." Mason agreed fervently. "It is very difficult to think when she has it on. Even for us who know her. Right after we got her back, she went and had to hug and kiss us all. I could hardly concentrate on my own job."

Sienna smiled. "I can usually do pretty well without the pheromones; it is just harder and requires a lot more work. Remember that time in Argentina when I did the strip-tease at the one bar to distract all the patrons?"

"Oh, my God, yes!" Juan said loudly. "I don't even know what I

286

drank! I never even looked at the goddamn cup, just chugged! I couldn't fucking look away and I knew it was going to be happening!"

Sienna's smile turned very naughty. "Want to see it again? I can probably do a good one here. Just let me get some room..."

"Fuck no!" Juan said, covering his face. "I was so shit-faced that night I couldn't even walk. Michael had to fucking carry me out. And he was tipsy as hell too. When you dropped the shirt, it was like a fucking bomb went off in there. You could kill a man like that."

She shrugged. "Well, I didn't. Perhaps I just need to practice more."

Mason flushed slightly. "Not here and not around me. Ever."

James was blushing furiously. "Please don't ever do that, Miss Sienna!" He begged. "I could never look at you the same and I would feel terribly guilty."

"I won't, James. I like teasing my friends, but I would not wish to make anyone uncomfortable."

Callie and Karen came into the room. Callie looked at James with a curious expression. "Is something wrong, James?" She asked.

Sienna smiled at her. "I was just threatening to do a strip-tease and he was a bit upset with the idea for some reason. It's not what you take off, you know; it's what you leave on. You just have to give everyone enough to imagine everything else and then you don't have to take it all off."

Mason raised his hand. "You're upsetting me, too! Stop, please!"

Callie blushed slightly herself. Then she gave James a calculating, sidelong glance through her eyelashes. "Hm, Miss Sienna, do you suppose you could teach me? I am always open to new skills and that seems like a good one to have. Right, James? Can't you just picture that?"

"Oh my God!" James, who rarely ever swore, shouted. He almost ran from the room.

"That was perfect." Sienna laughed.

287

"You women are diabolical!" Mason chided.

"So?"

Porter came in. "What the fuck did you do to James, Sienna?" He asked curiously.

"Me?"

Porter looked at her calmly. "My dear, I recognize the symptoms. Yes, you."

Callie smiled. "I might or might not have asked for some tips on stripping."

"That would fucking do it. Just imagining it is almost more than enough. Seeing it probably causes heart attacks."

"That's why I asked. I only want the best. But haven't you seen her do it?"

Porter smiled slowly, his eyes twinkling. "I think James is in for the time of his life. Both good and bad. Possibly at the same time. No, I have never seen Sienna strip, which is just as well, since I can hardly keep my fucking hands to myself as it is. I can imagine it though, and that is enough, for now."

Sienna inclined her head with a mocking smile.

Mason stood up. "I am going to get something else to drink. Anyone else?"

"Me." Juan said, going back to his phone. "Just half a shot."

"All right." No one else wanted anything.

Porter followed Mason into the kitchen area. He poured himself a shot of vodka and tossed it.

Mason poured three other drinks.

"Who's the other one for?" Porter asked.

"James. He's gonna need it. He was pretty upset by the suggestion of Callie stripping for him."

"Poor guy. He didn't have a chance in the world when they ganged up on him like that."

"No, it was pretty funny to see him charging out of there though. I think he will be a good asset. I am just not sure on Callie yet."

Porter nodded. "I understand, Mason. I don't tell you what to do."

"No, you only try to tell me what to think."

"Yes, but I do that to everybody. I know you can't say much, but what is with Juan?"

"He's trying to break into something for a job that might come up or might not. If he gets in, it will be him on his own."

Porter whistled softly. "That's hardcore."

"Yes. We'll see what materializes."

Michael came into the kitchen. As usual, the room seemed to shrink.

"You ready?" Porter asked.

"I don't know. I am fucking nervous." Michael said.

Porter passed him a shot of vodka and Michael drank it. James followed and Mason handed him the third glass.

They all went back into the living room. Michael signaled for silence. "I have an announcement to make. I know that you have all met Karen and you know that I have been sharing this apartment with her. Well, tonight, I wanted to offer something to you, Karen. I have a deed to a small house outside the city a little. I want you to have it, if you want it, for as long as you want it. It is yours."

Karen covered her mouth with her hands. "Oh, Michael!"

He held up his hand. "It is a gift from Porter, Mason, Juan, James, and me. We all contributed. We want you to be happy wherever you are."

Karen started crying. She stood up and hugged and kissed them all.

Mason smiled. "I think that means she agrees."

Karen nodded, still unable to speak.

Sienna looked at Porter. "I assume that was the big surprise? You did marvelously, all of you."

Karen had regained some of her dignity. "Wait. Okay, I will take it, but only on one condition."

289

"What is that?" Michael asked a bit warily.

"That you come with me."

Michael looked taken aback. Then he suddenly grinned. "Of course!"

Karen threw herself into his arms and kissed him very enthusiastically.

Porter winked at Sienna with a grin. "No, my love, that was the surprise."

She laughed. "Perfect!"

James looked confused as Callie put her arm around his waist and he put his arm around her shoulders. "I'm missing something. Why is it perfect?" He said softly to Mason.

Mason smiled. "It has to do with Michael and his own inability to accept who he is. He has made a conscious choice to be defined by being with Karen, and that is a big step for him."

James thought about that. "This is one complex group."

"Yes, so make sure it is what you want before you throw in your lot with us."

James grinned at him suddenly. "Are you kidding? You all make me feel alive and special in ways I never have before. You challenge me. Why wouldn't I want to throw in there? Even if Sienna throws me a curve ball every once in a while."

Mason laughed. "I like you, James. We'll have to see if we can find something for you to do some time. To be fair, she throws them at me sometimes, too. I am not totally comfortable with it, either. But then, that is the charm of her; no one is ever totally comfortable with her. That's how she can do what she does. If we got used to her that would diminish her for us. So, it's a good thing, maybe."

Karen and Michael were finished congratulating each other, so everyone else was grouped around them to offer their own comments. Mason winked at James. Callie had joined the group around the other two. "Just make sure of Callie. I trust your feel of the situation. But if it's not going to work for her, trust me; you are better off not joining us for jobs. We still will be your friend and hang out with you, but maybe not for jobs. The strain can become extreme on relationships."

James nodded. "I understand, Mason."

"Good." Mason moved to offer his own congratulations to Michael and Karen. He was very satisfied with how both things had worked out tonight.

The future looked very promising indeed.